1

The Girl from Berlin

Book Two

Gruppenführer's Mistress

Chapter 1

I was taking my earrings off under the steady look of my husband. He was leaning on the door, with his arms crossed on his chest. He didn't look happy.

"What?" I finally decided to meet his eyes in the mirror of my dressing table while taking hairpins out of the complicated bun in the back of my head.

"You went to Vienna, again."

I said nothing and just kept un-braiding my long, dark blond hair, letting it fall all over my shoulders and back. What was the point in stating the obvious? Of course I went to Vienna. I'd been to Vienna at least four times in the past couple of months, and Heinrich knew it perfectly.

"You went to see Kaltenbrunner, didn't you?"

"I'm not sleeping with him, if that's what you're asking about," I answered coldly.

I really wasn't. It would be monstrous to even suggest something like that, especially after all the pain we both were still suffering from: there's nothing more devastating for parents than losing their first child. We'd lost ours before we even had a chance to hold him in our arms and tell him how much we loved him. I was still blaming myself for that, even though the doctor said that such a tremendous shock caused by the death of my only brother Norbert was responsible for the miscarriage.

The doctor tried to comfort me by saying that it happens a lot during the first pregnancy, and that it was nothing to kill myself about. We were both still young and healthy, and could have a million kids in the future. *I don't want the millions, I wanted that one*, I wanted to tell him. But there was nothing I could do. Just like there was nothing I could do about my big brother laying six feet underground, together with my unborn baby. The only thing I could do was to plan my revenge, revenge on the man who was responsible for their deaths. That man's name was Obergruppenführer Reinhard Heydrich, the Chief of the Reich Main Security Office, mine and Heinrich's immediate boss. And that's exactly why I kept going back to Vienna almost every two weeks, because in Vienna lived the only man who could help me carry out my plan. And that man's name was Gruppenführer Dr. Ernst Kaltenbrunner, the leader of the Austrian SS.

"I know that you're not. Even if you were, that would still bother me less than thinking that you're getting involved in something dangerous." Heinrich frowned at me. "You're up to something, and I don't like it. Especially when you're not telling me what exactly you're up to. And considering that you're dealing with Kaltenbrunner, I know that whatever it is, it can't be good."

Heinrich was right of course. He was always right about everything. But I just couldn't talk to him about what I was about to do, and that was the only secret I was keeping from my husband since we got married. Before we knew everything about each other. Before, without hesitation, I revealed to him the biggest secret I had – my real origin. I told him that my whole family and I were Jewish even though he was an SD Standartenführer and could have easily sent us all out of the country (if we were lucky) or directly to the camps. But I still told him that. Because I trusted him. Because I loved him. Because I knew he loved me too.

Before he trusted me too. He had to trust me to say that he had been working for the American Secret Service for years before I'd even met him. Before there wasn't a thing that would be left unspoken between the two of us. But it was all before – before Heydrich killed my brother.

He wasn't the one who pulled the trigger, but it doesn't lessen his fault. When I came to him begging to transfer my brother from the position of a guard in Auschwitz, the position that was the beginning of the end for my poor Norbert, with the everyday evil and atrocities he had to witness applied to his own people, the Chief of SD simply refused to listen to me. He could have saved Norbert's life with one little signature. He decided not to. Just because he liked playing God. Just because he didn't care about anybody's life. And that's why he'd lose his soon.

A grin crossed my face. The plan that the leader of the Austrian SS Dr. Kaltenbrunner outlined for Heydrich was almost flawless. And the best thing about that plan was that in the case of investigation, which would most definitely follow, nobody could possibly find out that the two of us were in any way involved.

"Heinrich, you know how much I love you, right? I promise that it'll be all over very soon. Just give me a little bit more time and don't worry about me, I know exactly what I'm doing."

"Why won't you tell me then? Don't you think I would listen to you and help you?"

He sounded a little offended. I understood him perfectly: when your own wife goes to some other man for support and more than that, keeps it a secret from you, you have all the right to be offended. I turned around in my chair to look him straight in the eye.

"Sweetheart, I can't. You're just… too good of a man for it. And I need the help of the one who is not."

That's why Gruppenführer Kaltenbrunner was the most obvious choice. As a counterintelligence agent Heinrich was trying to save as many lives as he could. In comparison, Dr. Kaltenbrunner was able to stand over a dying man who he'd shot in the neck and watch him bleed to death.

"I don't like it, Annalise. You're putting yourself in big danger, I can sense it."

It didn't matter if I was. Since I lost two people who were so close to me, since I watched them being put in the grave, a part of me died too. The good part, the one that was taught to forgive and forget throughout her whole life. I wanted to die right before the funeral. Right after I decided to live, to live with one purpose only: to put Heydrich in a grave as well. It's a terrible and miserable existence when you live only for your revenge. But I couldn't imagine any other way for me. I just *had to* do it.

"You have nothing to worry about, darling. Whatever Dr. Kaltenbrunner is helping me with, he's in it too. And he wouldn't risk his life or incriminate himself."

It was partly true. But the other part I didn't want to say aloud. Dr. Kaltenbrunner wouldn't allow anything to happen to me. He needed me alive. He wanted me alive. He wanted me for himself; but that was something Heinrich didn't have to know about.

Two months earlier, Vienna, 1942

"That's a very interesting proposition, I have to say. It's not every day a beautiful woman shows up at my door asking for my assistance in the assassination of one of the top Party members." Gruppenführer Kaltenbrunner paused for a second and then added with a grin, "But you certainly have come to the right place."

We were sitting in his car in a secluded area near the park, where no one would be able to overhear us. Of course we couldn't talk about it in his office, and that's why he told his adjutant to cancel his further appointments and instead decided to take a ride with me.

"So you'll help me then?" I held my breath expecting his answer.

"What did he do to you that you want him dead?" Dr. Kaltenbrunner asked instead. "Pinched your behind while you were serving him coffee? Because I'd personally shoot him for that."

"He's responsible for the death of my brother."

6

"That's a little more serious than I thought." He wasn't smiling anymore; instead he put his hand on top of mine and slightly squeezed it. "I'm very sorry for your loss, Frau Friedmann. Please accept my sincerest condolences."

I nodded. "Thank you, Herr Gruppenführer."

"Was that the same brother who I saw you with in Paris?"

"Yes, it was him. He was my only brother. I don't have any other siblings."

"I understand. It's very sad."

"It is, Herr Gruppenführer."

He was still holding my hand and I was glad to feel that silent support. I only wished that we both weren't wearing gloves so I could feel the warmth of his hand on top of mine.

"So what happened exactly?"

"What happened was that Heydrich refused to transfer Norbert from the position of a guard in Auschwitz back to *Waffen-SS* on the Eastern front. My brother was never a coward, Herr Gruppenführer, he loved his country and was ready to fight for it. He was highly praised by his commanding officers after the Warsaw siege, but he was not made to be a prison guard. He was sick of it all. And I've been there and I can understand why. It's disgusting what they do to people there, and he never wanted to be a part of it. He wanted to fight against the real enemy, not torture innocent people for no reason."

I paused for a moment. I suddenly realized that I wasn't talking to my husband who was very much against the whole Nazi Party politics in relation to the 'Jewish problem,' but to the man who was most likely supporting it. I glanced at Dr. Kaltenbrunner, wondering if I had said too much already, but couldn't tell from the look on his face what he was thinking. I decided to continue.

"The official version that they gave us was that Norbert 'accidentally' shot himself while cleaning his weapon. But how can you accidentally shoot yourself in the temple? I know that he just couldn't take it anymore, and… he took his own life."

I tried really hard not to cry after those last words, even though my chest was burning from all the tears inside.

"Heydrich could have saved him if he wanted to. All he needed to do was to put his signature on the transfer order, and my brother would still be alive. I begged him to help me, and told him that I would do anything; that I would be in his debt forever… But he still said no. Not because it was something that was out of his power, not because it would jeopardize his image... Just because he didn't want to." I felt that poisonous hatred spreading through my body again, which was always there since Norbert died. It was a part of me now, and I felt like I'd never get it out of my system again. "That's why I want him dead, Herr Gruppenführer. He deserved it. He must die."

7

After a minute pause Dr. Kaltenbrunner finally said, "I'll help you, Frau Friedmann. And I think I already know how."

I couldn't contain a smile after hearing his words.

"Thank you so much, Herr Gruppenführer. You don't know how much it means to me."

"Don't thank me, I haven't done anything yet." He grinned at me. "But I'm going to need something from you though."

"Anything."

"Anything?" Gruppenführer Kaltenbrunner raised an eyebrow and laughed. "You're tempting me to ask for a completely different thing from what I had in mind, but I will try really hard to remain a gentleman, especially taking into consideration your vulnerable position."

I caught myself smiling and blushing at the same time. One thing Heydrich was right about: Gruppenführer Kaltenbrunner really needed to have his mouth washed with soap several times before he could talk to a lady.

He finally got serious again. "I'm going to need you to snatch up Heydrich's travel schedule from his adjutant's table. Is it possible for you to do that?"

I thought about his request for a second. It was next to impossible, but I was sure I could find a way, I *had to* find a way.

"Yes, I can do it."

"On second thought, don't take it, it'll be very suspicious if it suddenly disappears. Just copy it for me, will you?"

"Yes, but I'm going to need some time."

"That's fine. I'll be out of town anyway, so let's meet on Saturday, in two weeks. I can pick you up right from the train station and then we'll go to some quiet place where we can talk. Sounds good?"

"Yes, Herr Gruppenführer. Thank you again for helping me."

He eyed me for some time and then asked, "Weren't you afraid to come and ask me something like that? You were risking your life by doing so. High treason is punishable by death."

I shrugged. "You're the only person who I could trust with that."

He liked that, I could see it in his eyes.

"I'm not the person who people normally trust, Frau Friedmann. I'm the Chief of the Austrian Gestapo, you know." He paused for a moment and then added with a smile, "But it's certainly nice to know that you think otherwise."

"After all the time that I've known you I've come to the realization that you're a much better man than people picture you, Herr Gruppenführer."

He liked that even more. He liked to know that I was thinking so highly of him, even though my opinion could be very wrong.

"I appreciate you saying that, Frau Friedmann. And don't worry, I'll make sure that bastard will pay for all the pain he caused you. I hate to see you like that. I want to see you happy and laughing again, like you used to be every time with me."

"I promise you, Herr Gruppenführer, that after his funeral I'll be more than happy."

He was looking at me for some time with his dark brown eyes and then finally said, "You know how much I care about you, right?"

"Yes, Herr Gruppenführer."

"You can always come to me if you need something. Anything."

"Thank you, Herr Gruppenführer."

He looked at me a little longer as if waiting for me to say something else, but I kept silent. He let go of my hand that he was holding all this time and asked, "Do you want me to take you to the station?"

"I can take a bus. I don't want to impose on you, Herr Gruppenführer."

"You never impose on me, Frau Friedmann. I'll drive you there and wait till you board your train."

He did. And already sitting in my coupe for some reason I started feeling very guilty, as if I did something very wrong.

Berlin, January 1942

The working day in the Reich Main Security Office was coming to an end, and I nervously shifted in my chair. I had just finished typing the transcript of the messages I recently exchanged with the British base. Several days ago the Gestapo got a hold on one Englishman working as a radio operator here in Berlin, and after the latter refused to work for them or give away any information, they ordered two especially ruthless agents to help him change his mind. The poor operator died the next morning from massive head trauma, but before that he told his tormentors where the code book he used for coding his messages was hidden. Now my new assignment was to pose as him and try to make the English drop their 'cargo' – several parachutists that were supposed to join the Allied underground spy net, where the Gestapo could easily intercept them.

But my mind was preoccupied with a completely different thing. Today I needed to get my hands on Heydrich's travel schedule just like I promised to Gruppenführer Kaltenbrunner, and it was now or never. In the past week I had found where his adjutant was keeping it, and now all I needed was two minutes alone in the anteroom. For this purpose I kept all the important correspondence together with my transcripts on my desk till I had a whole pile of them. Barbara, my fellow *SS-*

Helferin, gladly handed me her paperwork as well, since she was in awe of Heydrich and loathed going to his office.

At a quarter to five I finally got up from my chair, put together all the papers as neatly as I could and proceeded to Heydrich's office. His adjutant was at his table, doing some paperwork. I faked a guilty smile at him.

"I'm sorry there are so many of them today," I half-whispered to him since Obergruppenführer didn't like any noise in his anteroom, including conversations between his own adjutant and agents. He said it distracted him from his work. "I couldn't leave my table to bring them earlier, I was waiting for the signal from the British."

Heydrich's adjutant let out a suppressed grunt taking the pile of papers from me and shook his head. "He will not be happy."

"I know. I'm very sorry. I put the important ones on top, he wanted to see them as soon as they're done."

He walked to the door leading to his chief's office, and I whispered loudly before he opened it, "I'll wait here if he needs me to explain something."

He nodded and disappeared behind the door. I was finally alone. I waited for several seconds, listening to the voices behind the door, making sure that Heydrich wasn't busy with something else and wouldn't send his adjutant back to the anteroom. But as soon as I heard them talk, I rushed to the table where his adjutant kept all the paperwork, and as carefully as I could opened the top drawer. In the past several days I kept searching through his papers in thirty seconds intervals when he would go inside the main office to deliver my reports. And I already knew where he was keeping the schedule.

Still listening to the voices inside and hoping that no one else would enter the anteroom with their report, I opened the file and let out a desperate sigh. There was no way in the world I could copy so many dates and places in less than a couple of minutes. My mind was racing. I didn't know if I would have another chance like this.

I started thinking. February and March would be out of the question because Dr. Kaltenbrunner would definitely need more time to thoroughly plan and prepare everything. April and May then. I took out a piece of paper I brought in a pocket of my uniform, and thanked God for learning stenography at my *SS-Helferin* classes. Heydrich barked something at his adjutant behind the closed door. *I hope he didn't dismiss him.* There was a thick carpet under Heydrich's desk and I wouldn't hear his adjutant's first three steps, but then he'd have to make eleven loud ones on the wooden floor, which would give me exactly four seconds to put the file with the schedule back in the drawer, close it and move away from the table. But I didn't hear the steps yet.

I kept writing as fast as I could. I was only finishing April, when I heard Heydrich say something again. I heard his adjutant's loud '*Jawohl*, Herr Obergruppenführer,' but I didn't stop writing. I needed to finish May. Sweat starting breaking out in my temples. There were no steps yet. My eyes were jumping from the file to the paper, my hand moving with cosmic speed. Heydrich's voice, then his adjutant's '*Jawohl*' again, and then the first loud step on the wooden floor. I was halfway through. Second step. Almost done. Third and fourth step, closer and louder. I quickly put the paper away back in my pocket and looked at the final dates and places of the schedule, imprinting them in my memory. Fifth and sixth, very loud. I flipped the file closed and put it back in the drawer. Seventh and eighth, almost by the door. I closed the drawer very carefully in order not to make a sound. Ninth and tenth, I made a big step away from the table moving on tiptoes. Eleventh, the door opened. I was standing in the middle of the room, smiling at him. He smiled back.

"You can go, Frau Friedmann. Herr Obergruppenführer will let you know tomorrow if he needs any clarification or if he has any further requests concerning the paperwork."

"Thank you and good night."

"Good night."

I left the anteroom with a wide smile on my face and the copy of Heydrich's schedule in my pocket. Oh, it was a good night indeed!

Vienna, April 1942

We were driving for a good hour already way outside the city limits, and Gruppenführer Kaltenbrunner still wouldn't tell me where we were heading. He seemed to be in very good spirits from the time he picked me up at the train station, but to all my questions he kept saying that I had to be patient for my 'surprise.' I had no idea what he was talking about, but Gruppenführer himself seemed to be very excited about it.

I was still a little shaken up by two recent events both of which took place on the way from Berlin to Vienna: first I had met Max Stern on the platform. He was Heinrich's colleague from *SD-Ausland,* and married to my best friend Ursula. He was taking some paperwork to the office in Vienna and was very surprised to see me. I had to lie that I had some personal business to take care of in the Austrian capital. Another event was that we almost got derailed just outside Berlin.

When the train just started gaining speed, Max and I were walking through the second class car to his coupe (he nicely offered me to share one with him so I wouldn't feel bored). Suddenly the train stopped so fast that I almost fell on some

11

older gentleman if Max hadn't caught me on time. It wasn't just me, some passengers also fell on their neighbors seated across from them. Half of their suitcases fell on the floor, and I thought that we were lucky that they didn't hit us on the head. After everybody got over their initial shock, they started picking up their luggage and curse the brakeman, although we found out later that it wasn't his fault; someone had forgotten to change a railroad point.

Max was helping people behind me to rearrange their suitcases, while I picked up some young woman's bag; the woman was holding a baby in her arms and couldn't do it herself. Her suitcase was also on the floor and I tried to get it to the top shelf, but it was too heavy for me to lift above my head.

"What do you have in there, stones?" I smiled at the woman, still struggling with her luggage.

"No, my husband's books. He teaches philosophy. Don't worry about it, just leave it on the floor, it's too heavy for you."

Luckily Max came to my help and easily pushed the suitcase back on the shelf. The woman thanked us, and we went to our coupe. Thank God the rest of our trip was uneventful. Max offered me a ride as soon as we got off the train, but I told him that a friend was picking me up. Right now I was sitting in that 'friend's' black Mercedes. I don't remember how long ago I saw a car passing us by, but after he turned onto a dirt road leading somewhere inside the woods, I got completely lost.

"How long do we have to drive for?" I asked him again.

"Have some patience, my darling, we're almost there." Dr. Kaltenbrunner winked at me, smiling.

Even though I'd got to know him pretty well by now and could even go as far as calling him my friend (or at least co-conspirator), I was still aware of the true nature of this man, who was more than capable of absolutely terrible things. For a second a thought occurred to me that in my current position I was at his complete mercy, and if it came to his mind to rape and kill me right there in the woods, nobody would even know where to look for my body. What if he changed his mind about the whole Heydrich assassination idea and decided to get rid of the only witness – me? I shifted uneasily in my seat and kept looking at the scenery outside. It was pretty unsettling: we were driving in the middle of nowhere, but it seemed like Gruppenführer Kaltenbrunner knew the road perfectly. *How many times did he take a ride here*, I wondered, *and the main question is why?*

"Are you nervous?" His question took me aback. He must have really had some animalistic instincts, if he could sense my fear so fast.

"Should I be nervous?" I asked back, trying to smile brightly. I *was* nervous. Very nervous.

"You're with me, aren't you?"

That was supposed to sound reassuring, but to me it sounded more like the main reason to be afraid. Nevertheless I smiled even wider and nodded. In a couple of minutes Dr. Kaltenbrunner finally stopped the car and turned it off.

"That's it. We're here." He turned to me. "Time for your big surprise."

He's definitely going to kill me, I was sure of it now. At least I didn't see any other reasons why he would bring me in this wild forest. Meanwhile, he opened his door, walked around the car, opened my door and courteously offered me his hand. I was glad that I was wearing gloves, because he couldn't feel how cold my hands had become. *I wonder how he's going to do it though: is he going to shoot me or strangle me? I hope he'll shoot me.*

"Now you'll to have to close your eyes."

Right. The same reason why SS soldiers make their victims face away, so they wouldn't be looking at them. I never suspected that Gruppenführer was so sentimental though. *Oh well, I guess I haven't escaped the fate of my fellow Jews, previously executed by the members of the same organization, whose leader was going to finish me off now.* I took a deep breath and closed my eyes.

"Good. Now no peeking till I tell you to open them."

"Alright."

I heard his steps in the direction of the back of the car and the sound of the trunk being opened. He had both his gun and service dagger on him, so what was in the trunk? Thanks to all the horror stories about Gruppenführer Kaltenbrunner's favorite games in the Gestapo interrogation rooms told to me by my husband, I was now absolutely terrified. *Is he going to torture me before he kills me? What did I get myself into?*

Dr. Kaltenbrunner dropped something very heavy on the ground, and that something made an undistinctive noise. I was afraid to look and kept my eyes shut tight. His steps approaching again and something dragging on the dry leaves still covering the ground from last year. He stopped right next to me.

"You can open now."

I opened my eyes and involuntarily gasped. Smiling Gruppenführer was holding a man by the scruff of the neck, and judging by the black hood over the man's head and his tied hands and legs, he wasn't brought here by his own will.

"Who's that?" I definitely couldn't understand what was going on but silently thanked God for still being alive.

"Your big surprise."

Dr. Kaltenbrunner slightly shook the man and the latter let out another muffed grunt. I realized that he probably had a gag in his mouth.

"Don't be rude, say hello to this beautiful lady," Gruppenführer addressed the man. "Oh, right, I forgot, you can't talk. Let's take this thing out so we can all have a nice and productive conversation."

He lifted up the hood on the man's head just enough to get a cloth out of his mouth, and put the hood right down. Gruppenführer Kaltenbrunner clearly didn't want him to see us.

"What do you want?"

Those were the first words out of the man's mouth; he was speaking with a distinctive accent that I couldn't quite place. Gruppenführer Kaltenbrunner gave him a hard smack on the back of his head.

"I think I told you to say hello to the lady first, you dirtbag!"

"Hello," the man said without any enthusiasm.

"Hello," I replied, still completely confused about the whole situation, and then addressed Dr. Kaltenbrunner. "Who is he?"

"He is, my darling, your new best friend. Right, Marek?"

I figured that Marek was the man's name. Polish?

"I don't even know who you are and what you want from me."

Another smack followed, this time a harder one.

"Be nice, I'm trying to save your unworthy life here, you pig."

"I'm sorry," Marek replied with even less enthusiasm than before.

"That's better." Dr. Kaltenbrunner turned to me again. "Now your – and mine – new best friend here, our good buddy Marek, is a member of the Czech Resistance group, isn't he?"

"Are you from the Gestapo too? I've already told them everything."

"Of course you did. And in my inner pocket I have an order for your execution for being a member of the anti-government organization. Now you, my friend, have two choices: option one, you keep being rude and stubborn, and I execute this order right here and now with no problems. Option two, you agree to work for us, and I let you go."

"You'll let me go?"

"Not only will I let you go, I'll have my man drive you all the way to the border of your shitty country and even let you go back to your anti-governmental activities. On one condition, of course: your first anti-governmental activity will be appointed by me personally, and you'll find the way to do it."

"What's the catch?"

"The catch is that your wife and two kids are still in the Gestapo jail, and if you decide to mess with me, they'll be right here where you stand now, but six feet underground. Got it?"

Marek sighed. Even though Gruppenführer Kaltenbrunner gave him the illusion of having two options, he didn't leave the poor man a choice.

"What do I have to do?"

"Now we're talking!" Gruppenführer laughed and roughly patted Marek on the cheek with his gloved hand. I thought that it was good that he was wearing the hood over his head. "You'll have to form a group of your other Resistance members and assassinate Obergruppenführer Heydrich during his next visit to Prague."

"Heydrich?" The disbelief in Marek's voice was more than obvious. "Are you two Germans? Or you're from the Resistance too?"

"You can think either way. The only thing that matters is that we want him dead and your goal is to make this happen. Understood?"

"Yes."

Marek sounded much more cheerful now. He wasn't given the usual Gestapo requests to sell out his friends from the Resistance, neither was he in any way collaborating with the Nazis against his own government. More than that, he was given a chance to assassinate the worst enemy his country ever had, who they called 'The Hangman' because of all the executions and atrocities he brought on their territory since he got appointed on the position of the Protector of the Reich in Bohemia-Moravia. Marek was more than happy about the deal he just made.

"Good. Now listen to what I tell you and listen carefully. Heydrich's next visit to Prague will be on May 26, right after he comes back from Paris." Gruppenführer Kaltenbrunner winked at me in silent appreciation of obtaining this information he was now sharing with the Czech. "So it gives you and your friends about a month and a half to plan and prepare everything. From my intelligence source I also know about two of your buddies who interest me the most: Jan Kubis and Josef Gabeik, who are currently being trained in Britain for different diversion tasks."

"I only know Jan, not the other one," interrupted Marek.

"It doesn't matter, they know each other and that's all we need. According to the intercepted messages, which your Resistance and the British have been exchanging lately, very soon they will finish their training and will be dropped on the territory of Czechoslovakia by a British plane."

"Excuse me for interrupting, Herr... I beg your pardon, I don't know your name..."

"You can call me Herr Himmler, if you like. After Heydrich reached a position of being a Minister and succeeded him in rank, he wants Heydrich dead as much as I do."

I could hardly suppress my laughter. I finally relaxed a little, realizing that I would most likely survive this day. Marek appreciated a joke as well and let out a little chuckle.

"Excuse me for interrupting, Herr Himmler, but if your source of information is the Gestapo, which I think it is, you sure understand that both parachutists will be immediately intercepted as soon as they land..."

"Let *me* take care of that," Gruppenführer confidently promised. "Now after they land you take them in and make sure they have everything necessary for the assassination. I understand that they're bringing some good quality British

15

equipment with them, a couple of bombs, guns and other ammunition, and we can definitely use all of it."

Marek nodded under the hood on his head.

"Now you realize that it's a one-time opportunity and you can't possibly fail?" Gruppenführer's voice now sounded borderline menacing.

"Yes, sir."

"Good. Because if you do, I'll find you even in the North Pole and will make sure that your death will be slow and agonizing. But before I'll personally execute all your family members all the way to the most distant cousins twice removed. Got it?"

Marek nervously gulped. "Yes, sir. I understand."

"I'm glad we're on the same page." Dr. Kaltenbrunner smiled. "Let's get down to our plan then. I was thinking for some time what would be the best way to get to Heydrich. And do you know who helped me find the decision? This beautiful lady over here."

"Me?" I was quite surprised by his words.

"Oh yes, my darling. You." I finally understood now why he kept calling me 'my darling' all the time: he didn't want Marek to know my name. Or maybe he just liked saying that. "It was you, who first gave me that idea when we were talking about his habits. It was you, who pointed it out that his worst attribute (God knows out of how many!) is his incredible arrogance. All the power that he recently gained definitely went into his head, and he started thinking that he's invincible, both for his political opponents and external enemies. It was you, who told me that he always drives around in an open car on the territory of his newly obtained Protectorate, just to rub Czechs' faces into his confidence in his terror policies. He started to think that nobody would ever dare to even think of an assassination."

Gruppenführer Kaltenbrunner suddenly burst into laughter.

"God, Marek, I envy you! I wish I could go with you just to see the look on his face. That would be such a priceless sight!"

I absolutely shared that last thought of his and grinned.

"And that's exactly how you, my good friend Marek, are going to get him with your two parachute buddies."

"In his car?"

"Oh yes. According to my source," Dr. Kaltenbrunner said with another wink in my direction, "Heydrich always takes the same route each time he goes from his villa just outside Prague to Hradschin, the old imperial castle, which he recently made into his headquarters. The road that he takes turns sharply right as it approaches the suburbs of Prague, so his driver will have to slow down to take the bend. And that's exactly where you will have him right in the open, ready to get shot, stabbed, thrown a grenade at or whatever it is you wish to do to him. Have several people

16

from both sides of the road, so you'll be able to finish your mission if one of you gets shot by him or his driver; don't forget, he's not stupid and will most definitely return fire as soon as he realizes what's going on. And he's a damn good shooter."

"I understand."

"One more thing. When my man drops you off at the border, he'll give you a small package with liquid substance in it. Do not touch it with your bare hands under any circumstances, and take care of the container as if it was your firstborn. And when your friends land with their ammunition, make sure to soak all the bullets, bomb parts and other weapons in it before you go on your mission."

"Why?"

"Some toxic thing I got my hands on not that long ago. Even if you hit him with one bullet with that substance on it, he'll slowly die of an ailment, which will be potentially unrecognizable to doctors. Even the autopsy won't reveal anything. The experiments proved it highly effective. That's all you need to know."

"I'll personally take care of all the ammunition," promised Marek.

"Excellent. Well, that about sums it up. Any questions?"

"After we're done… Will you release my family?"

"As soon as I see Heydrich's dead body with my own eyes, I'll personally open the door to their cell."

Marek nodded in satisfaction. "Thank you, sir."

"No, Marek." Dr. Kaltenbrunner smiled. "Thank *you*. Now get back in the trunk, I'll drop you off at the hunters' hut not too far from here, from where my man will pick you up. And don't try to run, if he doesn't catch you first, the wolves sure will. There are a lot of them around here and they're hungry as hell."

"I won't run, I promise."

"I know you won't. Just letting you know of the possible consequences."

With those words Gruppenführer Kaltenbrunner effortlessly dragged the tied man back to the trunk, and once again I was more than impressed with the immense strength he possessed; Marek was not a small guy, but Gruppenführer Kaltenbrunner handled him so easily if he was a five year old child. After closing the trunk, he walked up to me, smiling.

"Well, how did you like your surprise?"

"I must admit, you outdid yourself, Herr Himmler."

Laughing, he opened the door for me and helped me get back in the car. For a second I felt ashamed that just half an hour ago I was more than convinced in his sinister motives. Dr. Kaltenbrunner did care about me after all, and I realized that I shouldn't had been listening to all the repulsive stories about him in the first place. He grinned at me before starting the car.

"I never suspected that talking about killing someone would get you so excited."

"What? I'm not excited!"

"You're excited like a kid on Christmas, look at your eyes. You're very happy that he's going to die."

I looked away trying very hard not to smile but couldn't help myself. He was right; indeed, I was extremely happy that in the trunk of his car was the man who would help me revenge for my brother and baby. I *was* happy. It was a disgusting feeling, being so happy about somebody's death, and I was very ashamed of myself. But ashamed in a way like a child who secretly steals candies from the cabinet while his parents can't see. It was very wrong, but it felt so goddamn good.

I leaned back in my seat, already openly smiling at Gruppenführer Kaltenbrunner. He was smiling too.

"I never suspected that you had such a dark side in you, my darling. But I like it. I like you evil."

"I'm not evil. He deserved it, that's all."

"Yes. That's what I always say." I saw how his eyes sparkled when he said it. "We're very much alike, my darling. We're the nicest people... until somebody 'deserves it.'"

"I bet you had way more people who 'deserved it' on your way than I ever will."

"Don't forget that I'm seventeen years older than you. And let me assure you that you started way earlier that I did. When I was twenty one, I was busy with my law studies, not with planning a murder. You'll go far, my evil friend."

Gruppenführer Kaltenbrunner laughed again and started the car, and I got lost in my thoughts. *Was I really like him? Was I really evil? What if he keeps justifying all his actions by the same principle I did, that someone 'deserved it?'* Suddenly I got scared of myself and hoped to get home as soon as I could, so Heinrich would tell me that I was good, that I wasn't evil and that there still was hope for me.

Chapter 2

The nation was celebrating the Führer's birthday today, and it started to seem that this evening would never end. Yet another speaker was praising the Reich's leader for the past fifteen minutes, and I desperately wished they were serving drinks here. Judging by Heinrich's face, who was sitting next to me in this huge concert hall filled with the Reich military and political elite, he was thinking the same. I slightly pushed him with my elbow.

"How about some champagne when it's all over?" I whispered in my husband's ear as quietly as I could. He chuckled.

"I was thinking to start with double whiskey!"

I suppressed my laughter, and Heinrich meanwhile leaned to my ear and whispered, "How about we sneak out for five minutes and make out in the hall instead?"

"Standartenführer Friedmann, you're absolutely awful!"

"I'll go first and then you follow me in a minute. I'll be waiting for you in the hallway behind the curtains."

"Alright."

As soon as he left I looked around, hoping that no one would notice our quick disappearance. It was a very daring thing to do, especially on such a big occasion, but I was ready to take a risk to get a scolding from any of our superiors if they happened to catch us outside. We were finally starting to get back to the way we used to be before the tragic death of my brother and the loss of our baby, which absolutely devastated us both. We had finally got rid of the black clothes and started to learn how to laugh again, how to enjoy life and how to look in the future with hope. After all, we still had each other, and nothing would ever change that.

I looked at the front row where all of them were sitting: Reichsführer Himmler, Minister of Propaganda Goebbels with his wife, General Goering and the leader of the Reich himself – Adolf Hitler. Obergruppenführer Heydrich was sitting behind them with his pregnant wife. I silently hoped that the ceiling above them would collapse and crush them all. *When did I start wishing people to die on such a regular basis? That's definitely not how my parents raised me*, I chuckled.

After a minute I quietly got up and made my way out, trying to attract as little attention as I could. As I was walking down the hallway where Heinrich was supposed to wait for me, somebody grabbed my waist from behind and yanked me to one of the dark niches with tall statues inside; it was my husband. He pulled me behind the curtain covering the niche, turned me around and pressed me against the wall, making us completely invisible to everybody.

I felt like a school girl making out with her boyfriend in a school yard when the teachers don't see; it felt so silly and exciting at the same time that I started to giggle. Heinrich started laughing too, trying to hush me at the same time.

"Stop it, somebody's going to hear us!"

"I'm sorry, I just can't help it. We're two grown-up people, who work in the Reich Main Security Office, and what do we do on our Commander-in-Chief's birthday? We make out in the hall like two teenagers!"

"Screw the Commander-in-Chief!" Heinrich whispered, trying not to laugh too loud. "Let's have sex right here just to make a point!"

"Heinrich!" I tried to make my laughing husband stop pulling up my skirt. "We are not having anything here!!! Are you crazy?"

"Nothing like having sex with my Jewish wife on the Führer's birthday!"

"Heinrich, I'm serious! Stop! We're going to get shot!"

"I say, let's go on the stage and do it in front of him!"

"Heinrich!!!"

Still play-wrestling with him, I was laughing hysterically now. I almost forgot how it felt, to laugh like that until the tears started forming in the corners of my eyes and my stomach started hurting from laughter. I was so grateful to my husband for reminding me how great it was. We were both sitting on the floor now, squeezed in a tiny space between the statue and the wall, our knees pressing into each other. We weren't laughing anymore, we were just looking at each other, smiling. Heinrich took my hand in his and kissed it.

"You don't even know how happy it makes me to see you like this, Annalise. I thought that I lost you after all that happened."

"Oh, sweetheart, don't say that!" I pressed his hand to my heart and then pulled him closer, tightly hugging him. "You can never lose me, I'm your wife and I love you more than anything in the world!"

"I know. I love you too." He was gently rubbing my back, kissing my shoulder, neck and face. "I love you more than life, Annalise. I don't know what I would do if you would leave me."

His words almost broke my heart. So that's how he felt all this time while I was so preoccupied with nursing my revenge plans. That's what he was thinking every time I was away in Vienna. That's what he thought was going on. I was so consumed by my own feelings that I never even thought how much I was hurting the most important man in my life. What a horrible wife I must be!

"Heinrich, love, I'm so sorry for everything!" I took his pretty face in my hands and started covering it in kisses. "I'm sorry I was so selfish! I'm sorry I didn't tell you from the very beginning. But you really wouldn't be able to do anything and I didn't want to drag you into all this."

"Annalise, what did you do?"

"I asked Dr. Kaltenbrunner to help me kill Heydrich," I finally whispered after a pause.

"What?!" Heinrich looked at me in awe. "What have you done?! Are you insane?! You actually asked him that?!"

"Heinrich, I had no choice! I was so devastated because of Norbert and… the baby and… I swore on their grave that I would kill him. I couldn't help it, honey, I'm sorry! I was so mad, I had such hatred in me, I wasn't afraid of anything. I just wanted Heydrich to pay for everything."

"Do you even understand how serious it is? If you try to assassinate a political figure of his rank? He's more powerful that Himmler now! If he dies and they find out that it's you two who's responsible, they are going to hang you both together on the first gates! Oh God, I should have known! I knew that you were up to something, but this!" Heinrich shook his head and then put both his hands on my shoulders. "You will go back to Vienna next weekend and you will tell him that you've changed your mind. Tell him not to do anything."

"It's too late."

"What do you mean it's too late?"

"He can't do anything now. The man who's preparing the whole operation is in Czechoslovakia. And I don't even know what he looks like."

Heinrich was sitting quietly and looking at me. I took his hands in mine again.

"Don't worry, my darling, Dr. Kaltenbrunner thought everything through. He would never take such a risk if he wasn't one hundred percent sure of success."

"Promise me that in the future you will tell me about everything. Everything. I'm your husband, not him."

I willingly nodded.

"I promise, darling. No more secrets. Please, forgive me."

He shook his head and gently brushed my cheek with his hand.

"You're not guilty of anything. You were very upset and weren't thinking straight. I'm sorry that I wasn't as supportive as I should have been. I guess I didn't realize how hard it was on you. I made you go and ask the Chief of the Austrian Gestapo for help. What a good husband I am!"

I smiled thinking how I was blaming myself for being a terrible wife just five minutes ago. After three years of marriage Heinrich and I had become so incredibly close that we had started to even think alike.

"Kaltenbrunner wasn't trying to take advantage of the situation with you, was he?" Heinrich suddenly asked after a pause.

"Oh God, no. He was actually very courteous and polite."

"It's surprising to hear such positive attributes together with his name." Heinrich chuckled.

"He's always a gentleman with me. I wouldn't deal with him if he wasn't."

"He doesn't do charity, Annalise. One day he might ask something in return."

"Well, then I'll have to ask somebody else to kill him." I grinned at my husband. "Now let's go back inside before everybody starts looking for us."

Before getting up he leaned closer to me and kissed me one more time. I felt much better after I told him everything. *No more secrets between the two of us*, I promised myself, *never again*.

Berlin, May 1942

Ingrid, an American Secret Service agent who'd been leading an undercover life with her 'husband' Rudolf for almost seven years now, was pacing around their spacious living room. She always paced when she was thinking something over or when she was nervous, I'd noticed it by now. It helped her concentrate and think clear.

"I don't know about it, Heinrich." She shook her head at my husband, standing at the window with a glass of brandy in his hand. "I think it's too dangerous. Too compromising. You can get caught."

The reason why both husband and wife were so invincible for the all-seeing Gestapo for such a long time was this exact quality of theirs: they both were incredibly cautious. And what my husband had in mind was everything but a safe operation: he wanted to break into the office of the Chief of the Gestapo, Heinrich Müller, during the annual party held for all the commanding staff of the Reich Main Security Office, install a microphone under his desk and falsify the latest orders for the execution of the Soviet prisoners of war, which were arriving to the country in tens of thousands now.

The problem was that Herr Müller's boss, Obergruppenführer Heydrich, disregarded all the rules of the international war codes and demanded the immediate execution of all the Soviet commanding officers of more or less higher rank, considering them a menace to the security of the Nazi regime just because they belonged to the Communist Party, which in his eyes was even a bigger crime than being a Jew.

Heinrich, who had already copied Heydrich's facsimile with a little wax press (while the latter was cleaning up his uniform after Heinrich, pointing something out on the map spread on the table, 'accidentally' spilled Obergruppenführer's coffee), was hoping to steal the lists of the POWs from Müller's desk, attach the beforehand typed order (stamped with Heydrich's facsimile) to send them to the working factories instead of Mauthausen, also known as *Knochemuhle* or the 'bone-grinder,' the camp especially classified as the toughest camp for the 'incorrigible' political enemies of the Reich.

Gruppenführer Müller had a known weakness for vodka, and by the time he'd come back hungover to his office the next day, he most likely would be relieved to find out that Obergruppenführer Heydrich had already taken care of the POWs and most likely wouldn't trace where they had been sent to. After all, if an order carried Heydrich's signature, Heydrich could send them to the Moon if he wished, and no one would blink an eye. The perks of the centralized power was doing my husband a big favor – no one would ever check or question their superior's orders. And that's why he was so sure that the case was worth taking the risk.

"Ingrid, we are talking about almost two thousand people here, who are currently on their way to Austria. And that party is a God's gift to us, everybody's going to get so drunk that they won't even understand what happened. It's such an easy thing to do."

"How are you going to get into his office unnoticed? The guards always remain on their posts in the hallways, party or no party."

"Through the window. My office is on the same floor, I'll just have to walk on a ledge around the corner and I'm there."

"Someone's going to notice you from the outside."

"His office is on the fourth floor, Ingrid. Do you think those guards down there walk around looking at the roofs all the time? They couldn't care less, especially when their superiors are getting drunk inside. They will probably bring some booze and get drunk too."

Rudolf finally got up from his chair and went to the bar to freshen his drink.

"What about the microphone, Heinrich? Don't you think he'll notice it?"

"Of course he'll notice it eventually. But in the meantime we'll be able to hear every single thing he says, both in person and on the phone. And you know that even a couple of days of such conversations in the Chief of the Gestapo's office are priceless."

"He'll know someone from the office installed it there."

"Rudolf, how many people work in the RSHA? Hundreds. He won't be able to screen them all. Of course he'll check the immediate staff members who have access to his office, but it won't lead him anywhere. Besides, I'll install it inside the bottom drawer, on the top of the box, and it'll take him ages to even notice it. I'm telling you, it's a winning proposition. Let me do it."

Rudolf and Ingrid exchanged looks. I could swear they could communicate without words. Finally Rudolf broke the silence.

"Alright, Heinrich. Do it. But if you feel that something – anything – doesn't feel right, abort the operation right away and get out of there. Drop everything and go. We can't risk losing such a valuable agent as you are."

"I'd say that my life is a fair price to pay to try to save two thousand lives." Heinrich smiled.

He was never afraid of anything, my husband. And the more people his office killed, the more he wanted to save. I couldn't be more proud to call myself his wife, even though my heart was aching every time he would do something extremely dangerous. If something happened to him, I wouldn't be able to live. I couldn't imagine my life without this man.

"No, it's not." Ingrid crossed her arms on her chest. "Yours is way more valuable than those two thousand. If they die, nothing will change. If you die, we lose our best agent within the RSHA. You're the only one, Heinrich, and I hate to say it, but you're irreplaceable. So please, keep it in mind. You'll be way more helpful to all the other people we can help in the future if you play it safe. No dangerous tricks, be so kind."

"No tricks, I promise."

"Who's going to handle the transcription of the conversations in Müller's office?"

"Adam will, of course." Heinrich seemed to be a little surprised by the question. "He's the savviest kid we've ever had. He deserved a medal just for not getting caught with the radio for the past two years!"

"Yes, he's a smart kid." Rudolf nodded. "Let him do it. And tell him to bring all the transcriptions to us. The ones that we consider important, we'll give back to him so he can send them to our friends at home."

"Do you want me to do the coding?"

"No, we'll do the coding ourselves. You do your job in the office and look eager. Annalise will help us if we need something, right?"

I nodded.

"Of course I will."

"Then it's settled. Sunday after the mass, when you stop by for a tea, we'll give you the microphone to install. We'll be able to get it by then."

Heinrich was a Catholic, and after we got married I started going with him to the Catholic Church instead of the Protestant one, where I used to go with my parents. Of course we didn't go there to pray; it was a good excuse to meet with our fellow agents without causing any suspicion. But I still liked the church, I liked how peaceful it was, how grand, how holy. For me, a Jewish girl who'd never been to a synagogue in her life in order to keep a multi-generation Aryan image, it was the only house of God where I could talk to Him. It didn't really matter how that house looked like as long as He could hear me. This time I would pray for Heinrich to be safe.

Max, Heinrich's best friend and also an SD agent, was telling another story to the group of officers gathered around him. Max's wife Ursula, who by now was like a sister to me, was another reason for Max's colleagues to be around the couple. She lost all the weight after having her first baby two years ago and was more than happy to go back to the social life she so dearly missed. Tonight Ursula looked absolutely stunning in her blue evening gown and was gladly accepting compliments from her husband's co-workers.

I was laughing out loud at Max's stories, making believe that I was drunk. In reality I hardly sipped any champagne from my glass during the evening. Heinrich had just slipped away from our circle unnoticed, and I stayed to make sure that no one would notice his disappearance. Also I needed to keep an eye on the Chief of the Gestapo, Gruppenführer Müller, and prevent him from going to his office for whatever reasons. I had no idea how I could possibly manage that, so I was very relieved that Herr Müller looked more than comfortable in his chair talking to one of his subordinates and didn't seem inclined to leave it any time soon.

I glanced at the clock on the opposite wall and noticed the time. Heinrich said that he needed about five minutes inside Müller's office and about another five to get in and out. The part of the plan that worried me the most was that he had to walk on a thin ledge at the fourth floor's height, and I kept praying to God that the construction of the building was a strong one. If the window wasn't open, like Gruppenführer Müller liked to leave it for the night for the fresh air, Heinrich would need another couple of minutes to open the lock from the outside with his service dagger. Plus two minutes to ascend and descend the stairs from the big reception hall where we all were right now to the fourth floor where the offices were. So after precisely fourteen minutes I should start worrying. Only one passed.

Ursula whispered in my ear that she was going to the ladies room and asked me if I wanted to go with her. I just smiled and shook my head, whispering back at her that all these officers would be bored to death if both of us leave. The argument that they needed their female audience made a lot of sense to my friend, and she left me without any suspicions. I couldn't leave my post: I needed to watch Müller.

Two minutes passed. Heinrich probably just opened the door to his office. I was impatiently tapping my index finger on the glass I was holding. Picturing my husband getting out of the window and stepping on a thin ledge underneath, I started to think that Ingrid and Rudolf were right and the whole operation was a bad idea. But it was too late to do anything now. Someone said a joke and I laughed along with everyone, even though I didn't even hear what they were laughing about. Müller was still sitting in his chair.

Ursula came back. Too nervous about Heinrich playing a circus acrobat on the top floor, I told her that I needed some fresh air and quickly glancing in Müller's direction once again, I walked through several long hallways to the glass door leading to the backyard. SS guards standing next to it like statues didn't seem to pay any attention to me; I already saw several officers walking out through this very door to enjoy their cigarette outside, so there wasn't anything suspicious about me doing the same thing. The SS guards didn't have to know that I didn't smoke.

Already in the back yard I quickly closed the doors behind me and, making sure that I was alone, I took several steps so I could see the roof. No one was on it. I sipped a little more of my champagne and looked up again, trying not to lift my head too high. No one appeared, which meant that Heinrich was already in Müller's office. I let out a little sigh of relief and quickly walked back inside to keep my surveillance on the Chief of the Gestapo. But before I could make my way back to the reception hall, an officer passing me by suddenly grabbed my arm and pulled me to the wall, pressing his hands on both sides of my body, completely restraining me from any movement. In the dark hallway I couldn't see his face, but there was something very familiar about him, something very threatening.

"What are you doing?" I asked him as loud as I could. Too bad the music inside was louder.

"Haven't seen you in a while, Annalise."

I recognized him now. I could never forget this voice, the voice of the man who almost raped and killed me after I refused his advances several years ago, the man who filed a report on me to the Gestapo, which almost costed me my freedom and maybe even my life; the man who, thanks to his girlfriend Gretchen, who used to dance in the same ballet company with me, found out that I was Jewish. Sturmbannführer Ulrich Reinhard.

"Let go of me. Now!"

I tried to push him off me, hoping that someone would pass by and notice us, but it was just him and me in the dark hallway. Last time it happened, he almost choked me to death. Needless to say, I was terrified.

"Why? Don't you want to say hello to an old friend? Where are your manners?"

26

He grabbed my hand and pulled it behind my back, making me drop my champagne glass on the carpet. I tried to scream but he pressed my mouth shut with the other hand. I knew that he wouldn't actually do anything to me at least during the party and that he was just trying to scare me, but I hated to admit that he succeeded.

"You little Jewish whore, do you know that I lost my office position because of you?" The hateful expression of his face was leaving me no doubts: he did want to hurt me, one way or another. "Do you know that I was transferred to the goddamn *Waffen-SS* thanks to you? Do you know how many Jews I had to round up and execute on the Eastern front to get my position back?"

I couldn't answer even if I wanted to: he was still holding my mouth shut. Last time I got away by kicking him in the groin, but he was smarter now and was pressing me against the wall with his body. From the side we probably looked like two lovers hugging in the hallway. In reality Reinhard twisted my wrist even harder.

"Good thing that Obergruppenführer Heydrich appreciates people like me," he said looking me straight in the eye; then another menacing smile crossed his face. "I'm back now, I'm an official Gestapo agent and you'll be seeing a lot of me in the nearest future. Till I find the way to destroy you. And this time no one, even your husband, will be able to help you."

My husband! I needed to go back to the reception hall to see if Müller was still there. Only I couldn't. He was still holding me.

He leaned closer to me and said in a voice that sent shivers down my spine, "How does it feel to know that your worst nightmare is back, huh, Jew-girl?"

Then he laughed and finally released me from his grip, but as soon as I tried to make a run between him and the wall, he stretched his arm against the wall to prevent me from escaping. He obviously liked playing cat and mouse with me.

"Going so soon? One more question I wanted to ask, as an official now: what happened to your parents? Why did they have to leave the country so hastily?"

I froze where I stood, afraid to take another breath. *How did he know?*

Reinhard smiled even wider and more evil. "Did someone find their real birth certificates?"

A tall figure just entered the hallway, and I saw the red tip of the cigarette being lit in the dark. A tiny light of hope appeared in my heart; but there was no way it could be him. However, the closer he was getting to us, the more I was sure of it. I pushed away Reinhard's hand and rushed towards my unexpected savior, Dr. Kaltenbrunner.

"Herr Gruppenführer!" I screamed as loud as I could.

He caught me by my shoulders, obviously surprised by my sudden appearance.

"Frau Friedmann? What happened?"

I clenched onto his uniform as if my life was depending on it and pointed to Reinhard's direction.

"That man was threatening me!"

Even in the dark I could see the expression of his face change from pleasantly surprised to visibly menacing. He let go of my arms and slowly walked up to Ulrich Reinhard, who froze on his spot with his hands pressed against his body.

"Did you threaten her?" A nod to my direction.

"Absolutely not, Herr Gruppenführer. We were just talking."

"You almost broke my arm!" I screamed at him. I saw how ominously Reinhard's eyes sparkled as he met my gaze.

"You dared to lay your dirty hands on this woman?" Gruppenführer Kaltenbrunner asked very quietly, with hardly masked fury.

"She's exaggerating. I only…"

But Gruppenführer Kaltenbrunner didn't let him finish; he grabbed Reinhard by the lapels and with immense force threw him against the wall, after which Reinhard hit the floor. I yelped and covered my mouth with my hand. Reinhard tried to get up on his feet, but Dr. Kaltenbrunner gave him a hard kick under the ribs, which made the former lose his wind and start coughing, gasping for air.

"What's wrong with you? Are you hurt?" Gruppenführer Kaltenbrunner leaned over Reinhard's body. "Let me help you get up."

With these words he grabbed Reinhard's left arm and twisted it hard, forcing it behind Reinhard's back. Reinhard screamed and bent backwards towards the hand, trying to somehow alleviate the pain.

"Oh, I'm sorry, did I hurt your arm? I think you're exaggerating though. I haven't broken it. Yet."

"No, please!"

Gruppenführer Kaltenbrunner pulled his hand even higher to an almost unnatural position. Reinhard's face was distorted with pain.

"Herr Gruppenführer, please let me go, I'm sorry!" he cried out.

"Damn right you are, you piece of shit!" Dr. Kaltenbrunner finally let go of Reinhard and the latter pulled the hurt hand to his chest, still standing on his knees in front of Gruppenführer. "That was a warning. One more time I see you near her, I'll break your fuckin' neck! You got it?!"

"Yes, Herr Gruppenführer. Thank you, Herr Gruppenführer."

"Get the hell out of my face and make sure I don't see you for the rest of the night."

"*Jawohl*, Herr Gruppenführer."

Reinhard got up on his feet and walked a little unsteadily towards the exit. The gaze that he threw at me passing me by was withering. I was alone with Dr. Kaltenbrunner, who came up to me and gently lifted up my chin.

"Are you alright?"

"Yes, Herr Gruppenführer. Thank you so much."

"Who was that son of a bitch?"

"Remember the man who put all the incriminating information about me in the file that they gave you in the Gestapo jail when you were interrogating me? That was him."

"Interrogating?" Gruppenführer Kaltenbrunner finally smiled. "I always thought that we were just talking, no?"

I was glad that he couldn't see me blush in the dark.

"I'm sorry. Yes, we were just talking. And you were very kind to me over there. Thank you for that."

"The pleasure was all mine, Frau Friedmann. And you know, you shouldn't be walking around alone in the deserted parts of the building at night; see what can happen?"

"Yes, I know. I just wanted to get some fresh air outside."

"What if I didn't happen to pass by? Your husband is not doing a good job watching you. Where is he, by the way?"

My husband!!! Cold sweat broke on my forehead right away; between Reinhard and Dr. Kaltenbrunner I absolutely lost track of time. *What if Müller went back to his office for some reason? What if Heinrich fell off the ledge coming back to his office?*

"He's supposed to be with his friends in the reception hall."

"Let me take you to him then. I can finish this later."

With those words he threw an unfinished cigarette to the tree pot standing on the floor and wrapped my hand around his arm. I still couldn't believe that he was here and he just saved me, once again.

"What are you doing here, Herr Gruppenführer? I mean, in Berlin?"

"I'm supposed to exchange some people with Gruppenführer Müller. He wants my Austrian Jews for his Auschwitz, I need his prisoners of war for my Mauthausen. We're expanding granite quarries according to the Führer's wish. He wants to lay the streets of Berlin with it, so Paris would be nothing compared to the capital of the Reich." He chuckled. "The funniest thing is that it's Austrian granite, but Vienna won't get nothing. And that's actually the main reason why I'm here. I want to have a serious conversation with Reichsführer Himmler and let him know how much I'm displeased with the current situation, to say the least."

Prisoners of war for Mauthausen. I was praying to God that they weren't the same prisoners of war that Heinrich was currently trying to falsify the papers regarding their new destination. *If this comes out, we'll be in big trouble.* As we walked inside the reception hall, I took a quick look at the clock. Only ten minutes had passed. I looked around; Heinrich was nowhere to be seen. The good thing was that Gruppenführer Müller was still enjoying his drink in his chair.

"Your husband is not here. I told you he's not doing a good job looking after you."

I couldn't understand if Dr. Kaltenbrunner was joking or if he was serious. I smiled at him.

"He probably noticed that I was gone and is looking for me somewhere outside. Why don't you keep me company instead?"

First, I didn't want him to go talk to Müller because they could have decided to go up to Müller's office. Second, I wanted to find out more about those prisoners of war he was talking about.

"On one condition." Gruppenführer Kaltenbrunner grinned at me.

"What condition?"

"You'll have to dance with me. I think you owe me after all those times I got you out of trouble."

I smiled but followed him to the middle of the room where we joined the rest of the dancing couples. He took my hand in his and put another one on my back, while I rested mine on his shoulder. For the first time we were so close to each other, and I suddenly forgot what I was supposed to ask him about. I thought that it was just adrenaline still messing with my head. Meanwhile Gruppenführer Kaltenbrunner leaned even closer to me and whispered in my ear, "I have some good news I wanted to share with you."

"What is it?" I whispered back, suddenly noticing that my heart was beating way faster than it should.

"Our friends landed in Czechoslovakia several days ago. Marek took them in, and they're already working out the last details of the plan."

He was looking at me with his dark brown eyes, smiling and waiting for my reaction. I didn't know what to say.

"Thank you," I finally whispered, fighting the urge to hug him tightly.

"You're welcome, my beautiful friend." He pulled me a little bit closer, his hand slightly caressing my back through the silk of my dress. "You know that I'm always more than happy to kill for you."

I shook my head at that last joke of his and desperately tried to remember what I needed to find out from him. Instead for some reason I remembered how we got drunk in Paris and I touched his face, tracing the outlines of the dueling scars on his left cheek. I suddenly wanted to do it again. I wanted to touch his face. I wanted him to lean to me again and kiss me.

Oh God, why on Earth am I thinking this? I'm not even drunk! My husband is risking his life right now and I'm fantasizing about another man kissing me? What is wrong with me?! He helped me out, that's it. It's just a common victim's psychology, we gravitate towards our saviors, simple as that. Just a regular scientific fact. I am not attracted to him in real life. It's just adrenaline.

I blinked several times trying to get rid of his hypnotizing gaze and smiled as innocently as I could.

"So, prisoners of war, huh? How many of them do you need for your granite quarries?"

"The more the better. One can never have too many workers."

"Right." He was still holding me too close, and it was breaking my concentration. "But... Some of them are not good for work, right?"

"What do you mean?" His brow slightly furrowed.

"I mean that... I heard about the special directive from Obergruppenführer Heydrich. About the Soviet commanding officers. About... the 'special treatment.'"

"Oh that." He finally smiled again. "Yes. Them I don't need. A major waste of time. I hope that Müller doesn't include them on the lists, but knowing what a scheming bastard he is, and that he most likely wouldn't want to deal with them himself, I can expect anything."

All the euphemisms in the world couldn't cover the ugly truth: Gruppenführer Kaltenbrunner didn't want them just because it was a waste of time for the Kommandant of Mauthausen – to transport them to the camp, to gas them upon arrival and then kill the whole day for the cremation. That's how they saw those people. 'A major waste of time.' I sighed. Good thing I was married to Heinrich.

I glanced at the clock on the wall. It was time for my husband to come back already. I looked back at Dr. Kaltenbrunner. He was still smiling at me, confidently leading me in a slow dance. I thought that it was amazing how comfortable I was feeling in his arms. What if I told him that I was a Jew though? He would have probably sent me to the same Mauthausen and personally wrote 'for special treatment' on my papers.

"Why are you so interested in my inmates?"

"No reason. Just curious."

"Curiosity killed the cat."

"That's why I'm asking you about it and not somebody else."

Gruppenführer Kaltenbrunner suddenly stopped, put both hands on my waist and whispered in my ear, "Your husband is back, little kitty. Try not to get yourself in any more trouble, will you?"

He then brushed his cheek on mine, kissed me on the corner of my mouth, gave me yet another grin and left me absolutely smitten in the middle of the dancefloor. I followed him with my gaze and saw how he exchanged handshakes with Gruppenführer Müller. Only then I turned around and slowly walked towards the group of the already familiar officers, which Heinrich joined again absolutely unnoticed.

I came up to my husband and awkwardly hugged him by the waist.

"Is everything alright?" I lifted my eyes to his.

"Can't be better, sweetie." He was smiling brightly at me. I guess he didn't see me dancing with Dr. Kaltenbrunner. Thank God he didn't. I let go of him and joined the conversation, all of a sudden feeling very tired. There had definitely been too many events for one night. I just wanted to go home.

Chapter 3

Ingrid and Rudolf couldn't be happier. It had already been a week since they had begun regularly sending messages to their superiors in the United States based on the transcriptions of Gruppenführer Müller's conversations, always timely and accurately done by Adam. The Soviet commanding officers were also safe and relatively sound, working at the ammunition factory somewhere in South Germany. I thought that both Dr. Kaltenbrunner and Müller were more than satisfied with that fact, former – because he didn't have to deal with such a 'waste of time,' latter – because he didn't have to find excuses why he needed to attach them to the rest of the regular soldiers instead of taking care of them himself.

It was Sunday, and we were having one of our 'after mass tea parties' at Rudolf and Ingrid's. This time Adam was with us as well, since he brought the whole file full of transcripts, which Rudolf was going through as we were speaking. Sometimes he would even click his tongue in satisfaction and say, "This is priceless! Great job, Heinrich! Great job!"

Heinrich would just smile and wink at me. I wasn't even trying to hide a proud smile: not too many Aryan Germans, if any, especially occupying such a high rank in Nazi Germany, would risk their life for the people considered to be the enemies of the Reich. But he did. Because to him they weren't just Jews or Communists, they were people, same people like he was, with families and friends, with someone waiting for them at home, people who deserved to live as much as he did.

I could understand why Adam was working for the Allies – he was a formerly persecuted Jew and wanted to prevent his people from following his fate, the same reason why I joined the team. I understood why Rudolf and Ingrid were playing spy games for the past seven years – they were Americans and it was their job, to help the Allies fight the Nazi regime from within.

But Heinrich didn't have to do what he was doing by any means. He was a German. A purebred Aryan German, from a purebred upper middle class German family with no black sheep amongst them whatsoever. He had quite an impressive resume within SD, a long list of appreciations and awards from his superiors, and could have just enjoyed his life like the rest of them did. But instead he joined the US counterintelligence team, married a Jewish girl and swore to keep fighting for every single life he could possibly save. That's who he was, my husband. My rebel. My hero.

I smiled at him and took his hand in mine. He smiled back at me and put his cup back on the coffee table. Adam shifted uncomfortably in his chair; I noticed that he always felt awkward whenever Heinrich and I would display any kind of affection towards each other. I guess he still wasn't used to the thought that I was married to the German officer, even though that officer was working for the Allies. When he, Adam, was leaving the country after the decree of the elimination of Jews from basically every sphere of economic life came into power, I wasn't even dating anyone and despised everything concerning the Nazi Party. Being my dancing partner, he was my closest friend back then, and we spent more time working together than with our families. Maybe he thought of me more than just a friend, I didn't know and I never asked. He would never say anything either.

"How much time do you think will pass till Müller notices the device?" Ingrid asked Heinrich.

"I hope he never does." He laughed and then became serious. "We have to be very careful with all the messages we send though. I know the Gestapo from within, and they are anything but stupid. If Müller notices it, he might not even say anything and keep making believe that nothing happened. He might trick us and start spreading disinformation without us knowing it. That's why we have to double check everything suspicious coming from his office. He might want to give us a bait and as soon as we swallow it, we're done for. Be very, very careful with screening all of this information you're getting."

"We always are," Ingrid said confidently.

"Is there any way for me to know that he found the device?" Adam asked. "After all I'm the one who can actually hear all the sounds in the office, are there any pointers I should look for?"

"Yes." Heinrich nodded. "If you hear a very loud noise and scratching right near the speaker as if someone's touching it, that's number one and the most obvious one. Another one is if you hear a click and the sound disappears for some time and then comes back, which means he turns it off and on. And then just pay attention to his manner of speech and intonation, if it sounds too rehearsed and unnaturally loud, he's putting on a show for us. That's about it."

"All right, I'll listen very carefully to everything going on there and will let you know right away if something doesn't sound right."

"We really appreciate your help, Adam," Heinrich said very seriously. "You know, you're the best radio operator we've ever had. And you've become our very good friend."

Adam smiled shyly at him and lowered his eyes. "Thank you, sir."

He never left the habit of addressing both Heinrich and Rudolf 'sir' and Ingrid 'madam.' Only me he was calling by my first name, just like he used to when we still danced together.

"Well, I'd better get going then," he said, quickly getting up from his chair. "I still have to send out yesterday's mail."

'Yesterday's mail' meant the coded messages that Rudolf prepared for him to transmit today.

"Do you want me to give you a ride?"

I quite often offered Adam my services as a personal driver whenever he needed to go someplace far to use his radio. Normally I would drive him either to some secluded area but not too far from a busy road and he would exchange the messages with the US agents right from the car, or to some building in the former Jewish ghettos where no one would pay attention to us.

"If it's not too much trouble." Adam smiled at me.

"Don't be silly, of course not." He did have his own car, but mine (or better say Heinrich's) was way less suspicious. SS plates on it had a tendency to make it invisible for the possible Gestapo agents searching the area. "Let me just finish my tea."

"Sure, take your time. I'll wait for you downstairs."

Adam said goodbye to everyone in the room and left. Ingrid meanwhile turned to my husband.

"Try not to befriend any of your co-workers."

Both he and I were very much surprised by such an unexpected statement coming from the American agent.

"Why not?" Heinrich frowned at her.

"Affection and any personal attachments are the qualities that should be completely disregarded by any good agent. They quite often lead to failure."

"I don't understand what you mean."

Ingrid sighed.

"You can't allow any personal feelings to stand on your way while doing your job with the Secret Service. They create weak spots. See, Rudolf and I, even though we pose as husband and wife, never allowed any kinds of feelings to be between us except for the mutual respect for each other. This way if one of us gets compromised, the other one will get a chance for survival. We wouldn't give away any information if someone from the Gestapo would hold a gun to the other's head. Can you say the same about your wife?"

Heinrich and I exchanged quick looks. Ingrid just nodded.

"That's exactly what I'm saying. Your wife is your weak spot as it is, don't make any more of them befriending our subordinates, especially radio operators. They tend to die way more often than the rest of us."

Still thinking of Ingrid's words I was driving towards the former Ghetto, following Adam's instructions since I didn't know it as well as he did. His wireless radio was in the trunk of my car, neatly packed in the suitcase. When we finally pulled up to the building he planned to use, we made sure that the narrow street was absolutely deserted, and only after that Adam got out of the car and took the suitcase from the trunk.

"Don't wait for me here, there's another exit on the other side of the building that you can use. It's quieter in there," Adam told me through my driver's window.

"I'll park the car and come upstairs with you." Sometimes I would do that so while he was exchanging messages with the Americans I could look out the window for any possible suspicious activity. This time I decided to do the same.

"You don't have to."

"I want to. What's the number of the apartment?"

"Thirty six. I won't lock the door."

"I'll be right there."

After watching Adam disappear behind the front door, I circled around the shabby building and found myself in a small yard with the dirt road leading back to the main street as I figured. Judging by the bushes surrounding it, no one had driven a car here since the time when Germany was still a republic. I shook my head as I stepped on the ground covered with dirt and garbage, and proceeded inside the building trying very hard not to scrunch my nose. The smell here well suited the look, and I wouldn't be surprised if the back yard was sometimes used as a lavatory by the new habitants of the area.

When I opened the door to the apartment with my elbow (I forgot my gloves in the church, and now gave myself a mental note not to touch anything inside the apartment), Adam was already working with the radio with his headphones on. I decided not to bother him and went directly to the window, leaning on the wall next to it and slightly moving the stained and moth-eaten curtain away. Everything seemed quiet. For two years already we would perform the same routine in different places, and they were just not fast enough to get us. Adam always worked with an incredible speed.

But this time was different. My eyes widened as soon as I saw a black car quickly approaching the building from the front. There was no way it could be the Gestapo so soon! But I didn't want to take a risk. I rushed towards Adam and shook his shoulder.

"Adam, let's get out, quickly! The Gestapo's here!"

He took the headphones off his head and stared at me.

"What???"

"Let's split up." I already stuffed the sheet with the coded messages in the pocket of my dress, shut the suitcase with ice cold hands and grabbed the handle.

"I'm the one with the car, I'll try to get this thing out from the back and you try to get away through the roof. The next building is very close, jump on its roof and try to make it out."

I was already at the door when Adam tried to take the radio away from me.

"Annalise, wait! Leave the radio, get out alone!"

"Just go, Adam!!"

"No, leave it to me!!!"

He yanked the handle out of my hands and ran upstairs, while I rushed downstairs as fast as I could. The apartment was on the third floor and the only chance to outrun the Gestapo was by taking the back exit, jump into my car and pray to God that they didn't send a second car to block the backyard. But if they caught me in the hallway before I could escape through the back exit, I'd be dead.

The adrenaline was pumping in my blood as I almost jumped the last three steps leading to the hallway. I could see them running towards the building within twenty steps of me; I quickly turned to the back exit, run outside, got into my car and clenched onto the steering wheel, praying that the dirt road was clear. I saw one of them running after me in the back yard in the rear view mirror and getting his gun out. Then I floored the accelerator and turned the wheel all the way to the right, surprisingly safely making it to the main road despite all the gun shots behind my back.

I was driving way too fast through the backstreets of Berlin feverishly thinking where to go. Hopefully that agent who was trying to shoot at me didn't see my license plates. Hopefully Adam could escape through the roofs. Hopefully he'd get rid of that goddamn suitcase before someone would catch up with him. We could have just left it in the apartment of course, as if one of us would get caught with it, the Gestapo would have the biggest evidence they could possibly use against us. Without the radio on our hands it would be very difficult to prove anything. Unless, of course, they decided to torture us. I shuddered.

"Shit!!!" I never cursed but this time was appropriate. I just remembered that I had a coded message stuffed in my pocket, the message that Adam was supposed to burn as soon as he would be done with transmitting. Normally he would learn them by heart, but this time they were extremely lengthy and he had to use the paper. The paper with Rudolf's handwriting on it. With his and probably Ingrid's fingerprints on it.

With a shaking hand I got the piece of paper out of my pocket and not knowing what else to do, started tearing it piece by piece and stuffing it in my mouth. The paper tasted very weird and was very difficult to swallow without water. I tried to chew it in smaller pieces. Now all I could do is drive home and hope that Adam was able to escape.

I was sitting on the bed while Heinrich was pacing the room from time to time running his hand through his hair. His gun, fully loaded, was laying on the nightstand next to me. I took another sip from the glass he gave me. I hated brandy but at least it stopped me from shivering uncontrollably.

"Did they see you?" He asked me once again.

"They were running towards the building. There was no light inside the hallway, so I don't know. Maybe they just saw that it was a woman. I don't think they saw my face."

"Do you think they remembered your plates?"

"I don't know, Heinrich. I really don't know anything."

I put the glass aside and covered my face with my hands, feeling absolutely helpless and desperate. The unknown was the worst part. He sat on the bed next to me and pressed me to his chest.

"It's alright, sweetie, everything's going to be alright. If they come here, I'll shoot them all. They won't get you, I promise."

"You can't shoot everybody in the Gestapo."

"I know I can't. But that'll be enough to get you out of the country. I'll drive you to the border of Switzerland, you'll go get your parents and all of you will go to New York. As a matter of fact, let's go now. Pack a small suitcase and let's go. Why wait?"

I lifted my head and looked him in the eyes.

"I'm not going anywhere without you."

"Annalise, I'll have to stay here. If I leave together with you, they'll go after my family. You know how things are done in the Reich."

"Then I'm staying too."

"No, you're not. Let's go." Heinrich got up and tried to pull me on my feet, but I pulled back with all the resistance I had.

"No, Heinrich. I said I'm staying here with you."

"Annalise, they're going to kill you! Don't you understand?!"

"Maybe they won't! Maybe they won't find out that I have anything to do with it. Besides, even if they do, at least I'll be able to save you. I'll tell them that you never knew of my connections with the Americans. You have an impeccable reputation here, they'll believe me."

He frowned at me, shaking his head.

"Don't even think of it! Don't even think of sacrificing your life for me. You should save yourself."

"The Allies need you, Heinrich. You're the one who should save yourself. Think about the importance of the job you're doing."

"Screw that job! It's not worth my wife's life for God's sake!"

I got up from the bed, walked up to my husband and put both hands on his face. I saw tears in his eyes and it made me start crying.

"Heinrich, I love you more than anything. I'm staying with you, no matter what. If we die, we'll die together. But there's no way I'm leaving you!"

Then we grabbed each other into the tightest embrace and just stood like that for what seemed like an eternity. Neither one of us wanted to let go first.

They didn't come for me that night. They didn't come for me for the next couple of days, and I started to hope that maybe I was safe after all. But then they stopped right in front of my desk, and as soon as I lifted up my eyes at them, I knew that was it.

"Frau Friedmann, you're going to have to come with us."

Barbara was looking at our colleagues from Amt IV, simply known as the Gestapo, with her eyes wide open. It was not every day they came to arrest their co-workers. I sighed, put away my pen and slowly got up from the chair. Well, it happened after all.

I followed them through the familiar hallways of the Reich Main Security Office building, wondering what they had on me. *If someone thinks they identified me from the picture, that's one thing. They can be mistaken and I can argue that. But if they found my fingerprints on the suitcase that I so recklessly touched or followed up my license plates, I'm done for.* I clasped the cross on my wrist with cyanide hidden in it in my hand, hoping that they would leave me alone so I would be able to put the capsule in my mouth, just in case. Then if something went wrong, all I'd have to do was to bite on it.

They brought me to the basement, and I suddenly caught myself experiencing the most terrifying deja-vu: several years ago I was brought to the same basement, but my charges of concealing a Jewish identity was a walk in a park compared to the charges of high treason and espionage. They took me to the already familiar hall with several interrogation rooms and, after the guard locked the door behind us, they walked me inside one of them, right to the hands of my menacingly smiling interrogator – Ulrich Reinhard. I wasn't surprised that he probably jumped on my case as soon as he saw it. After all he swore to kill me.

I sat down on one of the iron chairs and crossed my hands on my chest, waiting for him to speak first. Compared to my first time in the infamous Gestapo jail, I felt a little more confident. Reinhard walked towards another chair across the table from me, still intentionally slowly turning pages of the file he was holding.

"Well, it sure is nice to see you. Especially here." He lifted his ice cold blue eyes at me. He reminded me of a shorter version of Heydrich. Needless to say that I hated him as much.

"And why exactly am I here?" I decided to play an offended victim until I found out all the facts.

He laughed.

"Playing dumb won't help this time, Jew-girl. We found your fingerprints on the wireless radio that used to belong to one of the Resistance members. You have one way out of this jail now – right to the gallows."

Shit. They have the radio. But he also said 'Resistance members,' which means Adam didn't tell them who he is working for. I hope they didn't do anything to him!

"I don't understand what you're talking about. And I demand a lawyer to be present at my interrogation. I'm a member of SS, not some street criminal, and deserve a respectful treatment."

"A lawyer?" Reinhard laughed even harder. "We can certainly do that! And I'll tell you what, I'll get you the best one here. How about Doctor of Law Gruppenführer Kaltenbrunner, who was so upset about our recent confrontation? I would enjoy so much to see what he's going to do to you when he finds out that you were working with the Resistance all this time."

"Dr. Kaltenbrunner is in Vienna."

"Oh no, he's not. He was just having a meeting in this very building with Reichsführer Himmler, Obergruppenführer Heydrich and Gruppenführer Müller. I'm sure that he would love to pay twenty minutes of his time to such a pretty spy."

I shrugged.

"Very well. Go call him then. I'm sure that with him here we'll clarify everything in less than five minutes."

I just wanted Reinhard to leave the room so I could put the cyanide in my mouth.

"You still don't realize what you got yourself into, do you?" Reinhard leaned towards me. "I don't know if you're sleeping with him or not, but when he sees this, he'll personally strangle you."

"I'm not going to argue with you about anything until I see Gruppenführer Kaltenbrunner *or* my lawyer."

"Fine. You asked for it, Jew-girl."

As soon as Reinhard left the room, I quickly clicked off the hidden section of the cross and got the little white capsule out. I had only looked at it once before, when I was putting it inside. That little thing contained such a lethal dosage of cyanide that it would kill me within seconds if I crushed it between my teeth. My hand slightly shivered as I was carefully placing it between my gum and back teeth.

I touched my cheek, making sure that the capsule was invisible from the outside. Now if someone would hit me on the face from that side, I'd be dead. I chuckled: they had my fingerprints on the radio, and as Reinhard said it, I only had one way out of this jail – to the gallows. So did it really matter how exactly I'd die?

I put my cross back in order, took it off my wrist, clenched my hands around it and rested my forehead on my hands, silently saying prayers that I learned when I was a little girl. Those were the Christian prayers of course, unfortunately I didn't know how to pray in Hebrew. I wasn't praying to God to take me to heaven – Jews don't believe in Christian heaven, we believe in heaven on Earth, but for some reason all of us now lived in a Jewish hell. I was praying to God to keep Heinrich safe, to take care of my parents and to help Adam. Talking to somebody, even though this 'somebody' didn't answer to me directly, was comforting.

The noise behind my door made me straighten in my seat. I put my hands down on my knees and was waiting patiently for the door to open. But even though I tried to look as calm as I could, my heart was racing inside my chest. I wasn't surprised to see Reinhard come in, and even Dr. Kaltenbrunner following him with a stern face. But the third man, which closed the door behind himself, I expected to see the least. Chief of the Gestapo, Gruppenführer Heinrich Müller.

"She demands a lawyer," Reinhard smirked, nodding in my direction.

"A lawyer?" The Chief of the Gestapo didn't look intimidating at all, especially standing next to the almost seven feet tall leader of the Austrian SS; Heinrich Müller looked more like a kind grandpa who you used to love visiting during the summer. Only I knew very well that his appearance was more than deceiving. "She can have a lawyer. We're not some kind of barbarians here after all, right? Herr Gruppenführer, would you be so kind to represent this young lady over there?"

"I still have no idea what is going on," Dr. Kaltenbrunner replied without taking his eyes off me.

"Neither do I," I added firmly.

Meanwhile Müller moved the chair for Dr. Kaltenbrunner.

"Herr Gruppenführer, please, take a seat, while agent Reinhard here will explain to us both the details of this very interesting case. As I understand the young lady is being accused of espionage and high treason?"

"That's right, Herr Gruppenführer," Reinhard replied with visible pleasure. "She was working with the members of the Resistance, and taking into consideration her position of an *SS-Helferin* here in SD, she most likely shared a lot of classified information with her friends from the Underground."

"Those are empty allegations, nothing else. I never had any connections with the Underground."

"Give me that." Gruppenführer Kaltenbrunner roughly grabbed my file from Reinhard's hand, which made the latter make a little step back. I guess he still remembered how his last meeting with the leader of the Austrian SS ended. Only this time my former savior would most likely take his side instead of mine.

"And what's the story with the fingerprints?" Müller asked Reinhard, who finally regained control of his voice again.

"We found her fingerprints on the wireless radio that one of her 'friends' tried to get rid of. He's currently in custody and is being interrogated as well."

"He told you it was her radio?" Müller continued.

"No." Reinhard frowned. "He insists that it was some other woman who was helping him. But he's most likely lying. Our best agents are working with him now, soon he'll tell us everything."

"Frau Friedmann." This time Müller was addressing me. "How can you explain your fingerprints on the wireless device?"

"My fingerprints can't possibly be on the wireless device, Herr Gruppenführer. The only wireless devices that I've ever touched are within the walls of this very office and if no one stole the radio from here, than the possibility of my fingerprints being on some other device is zero."

"You certainly sound very confident about it, Frau Friedmann." Müller slightly smiled at me. "But what about those pictures that Dr. Kaltenbrunner is holding in his hands right now? Are those her fingerprints, Herr Gruppenführer?"

"Yes. They are partial, but still identifiable." He wasn't looking at Müller, he was looking at me, and his eyes were almost black now with hardly masked anger.

"They couldn't possibly be taken off the radio. I can swear my life on it." I desperately needed him to believe me. "I've never touched any other radios except for the official devices here in SD."

He looked at me a little longer before going back to the papers in the file.

"Well, what does it say?" Gruppenführer Müller looked over Dr. Kaltenbrunner shoulder with interest.

"She's right actually. The fingerprints were taken off the handle, not the radio itself. And a partial fingerprint on one of the locks. Someone either tried to wipe them off or they were already there before someone else started using it."

"Well, that changes everything, doesn't it?" I crossed my hands on my chest. The cyanide in my mouth had given me the confidence of someone who was about to die any minute soon and therefore wasn't afraid of anything anymore.

"And how exactly does it change everything?" Dr. Kaltenbrunner mirrored my pose, leaning back in his chair.

"I could have touched that suitcase anywhere. By accident."

Reinhard laughed and Gruppenführer Müller just smiled.

"You touch a lot of other people's suitcases on a regular basis?" Dr. Kaltenbrunner asked me again with obvious sarcasm.

"No, of course not. But you have to admit that it could have happened."

"This is ridiculous." Reinhard smirked. "She's just wasting our time. Let a couple of my guys work with her for an hour, she'll tell you everything."

"I don't remember asking your goddamn opinion!" Gruppenführer Kaltenbrunner yelled at obviously intimidated Reinhard. "Get the hell out of the room, you're annoying the crap out of me! God dammit!"

With those words he smashed his fist on the table with such force, that Reinhard decided to leave before the second hit would land on his face. Even I jerked in my seat, for the first time seeing Dr. Kaltenbrunner *this* angry. I was glad that he at least took his emotions out on an unanimated object instead of hitting me on the head, and I had a feeling that he was very close to it. I know I would be, if I suddenly found out that someone who I was basically risking my life for (and that's exactly what he was doing while planning Heydrich's assassination) was all this time lying to my face.

Even Gruppenführer Müller didn't feel too comfortable in the presence of this giant with such a volatile temper, and decided to step outside 'for a smoke.' Meanwhile Dr. Kaltenbrunner took a deep breath, obviously trying to take his emotions under control, and then looked at me again.

"Let's pretend for a second that there is such a miraculous possibility. Where could you have possibly touched the handle of the suitcase which by quite a wondrous coincidence belongs to the member of the Resistance?"

"I couldn't possibly remember it now. I need time to think about it."

"You have five minutes. Think."

I shuddered in the inside from the thought of what he was going to do after five minutes were up and covered my eyes with one hand. I couldn't concentrate under his stare.

Where could have I touched the suitcase? I couldn't just make some story up, it had to be a real occasion which could be proven by somebody. *Suitcases. Where were most of them normally found? Train stations. I took a lot of trains in the past several years, but I definitely didn't touch anything during my trips. Besides, it had to be within a certain time frame, because my fingerprints were still fresh on it. Lately I've only been going to Vienna to meet with Dr. Kaltenbrunner.* I could feel how his eyes were burning a hole through my head. *Oh God, he's going to kill me!*

Stop it. Concentrate. Vienna. Train. Train station. And suddenly it hit me. *Train!!! The train that almost got derailed and I helped a woman with her suitcase! Max was with me, he can confirm it! Yes!!!*

I lifted my head high, hardly concealing a smile.

"Herr Gruppenführer, I remembered."

I saw how he straightened a little in his chair and leaned towards me.

"I'm all attention, Frau Friedmann."

Before saying anything that could compromise us both I leaned closer to him over the table and whispered, "This conversation is not being recorded from the outside, is it?"

I knew that the Gestapo would sometimes record an interrogation with someone who they felt had important information, and then attach it to their file as reason for their execution.

Dr. Kaltenbrunner shrugged. It wasn't his Gestapo and he didn't know. I decided to speak as secretly as I could considering the situation.

"When I went to Vienna about a month, maybe two months ago, we had a little accident with the train. It almost got derailed as I was walking towards my coupe, and all the luggage fell from the top shelves. There was a woman with a baby there and I saw her struggling with her suitcase, so I decided to help her because she had her hands full. I tried to pick up her suitcase, but it was very heavy. And then Hauptsturmführer Max Stern, who also works here in *SD-Ausland*, he by accident was on the same train as me, he helped me with that suitcase. I remember it so well because it was very heavy, and I even jokingly asked her if she had rocks in it. She said it was her husband's books. She said he was a professor of philosophy. That's the only suitcase I've touched recently."

"What were you doing in Vienna?" he asked me slowly. I knew that he had to ask me that if the conversation was indeed being recorded. It would be suspicious if he didn't; so I had to be very careful with my response.

"I have a lover in Vienna. Please, don't tell my husband."

A slight grin finally touched the corners of his lips.

"I won't. What was your witness's name again? Max Stern?"

"Yes, Herr Gruppenführer."

He pressed the button under the desk, and one of the SS guards opened the door waiting for his orders.

"Call here Hauptsturmführer Max Stern. He works in *SD-Ausland*."

"*Jawohl*, Herr Gruppenführer!"

After the SS guard disappeared behind the door, Dr. Kaltenbrunner walked behind my back and started to get hair pins out of my braid, until it fell down to my waist. He checked for any other pins, then took the cross from my hands, undid my belt and checked my pockets.

"What are you doing?" I finally asked, very much confused by such odd behavior.

"If your story doesn't prove itself and we find you guilty, you won't be able to kill yourself before the real interrogation takes place. And take your stockings off, too. Some women strangle themselves with them."

Thank God he didn't check inside my mouth, I thought.

"I'm not going to kill myself. I'm not guilty of anything. How stupid would I be to try and wipe my fingerprints off the radio but then leave some on the suitcase?"

Judging by his look he was also thinking of this little dilemma, which was now doing me a big favor. I started to hope that maybe I'd be able to persuade him to my innocence after all. But Dr. Kaltenbrunner was a very hard nut to crack.

"Are you going to take off your stockings yourself or do you want me to do it?"

His smirk and steady gaze made me blush as I was undoing the clips holding my stockings under my skirt. Of course he didn't even think of turning away.

"And the garter belt, please."

"Are you serious?!"

"Absolutely." He grinned even wider. "You have no idea how inventive you, women, can be, trying to escape prosecution."

"Well, turn away at least."

"Unfortunately I can't." He was almost laughing at my embarrassment. "According to the rules I should be facing you. Or you can attack me from the back."

"*Me*? Attack *you*?" I couldn't believe my ears. He was definitely playing one of his sick games with me.

"Take it off." He made a move towards me. "Or I'll help you take it off."

"Alright!" I almost screamed jumping to my feet.

I was so glad that the official *SS-Helferin* uniform skirt was pretty long, and was allowing me to at least cover half of my legs while I was struggling with my garter belt under it. Finally I took it off and threw it into Gruppenführer's hands.

"Mm, still warm," he said, feeling it with his fingers.

"You're such a…" '*Dirty pervert,*' I thought, but decided not to finish the sentence, and just sat on my chair with my back to him. He laughed.

Finally the door opened and the SS guard let Max inside. Seeing me in the chair next to Gruppenführer Kaltenbrunner obviously astonished him. Dr. Kaltenbrunner meanwhile gave all my belongings to the guard and motioned him to close the door.

"Your name is Max Stern, right?"

"Yes, Herr Gruppenführer."

"Do you know this woman?"

"Yes, Herr Gruppenführer. Annalise and her husband are our good family friends."

"Our?"

"Mine and my wife's, Ursula."

"Did you take a trip with her to Vienna recently?"

"Yes, only... We didn't take a trip together. We accidentally saw each other on the train and separated as soon as we arrived. I had to deliver some documentation to the office in Vienna, and Annalise said she had some personal business to take care of. I offered her a lift, because I had a car with a driver waiting for me, but she said someone was picking her up."

That someone was Dr. Kaltenbrunner. He looked at me. *So far, so good.*

"And what happened inside the train?"

Max's brow furrowed.

"I don't understand what exactly you mean, Herr Gruppenführer."

"Something unusual happened? Something worth noticing?"

"Oh yes, our train almost got derailed as we were leaving Berlin. Someone forgot to change the railroad point, and the train had to make an emergency stop. That was it."

"What happened as soon as the train stopped? Second by second, please."

Max looked very confused by such a strange question, but nevertheless proceeded.

"Well, as soon as it stopped, all the passengers almost fell onto each other. We almost fell too. The luggage fell down, and I helped some passengers to get it back up. Then we went back to our coupe."

"Did Frau Friedmann touch any suitcases?"

"Yes, she actually did. She tried to help a woman with a baby to put her suitcase back up, but it was way too heavy for her to lift it above her head, so I helped her."

"What was in the suitcase?"

"I don't know, Herr Gruppenführer, I didn't ask her to open it. She said it was her husband's books."

"A woman travels with a suitcase full of her husband books and it doesn't cause your suspicion? You're an SD agent, for God's sake! You should open any heavy suitcases that seem suspicious!"

"I'm sorry, Herr Gruppenführer. I didn't think of it."

I held my breath for a second, trying not to smile. It looked like Dr. Kaltenbrunner started to believe me.

"One more thing: were you wearing gloves?"

"Umm, I'm not sure. I did have them with me... Oh, that's right, I was! I put them on right after I finished smoking on the platform."

Gruppenführer Kaltenbrunner's eyes sparkled.

"And Frau Friedmann? Was she wearing gloves?"

"No, she wasn't. I remember it so well because I made fun of her cross that she always wears on her wrist. I told her that her husband converted her into Catholicism faster than he would convert a Jew before *Kristallnacht*."

Dr. Kaltenbrunner chuckled at the racist joke. He was in a relatively good mood now.

"That'll be all, Hauptsturmführer Stern. Go back to work, you've been very helpful."

After giving a salute to Gruppenführer, Max looked indecisively in my direction.

"Is Annalise in some kind of trouble?"

"It's still difficult to say."

Max looked at me once again and left the room. I was left one on one with Gruppenführer Kaltenbrunner. I was waiting for him to speak first.

"Well, that was a good one, Frau Friedmann. A woman with the suspicious suitcase. Proven by an unrelated witness from SD. I don't know how you do it, but I must admit, I admire you."

"I'm innocent, that's all."

"Are you really?"

"I can't prove it beyond the point that I just did, Herr Gruppenführer."

"Oh, allow me to disagree with you. There's one very simple test that always makes even the most stubborn people tell the truth."

Everything tightened inside of me as he slowly got up from his chair, took his service dagger out and walked behind my back. I decided not to breathe just in case, frozen in my seat with sweaty palms resting on my knees and a rapidly beating heart. He leaned his tall body over me until his face was next to my shoulder and pressed the cold steel of the dagger to my neck.

"Let's try this again. Do you have anything to do with the Resistance?"

"No."

"I'm not convinced." He started to turn the dagger from the flat side to the sharper one, the edge of it slightly cutting into my skin. "Try again."

"I've already told you, no!"

Every word I pronounced was hurting because of the sharp metal pressing hard against my throat. He turned it a little more and I felt how a thin streak of blood started slowly moving down to my chest.

"Strike two, as our American friends say. Last chance, sugar."

I knew how it worked. During the first two times he would ask them, the interrogated people would keep to their version, but on the third time they would start speaking the truth. The chance that he could slit my throat was fifty-fifty, and I had to think of something that would make Gruppenführer Kaltenbrunner break the traditional pattern.

I turned my head to him and slightly pulled forward, looking him straight in the eye. His brow furrowed, but the steel of the dagger wasn't pressing too hard into my neck anymore. I leaned even closer to him, slowly raised my hand to the back of his neck and, terrified inside and hardly breathing, slightly touched his lips with mine. Dr. Kaltenbrunner didn't move. I moved a little closer almost cutting my own neck, and pressed my mouth harder to his, praying to God that he wouldn't push me away. He didn't. I held the back of his neck stronger, so he wouldn't feel that my hands were shaking. My heart was beating so loud that I could hear it even inside my head. I finally understood what the expression 'to walk on a sword's blade' meant: that's exactly what I was doing right now, with another, actual blade still across my neck. I closed my eyes and kissed him again, more persistently, desperately hoping inside that it would work.

Suddenly the leader of the Austrian SS grabbed me by my braid and pulled it down, making me bend my head backwards. He dropped his dagger on my knees and pressed his mouth hard against mine, making me open my lips and forcing his tongue inside. I didn't push him away, on the contrary, I was looking to meet his every move, even though his grip on my hair was very painful. My fingers brushed the dagger laying on my knees, but just for a second; I moved my hands to his neck and pulled him even closer.

He bit my lip to hurt me, but I kissed him again; he pulled my hair harder, but I just gently placed both of my hands on his face. He soon got tired of fighting me, meeting no resistance at all. He let go of my hair and was holding me by the back of my neck, not hard, just enough to keep my face close to him. He wasn't rough with me anymore, just still very insistent and hungry. I was finally giving him what he was so long waiting for, and he was readily taking it from me.

I started thinking that he would want to go all the way; after all how was I different from all the other women he had probably raped in these same Gestapo interrogation rooms? But surprisingly he stopped kissing me before I even had a chance to put up with my fate. He let go of my neck and picked up the dagger still laying untouched on my knees. I could have easily stabbed him with it, and he knew it. He grinned at me, very differently this time.

"Congratulations, Frau Friedmann. You passed your test."

Chapter 4

When Gruppenführer Müller came back to follow up on the course of the investigation, Dr. Kaltenbrunner surprised him by saying that he was sure of my innocence, and that the presence of my fingerprints on the suitcase with the radio was purely coincidental.

"The suitcase belongs to the woman who Frau Friedmann and another SD officer, Hauptsturmführer Max Stern, by chance saw on the train. I'm convinced that it was her, who your agents saw leaving the building, from which that man that you're currently interrogating was trying to transmit messages."

The Chief of our Gestapo was staring at the Chief of the Austrian Gestapo for some time, and then finally spoke again.

"I absolutely trust your professional opinion, Herr Gruppenführer, but in a case like this it would be better if the *suspect* had some kind of an alibi, if you know what I mean. After all, *her* fingerprints are on the suitcase."

Gruppenführer Kaltenbrunner frowned.

"Well, let's see if she does. What timeframe are we talking about?"

"Last Sunday afternoon."

They both turned to me. For a second I didn't know what I should say: I could have said that I was having tea with my friends after the mass (and if asked, I knew that they would have confirmed it), but at the same time I had big doubts if I should drag them into this at all.

"Frau Friedmann?" Dr. Kaltenbrunner asked impatiently. Less than anything I wanted to see him angry again.

"I was with my husband and friends all afternoon. We were having tea by their house after the Sunday mass. They go to the same church as we do."

"Can we have your friends' names, address and phone number, if they have one?" Gruppenführer Müller asked.

"Yes, of course. Rudolf and Ingrid von Werner, they live in a townhouse on Blumenstrasse, right next to the bank, Rudolf works there. I don't remember the number of their house unfortunately, but you can ask my husband, he has a better memory than I do." I tried to smile at them. "I'm sorry, I don't remember their phone number either."

"Don't worry about it, we'll find them." Heinrich Müller smiled back at me. I was sure that they would, and very soon.

"How's the interrogation of the radio operator going?" Dr. Kaltenbrunner asked his colleague in the meantime.

"Not so well." Müller cringed a little. "Looks like the boy is pretty determined to take all his secrets to the grave. Keeps denying that he knows the woman who gave him the suitcase, insists that he doesn't know the code for the messages, doesn't say who his connection is... Our agents tried almost everything already, but the answer is still the same."

"That's a shame." Dr. Kaltenbrunner concluded.

"Maybe you could talk to him?" Müller suggested with a smile. "I've heard that you are pretty good at getting information out of even the most hopeless ones."

Gruppenführer Kaltenbrunner chuckled. "Maybe I could."

"What shall we do to the girl?"

"Nothing. Leave her here till you confirm her alibi, which I'm sure will be no problem at all, and then all you have to do is to let her go and apologize for the inconvenience."

They both looked at me again. I was thinking about Adam and what they had been possibly doing to him for the past two days.

"Alright." Gruppenführer Müller finally nodded. "Let's go pay a visit to the boy then."

They left me alone. I put my both hands on the table and rested my forehead on them. It looked like I got myself and people around me in such big trouble, and I had no idea how we all would get out of it.

They were gone for so long that I fell asleep. I woke up at the sound of the door opening, but instead of the two generals an SS guard walked in with a little tray with food and water on it, put it on the table in front of me and left. I was very much surprised by such a gesture, but still didn't touch the food: first of all, chewing on a sandwich with cyanide in your mouth is a pretty dangerous thing to do, and second, nerves completely killed my appetite, and I wouldn't be able to stuff anything in my mouth even if I wanted to. The mug of water on the contrary I drank with gratitude.

Before an SS guard could pick up the tray, Gruppenführer Kaltenbrunner came back with wide smile on his face.

"Frau Friedmann, I'm very glad to inform you that all the charges against you have been dropped."

I straightened in my chair. So Rudolf and Ingrid did confirm my alibi. *How mad Ingrid must be that I even mentioned their name! She'll definitely let me have it when I see her next time.*

"So... can I go now?"

"No."

"No?"

"No." He was leaning on the door with his hands crossed on his chest and still smiling at me. For some reason I didn't like that smile of his. "I have some other plans for you."

Whatever it was, it didn't sound too good. I started to get nervous again.

"What plans, Herr Gruppenführer?"

"I need your professional services as a stenographer, if it's not too much trouble."

Stenographer? What the hell is he talking about?

"Sure… What do I have to write down?"

"An interrogation."

I was looking at him with my eyes wide open.

"You're not actually suggesting that I will be in the same room while you…"

He smirked.

"While I'm what? Will be torturing that guy? What kind of a sick person do you think I am? I'm not going to torture anybody. We'll just talk."

"But why me? You can have any stenographer from Amt IV, they specialize in that. I would really rather not do it."

"I'm afraid you don't have a choice, Frau Friedmann. You see, while Gruppenführer Müller was giving me the personal profile information on our radio guy, a very interesting fact surfaced." He paused for a second looking me straight in the eye. "He knows you."

"He knows me?" I asked carefully, still not sure of what he was leading toward with that comment.

"Yes," Dr. Kaltenbrunner answered not without pleasure. "I have a very good memory. You have to have a good memory if you're a lawyer, you know? So when Herr Müller told me that boy's name, I thought to myself, 'Wait, I've heard it somewhere before.' But when I read his previous employment history from the file, all the pieces of the puzzle finally came together."

"I'm not sure I understand, Herr Gruppenführer."

"His name is Adam Kramer. Sounds familiar?"

So Gruppenführer Kaltenbrunner knew who Adam was. The question remained if he knew about our current and very illegal affairs.

"That was the name of my former dancing partner. But he emigrated to the United States four years ago. How can he be in Berlin?"

"I guess he came back."

"But why?"

"I have a theory why, but whether I'm right or wrong we're going to find out very soon. Let's go."

51

As I was following Dr. Kaltenbrunner through the labyrinth of hallways, I was trembling inside at the thought of what they could have already done to poor Adam. But when we approached the room the door to which an SS guard started to open, I all of a sudden couldn't make another step and just stood in front of it, till Gruppenführer Kaltenbrunner had to take me by my elbow and almost drag me inside.

I understood why we had to go so far: my interrogation room was in fact a pre-interrogation room, where only the questioning took place. This one was designed for getting every single word out of a suspect, and all the instruments on the side table looked terrifying enough for anybody to start speaking even prior to his executors using them. I still had no idea how my brave Adam managed to keep quiet for so long. I finally found the strength to lift up my eyes to his motionless figure in the corner of the room, sitting handcuffed to the chair with his head hanging low. I couldn't see his face, but his white shirt was soaked in blood. I looked away again, trying my best not to start crying. I didn't remember being so scared in my life before.

"Hey! Jew-boy! Wake up! You have a visitor." Gruppenführer Kaltenbrunner called out Adam.

Adam didn't move. He was so still that for a second I thought that he was dead. But Dr. Kaltenbrunner obviously thought differently: he picked up a glass of water from the table that the interrogators most likely kept for themselves, made two steps towards Adam and splashed its contents into his face. Adam jerked his head and finally looked up; I wished that he didn't. I covered my mouth at the ugly sight of what those Gestapo bastards did to him: one of his eyes was almost completely closed, his nose was definitely broken and still bleeding, his lips were split in several places and the rest of his face was covered in hematomas and bruises.

My poor boy, my poor Adam, what did they do to you? Why did they have to catch you? I have just lost my brother, now I'm going to lose you as well?

"Hey!" Gruppenführer Kaltenbrunner snapped his fingers in front of Adam's eyes, making him focus his gaze. "Do you recognize her? Don't look at me, look at the girl. Do you know her, yes or know?"

Adam slowly shifted his eyes from the tall Austrian in front of him to me and the horror reflected on his face; he obviously didn't know that they were interrogating me as well, or thought that they hadn't started yet. I was standing behind Dr. Kaltenbrunner and he couldn't see me, so I silently nodded at Adam, hoping that he would get my hint. He did.

"Yes. We used to dance in the same company several years ago." He pronounced in a raspy voice. I suddenly realized that the water was yet another means of torture for the heartless Gestapo agents: they wouldn't let inmates drink on purpose, and leave the glass full of water on the table right in front of their eyes but out of their reach in the hope that it would break them.

"And what happened then?"

"Then I had to leave the country."

"And why did you come back?"

"I wanted to help the ones who stayed."

"Bullshit."

Adam looked at Gruppenführer Kaltenbrunner with confusion, and so did I. Meanwhile he pulled up a chair for me at the table across from which Adam was sitting and nudged me to it.

"Have a seat, Frau Friedmann. Here's a notepad and a pencil, and in the course of interrogation I'll tell you what I want you to write down."

Concern on Adam's face quickly changed to disbelief.

"What is she doing here? She's not going to stay to see all this, is she?"

"She is here to help me." Dr. Kaltenbrunner sat on another chair not far from me and put his long legs in shining black boots on the table. "And she will stay until you tell me everything I want to know."

"Please... don't do it in front of her," Adam begged quietly.

"Do what?" Gruppenführer Kaltenbrunner smiled at him. "Do you think I'm going to beat you up? How about this: I'm not going to touch a hair on your head and you'll still tell me who you're working for and with. How does that sound?"

Hard to believe, I thought, *that's how it sounds*. It seemed like Adam thought the same and frowned.

"You're thinking how it is possible, aren't you? You see, I'm very good at this. The interrogation process, I mean. And I know that sometimes all you need is to find one soft spot that will make people talk like it's their last confession. Sometimes it's the physical spot; but sometimes it's an emotional one. And I think I found yours."

With those words Dr. Kaltenbrunner took his gun out, aimed at my forehead and took the safety off. I froze in my place afraid to move, but Adam pulled forward in his chair as far as his handcuffs allowed.

"No, don't!"

"Aha. I guess I was right, wasn't I?" The leader of the Austrian SS laughed and put the gun back into the holster. "Don't worry, Jew-boy, I wouldn't shoot her. She's my very good friend, and if something happened to her, I would get very upset."

53

Right, I thought. *You would. It's the second time that you're putting a lethal weapon to my head today, and for some reason this fact makes me really doubt that last statement of yours!*

"But you just showed me, even though unwillingly, that if something happened to her, you would get very upset too. Am I right?"

He was looking at Adam without blinking, and I suddenly didn't like where he was going with this. Adam kept silent, so Dr. Kaltenbrunner got up from his chair and walked behind my back.

"I think I know the real reason why you came back to Germany. Do you want me to share my suggestion with you?" Gruppenführer Kaltenbrunner addressed Adam. Adam didn't reply, so he continued. "I think you came back because of her."

He put his hands on my shoulders. Adam frowned.

"I think you came back because you couldn't stay away from her. All the national pride of yours and the desire to help your people, I don't buy it. She is the main reason why you're here." He slightly squeezed my shoulders and pulled me to the back of the chair. "As a matter of fact, I think you're in love with her."

Adam swallowed hard but didn't say anything.

"You don't have to say anything, I'm a very good psychologist and can read people very well. That's why I'm the Chief of the Gestapo, I guess." Gruppenführer laughed. "And you know what, I don't blame you. She's a very, very beautiful girl. How can you not be in love with her?"

He lowered his hands to my uniform jacket and unbuttoned it.

"But do you know what your biggest problem is?" Adam frowned even more as Dr. Kaltenbrunner took the jacket off me and undid several buttons on my shirt. "You're a Jew. And she's Aryan. You can't have her. It's against the law."

The leader of the Austrian SS put his chin down on my shoulder pressing his cheek next to mine, hugged my waist with both hands and smiled at Adam. "But I can."

I finally realized what he was doing, and how exactly he was planning to make Adam speak: he was going to use me as bait. I could only hope that Adam would keep quiet.

"I can understand your feelings. You saw her every day at work, you spoke to her, you were even able to touch her during the dancing. But I bet you never touched her like this."

Gruppenführer Kaltenbrunner moved one hand from my waist to my chest and slid it under my shirt, firmly pressing my breast through my bra. Adam almost jumped in his chair in indignation.

"What are you doing?! Stop touching her!!!"

"You can make me stop." Gruppenführer Kaltenbrunner smiled at Adam, his fingers still caressing my breast and playing with my nipple until it got hard under

54

his touch. "Just tell me where the code book is and who supplies you with information."

"I've already told your people that there is no code book. I already get those messages coded."

"Alright. Who codes them then?"

Adam didn't say anything.

"No? Fine. I have all the time in the world and I'll be enjoying every minute of it. And so will Frau Friedmann here."

This time under Adam's terrified stare he moved his hand inside my bra. I inhaled sharply and tried to close my eyes in my humiliation, but now it was just the sensation of his warm fingers on my bare skin, his heavy head on my shoulder and the other hand still pressing against my stomach. I decided it would be better to keep my eyes open.

"Stop doing that!!!"

"Why? She likes it."

"No, she doesn't!"

"Of course she does. Her heart is beating so fast now."

"It's because she's scared!"

"No, she's not scared. She's excited. She wants me to do it."

"No, she doesn't! Get your dirty hands off her!!!"

"I will, as soon as you tell me who codes your messages and where they're getting the information from."

Adam looked at me in desperation. This time with Gruppenführer Kaltenbrunner's face right next to mine I couldn't shake my head or give Adam any other sign, so I just pursed my lips and frowned the best I could, silently begging him to keep quiet. For the rare exceptions when Rudolf did it, my husband coded almost all of them. Adam sighed and lowered his head, but didn't say anything.

"Still no?" Gruppenführer Kaltenbrunner raised his eyebrow at Adam. "Very well."

He took his hand out of my bra, and with a sinister smile put both palms on my knees, forcing them apart. Adam shifted in his chair, looking at the leader of the Austrian SS in disbelief. I clenched onto both sides of my chair, desperately hoping that it was just a psychological trick and he wouldn't actually do anything to me. He slowly picked up my skirt to my mid-thighs and started stroking my legs, still resting his head on my shoulder.

"She has beautiful legs, right, Jew-boy? Only ballerinas have legs like that. Look how shapely they are, how long, how perfect. The real embodiment of the Reich's idea of Body Beautiful, don't you think? But I still don't understand what you were hoping for. Did you really think that you would come back to Berlin on the white horse, defeat the Nazi regime singlehandedly, save the princess over here and live with her happily ever after?" Gruppenführer Kaltenbrunner was still caressing my bare legs with his fingertips, slowly moving his hands higher and higher, my skirt moving along with them. "You were hoping that one day she'll become yours, weren't you? You were going to sleep every night dreaming how one day you would be able to do what I'm doing right now. Never going to happen, Jew-boy. But I'll do you one favor though: I'll tell you exactly how it feels."

Watching Adam's expression closely, he unhurriedly slid his hand under my skirt, moving it along the inside of my thigh higher and higher. I pressed myself inside the chair holding my breath. He was not actually going to do *that*. Adam was breathing heavily, looking at the grinning Austrian in desperation and anger. The latter stopped his hand within an inch from my underwear.

"One last time I'm asking you, who's coding your messages?"

"Please, don't do that," Adam hardly whispered, already knowing that all the pleading would be in vain.

"Don't make me do it. Who's your connection?"

"I don't know him…" Adam finally breathed out with a pained expression on his face.

"Wrong answer."

He put his hand between my legs and moved his fingers up and down, pressing them firmly against the silk of my panties. I closed my eyes again; I couldn't stand to see Adam's face. I never felt more exposed and embarrassed at the same time. And now the leader of the Austrian SS put his other hand inside my bra again, squeezing my breast, caressing my nipple with his thumb, pressing his cheek closer to my face and his leg closer to my hip. I heard Adam struggle against his handcuffs, desperately trying to release himself.

"Stop that, you son of a bitch!!! I'll kill you!!!"

"No, you won't." Gruppenführer Kaltenbrunner laughed. "There's nothing you can do, except watch me do whatever I want to the girl you're in love with. How does it feel, huh? Seeing some other man touch her where you could only dream of touching her?"

"She has nothing to do with all this, let her go!"

"I'm not the one who's holding her here, Jew-boy. She could have long been home with her loving husband if you weren't so stubborn. And now, if you don't start cooperating, I'll fuck her right here on this table, right in front of you."

"You won't dare!"

"Oh yeah? You clearly don't know me."

I did. I knew him very well.

"Frau Friedmann likes silk underwear," he continued. With my eyes still closed his voice sounded so loud in my head, his aftershave lingering on my skin where he was brushing me with his cheek, and his hands everywhere on my body, so gentle and so ruthless at the same time. "I like it too. I like how it feels when I touch her through it. But do you know what I like more, Jew-boy? No underwear at all."

I involuntarily jerked when Gruppenführer Kaltenbrunner moved my panties to one side and put his hand on me, not a single obstacle on his way anymore, just his fingers on my skin. I could feel how much it excited him, because he started breathing faster now, pressing himself even harder to me, touching me more persistently.

"She's so goddamn fine, you couldn't even imagine something like this in your wildest dreams, Jew-boy! So warm, so tender... so wet already." I could almost hear him grin wider as he said that. I hated him, hated that he had the insolence to do something like that in front of another man, hated how he was playing me with his fingers, moving them in slow circles around the most sensitive spot on my body, and hated myself because it started to feel so good. "You know what, don't tell me anything, I don't want anything from you anymore. I just want to fuck her."

I gasped as the leader of the Austrian SS slid two fingers inside of me. "Oh yes, I'll definitely fuck her. I swear, Jew-boy, she's worth all of your secrets."

"You'll go before the tribunal, you dirty dog!" Adam said very quietly, with unmasked hatred in his voice. I could tell that he was almost broken at this point.

"Most likely. But I'll die a happy man!"

He was laughing. I heard Adam swallow hard. And there was nothing I could do. Absolutely nothing.

"Josef. His name is Josef. He's the leader of the Resistance here in Berlin. He codes my messages. The woman who delivered me the radio was one of his agents, I don't know who she is, but he does."

I opened my eyes wide in awe. Trying to help me, he sold the wrong man, the man who used to work closely with my father when the latter was still a lawyer before he had to move to Switzerland, and was helping Josef to falsify all kinds of documents for the Underground movement. The Gestapo's close surveillance on that very Josef was the reason why my parents had to leave the country so hastily, because if the Gestapo would have gotten him, all my family would be in imminent danger. I told Adam about Josef and that if he happened to come across him, he should stay away from the leader of the Berlin Resistance for the same reason, but didn't say anything about my father. And now that little mistake might cost Papa his life.

Dr. Kaltenbrunner finally let go of me and straightened up next to my chair.

"It wasn't that hard, was it? You told me everything, and I hadn't touched a hair on your head, just like I said I would. I'm a little disappointed though that you destroyed my plans for the evening with my pretty Frau Friedmann, but a deal is a deal, and I'll let her go. You'll stay here of course and will tell the agents who'll proceed with your interrogation all the details. I'm not going to say that I'll see you in the future, because most likely I won't. Unless they decide to send you to Mauthausen."

Gruppenführer Kaltenbrunner laughed again and pressed the button under the desk so the guards would open the door. Already at the door, while Dr. Kaltenbrunner was talking to one of the agents waiting outside, I turned around and mouthed 'I'm sorry' at Adam; he just shook his head with tears in his eyes, as if saying that it was him who was sorry. I was ready to burst into tears myself: my poor Adam had no idea what he had done, even though unintentionally. *I just buried my brother, and now my parents' life was hanging by a thread. As soon as Adam identifies Josef by the picture, the Gestapo will start a massive manhunt and then it'll be all over with.* I started shivering walking behind Gruppenführer Kaltenbrunner out of the jail. As the last door was locked behind us, I started walking fast towards the exit of the building, further from all of them, out to the street. He caught me by my forearm and turned me towards him.

"Where are you going alone? It's night out, I'll drive you home."

I yanked my hand out of his with a force I never suspected I was capable of.

"Don't you dare ever touch me again, you dirty bastard!!!"

He was visibly confused at such an outburst from my side, but it wasn't enough for me to yell at him. I pushed him in the chest with both hands, already crying. *He threatened me, he humiliated me, he made Adam talk, he will make them arrest Josef and Josef will tell them everything about my father, and they will get him too.* I pushed him again and again; he didn't even try to stop me and was just standing there, blinking at me.

"I'm sorry," he finally said, clearly uncomfortable with me crying in front of him, finally realizing what he had done. "I shouldn't have—"

"I hate you!!!" I screamed at his face almost at the top of my lungs; I didn't care that the RSHA workers could hear me yell. He stepped away as if I slapped him.

"I'm very sorry..." he whispered again. I turned around and ran out of there, right into the cold May night.

Chapter 5

I walked all the way home even though the building of the RSHA was quite far from my house. I think it was even raining out, but I'm not sure. I was too deep in my thoughts to care about things like rain or cold. Halfway home I finally stopped crying and instead started thinking what could possibly be done now to prevent Josef from being caught. But nothing was coming to my mind.

I never picked up my belongings or my bag from the office, and now I had to knock on my own door. Heinrich wasn't sleeping of course; hearing his hurried steps in the hallway, I figured that he was waiting for me in the living room – close both to the door and to the phone. I guess Max had told him that I had been arrested.

My husband's look said it all as soon as he opened the door: I must have looked like a complete mess in wet clothes, with running mascara and loose hair stuck to my face.

"Oh my God, Annalise, are you alright?" He gently picked up my face with both hands, obviously looking for any marks on it. "Did they hurt you?"

"No, they didn't, I'm fine." I tiredly wrapped my hands around his waist and rested my head on his shoulder. I suddenly felt so extremely exhausted that all I could think of was going to sleep. "Take me to bed please, I can't walk anymore."

Heinrich effortlessly picked me up and carried me upstairs, not asking anything. He knew what the Gestapo did to people, if not physically, then emotionally for sure, and decided to let me rest first. Less than anything I wanted another interrogation, and I was glad that he understood that. Instead of talking, he just took my wet clothes off and covered me with the blanket. Almost half-asleep, I took the cyanide out of my mouth before I completely forgot about it and accidentally swallowed it in my sleep, and gave it to Heinrich.

"Here, take this too. I didn't have to use it this time."

Right after I fell into a deep sleep without any dreams.

I woke up with a start and saw that it was still dark out. I stretched my hand out to Heinrich's side, but the bed was made up where he was supposed to be sleeping. I quickly sat in bed, feeling anxiety taking over again. It all came back at once: the Gestapo, Adam, Gruppenführer Kaltenbrunner, Josef, my father. I rubbed my eyes with a moan; deep inside I was hoping that I dreamed it all.

"Sweetheart? Are you awake?"

I turned to the direction of Heinrich's voice and saw him sitting in a chair next to the fireplace.

"What are you doing over there?"

"I couldn't sleep. And besides I wanted to be up when you'd wake up. Do you want me to get you something?"

"Yes. An aspirin, a glass of whiskey and a gun loaded with one bullet."

Heinrich chuckled.

"Let me bring you the first two things, and then we'll talk about the gun and who you intend to shoot."

It took me two glasses to tell him everything that happened since two Gestapo agents stopped in front of my office table. Well, almost everything. For some reason I decided that it was a bad idea to tell him about kissing the leader of the Austrian SS and especially how he almost had his way with me right in front of Adam. Even though my husband was not a hot headed man (no spy can be, if he wants to survive for at least some time), he was still very protective of me and could easily go and shoot the man who dared to offend his wife in such a despicable manner. And then I would have most likely become a widow.

"Unfortunately there's nothing we can do for Adam at this point, but we'll try to get him out as soon as they decide which camp they will send him to. Right now we need to find this Josef before the Gestapo does," Heinrich concluded after I finished talking. "Ingrid and Rudolf can get your parents out of Switzerland through their people, but it'll take too much time that we don't have."

"How can we possibly get him before the Gestapo?"

"We have one big advantage: we have a lot of friends on the other side, who will gladly tell us where to find him. I seriously doubt that they will be as cooperative with the Gestapo as they will with us. But we mustn't waste any time: if we want to get him to him first, we have to do it now."

"In the middle of the night?"

"Night is the spy's best friend." Heinrich winked at me. "Get dressed in something dark and let's go."

Fifteen minutes later we were already driving on the empty streets of Berlin. Heinrich wasn't wearing his uniform this time, but still had his gun in his pocket.

"So what's the plan?" I asked him. "How exactly are we going to get Josef?"

"One of my connections that works both with us and the Underground might know where to find him. Or he might know someone who knows where to find him. We'll take it from there."

"And when we find him? Do you think he'll come with us? What if he refuses?"

"He doesn't have a choice. He'll have to come with us."

"Where are we going to hide him though? I mean before you get him out of the country."

"We aren't going to hide him. Too dangerous."

"I don't understand…"

"We won't have time to get him out of the country. No time and no resources, taking into consideration that the Gestapo have probably already made him number one on their most wanted list." Heinrich turned to me and looked me straight in the eye. "We'll have to kill him."

"What?" I honestly thought that I misheard what my husband just said.

"That's the only option we have."

"No! Heinrich, that's not right! You can't kill a man just like that!"

"Do you want your parents and Adam alive?"

"Yes," I finally replied.

Heinrich suddenly chuckled. "I'm surprised that you're so sensitive all of a sudden. Wasn't it you who asked Kaltenbrunner to organize Heydrich's assassination just a couple of months ago?"

"It's different." I frowned at him. "Heydrich deserves to die. And besides, I'm not the one who will have to physically do it."

"You won't have to. I'll do it."

There he was, another man ready to kill for me. The memories of the first one touching me everywhere in the most inappropriate way earlier that night were still fresh in my mind, and I shook my head trying to get rid of them. It was my own fault; both Heinrich and my late brother were trying to warn me about the true nature of that man, but I refused to listen. I sincerely hoped that Dr. Kaltenbrunner was the nice Dr. Jekyll, but he turned out to be the evil Mr. Hyde.

Lost in my thoughts I didn't even notice how we pulled up at one of the buildings until Heinrich opened my door and offered me a hand to help me out of the car.

"Are you sleeping with your eyes open?" He smiled at my confused look.

"No, I was just thinking."

"About what?"

"About how lucky I am to have a husband like you."

"You can express your gratitude when we get home." He grinned at me. "But now let's solve our little problem first."

He motioned me to follow him inside the dark hallway of the building. On the fourth floor my husband stopped by one of the apartments and knocked on the door using a certain pattern. It opened surprisingly fast, and an unshaved man with messy hair stuck his head through the opening. We obviously woke him up.

"Hello, Schtolz."

"Has something happened, sir?" The man immediately let us in and closed the door behind so no neighbors could overhear our conversation.

"Yes, something did happen. We need to find Josef and find him fast. Can you help us with his whereabouts?"

"Josef? Josef who?"

"The Underground leader Josef. Do you know where we can find him or no? We don't have much time."

The man slowly shook his head with a pensive look.

"I'm not sure, sir. I deal with some people from his circle, but never with him. Maybe you should ask Mark?"

"Who's Mark?"

"Mark the Bulldog, the one with the funny face, who used to help the Jews with passports."

"I've never met him directly, but I think my wife did."

I nodded. I didn't know his name back then, but I knew who they were talking about very well; at the very beginning of the war, when the repressions against the German Jews only started gaining their full force, I used to deliver him passports secretly stamped by Heinrich in his office, which allowed their Jewish owners to freely cross the border with Switzerland and escape an arrest or even forced deportation to the labor camps.

"He's the one who lives in the former Jewish area, right? Next to the market?" I asked just to make sure.

"Yes, that's him. He still lives there and might know where to find your friend Josef. He helps him with 'U-boats' now."

'U-boats' or Jews in hiding with fake papers were probably the only ones who were left in Berlin now. Underground people were helping them with getting those fake papers (exactly what my father used to do using his position as a lawyer), getting job placements that didn't require thorough papers checking, and sometimes providing housing or food. The jobs that didn't require paper checking were obviously not the top paid ones, and most of the families were struggling.

Heinrich shook the man's hand and opened the door for me.

"Thank you, Schtolz. You helped us a lot. Of course in case if anybody asks…"

"You were never here, sir. I know."

Heinrich smiled at his 'connection.'

"You're a good man, Schtolz."

"Good luck, sir. Frau."

I nodded at him and followed my husband out of the building and into our car. As soon as we got inside, he pressed the accelerator and we started making our way to the former Jewish area, hoping that Mark would be more helpful than Schtolz.

Mark was quite surprised to say the least to see us on his doorstep in the middle of the night, but nevertheless confirmed that he did know Josef personally and dealt with him on a regular basis, however, Josef's current address was unknown to him.

"You have to understand, he's the Resistance leader and he doesn't really list his name in the address book. I actually think he constantly moves from one place to another to avoid being captured."

"When is the next time you're supposed to see him?" Heinrich asked.

"Next week, around Wednesday. He lets me know through his men when and where."

Heinrich shook his head.

"Too long. They will definitely get him by then. Does he have any relatives who he might stay with?"

"Not that I know of."

"Close friends? A girlfriend, maybe?"

Mark finally nodded.

"He does have a girlfriend, she delivers me messages from him sometimes, and she's a member of the Resistance herself. Her name is Rebekah, and she lives somewhere around here as well, I see her at the market quite often."

"You don't know her exact address? A house or an apartment building at least?"

"No, sir, I'm sorry. I would have told you if I did."

"But you must have an emergency way of contacting him, don't you? If something suddenly goes down, you should have a way to get to him."

"Not really, sir. You should know better than the others how that goddamn Gestapo loves to kidnap people, pose as them and trick the others into revealing themselves. No, sir, Josef is smart in that sense, he only tells me where and when we're meeting. I have no means by calling him out. I'm sorry, but that's all I can help you with."

Heinrich remained silent for a moment, staring at the floor with a thoughtful look on his face, and then extended his hand to Mark.

"Alright. Well, thank you, Mark, it's still something."

"I'm sorry, sir."

After he closed the door behind us and we got back into the car, I looked at my husband.

"Now what?"

Heinrich shrugged.

"We can try a couple more of my people, but I'm starting to think that the result will be the same. Our Josef is definitely not stupid, I guess that's how he was able to stay alive for so long. That girlfriend of his, Rebekah, she's our main clue. If we find her, we'll find him."

"But how can we find her?"

"That's exactly what I'm trying to figure out now."

We both went quiet. I had no idea how to track people down, and was just desperately hoping that my husband would come up with something good. After all, that was a part of his profession. The worst part was that there was only two of us and a whole bunch of Gestapo agents against us. Time was quickly running out. Speaking of the Gestapo...

For a second I was blinded by the lights of a car unhurriedly approaching ours from the back. Heinrich lowered my head to the seat and covered me with his body as the black car passed us by and proceeded around the corner. Heinrich and I exchanged looks.

"Do you think...?"

"Yes." He nodded at me. "I think our friends know where to find Rebekah. Let's follow them."

Unnoticed by the Secret Police, we got out of the car and walked in the direction in which their car disappeared. We couldn't see it yet, but heard the noise of the motor running somewhere far in the distance. Trying to stay as close to the walls of the nearby buildings, we were slowly approaching the house by which they parked their car. Finally Heinrich motioned me to stop, and pressed me even closer to the wall behind his back.

"Stay here, I'll try to see what our colleagues from Amt IV are up to."

"Be careful!" I whispered back at him, and watched him disappear around the corner.

In less than a minute he came back, and motioned me to follow him.

"Don't make a sound and keep your head low, we'll hide behind that tree over there, see it?"

"Yes."

We quickly made it to the tree, the thick base of which happened to be the perfect hiding place to spy on the Gestapo. I chuckled at the thought: we were actually spying on the Secret Police, whose job was to spy on everybody in the Reich. Heinrich turned around and shushed me.

"Sorry. It's the nerves," I explained. He just shook his head at me.

Completely covered by the darkness of the moonless night, we crouched in our hiding spot and watched the two men leaving the private house. The third, who was smoking outside the whole time, finished his cigarette and got behind the wheel. In less than a minute they were gone.

"Why haven't they arrested her? Aren't they supposed to take her in for interrogation?" I whispered at Heinrich.

"I don't know. Maybe it's not her house. Or she isn't at home."

"What shall we do now?"

"Well, they're gone, so let's try and ask the owners of the house what did the Gestapo want from them."

Still staying as much in the shadow as possible, we quietly approached the private house and knocked on the door. An older man opened it and looked at us in surprise.

"Yes?"

"Hello." Heinrich smiled at him. "Can we come in for a second?"

"Who are you?"

My husband didn't wait for the man's permission and basically pushed him aside with his body, pulled me inside and closed the door behind us.

"We don't want those *other* people see us talk, do we?" He raised his eyebrow at the owner of the house.

"What other people?" The old man sounded a little unsure.

"You don't have to pretend with me. I'm on your side. Mark told us that Rebekah lives somewhere around here. You wouldn't be the one by chance to know her, would you?"

The owner of the house eyed Heinrich for a moment, then shifted his eyes to me and back to Heinrich.

"Who are you two?"

"We aren't from the Gestapo, and that's all you need to know. Rebekah's boyfriend Josef is in big danger as you probably figured out by now, and we need to find her to help him out."

Seeing that the man still wasn't convinced, but definitely knew something, I decided to step in.

"Please, sir, tell us where to find them. I'm Jewish myself, my father used to work closely with Josef before both my parents had to leave the country because of those Gestapo bastards. Please, help us help him before it's too late!"

The shade of uncertainty on the man's face became slighter.

"You know Josef?"

"Yes, I saw him by my father's house when he was picking up papers from him. He'll recognize me when he sees me. Please, just tell us where to find him."

The old man finally smiled. "They searched the house, the Gestapo. They knew that my daughter lives here with me, but I told them that she is currently in Poland with her relatives. You see, I'm a German myself, so they don't bother me too much. But my wife was Jewish and they killed her during the *Kristallnacht*. My daughter joined the Resistance right after. That's how she met Josef. Wait here, please. I'll bring her up from the basement."

"They didn't search the basement?"

"Of course they did. They always do. But they never find my hiding spot."

The owner of the house winked at us from under his bushy eyebrows and left us alone in the hallway. In less than a minute he came back with a young full figured girl who resembled him greatly, minus the beard of course. I couldn't help but notice that she was holding something behind her back, probably some kind of a weapon. She frowned at us.

"Who are you and what do you need Josef for?"

"I know Josef personally," I answered before Heinrich. I thought that the girl would be more inclined to trust another girl more than a man. "My father used to help him with getting different kinds of papers when he was a lawyer, but he had to leave the country soon after. We know that the Gestapo is looking for Josef and we're trying to find him before they can. We want to help him escape."

Those last words of mine almost got stuck in my throat. I was lying to the face of that girl just because I wanted to help my parents and Adam, because I wanted to save people dear to me. Only now that I met Rebekah face to face, I realized that Josef was a man dear to her, and I was going to get him killed; take away the man she loved to let the two men I loved live. Was that fair? Not at all. I felt absolutely horrible under her hopeful stare.

"He won't run. Not at least for a long time." Rebekah finally shook her head. "He's a fighter, not a coward. There's no way he'll leave the country."

I could hear pride in her voice when she said that. My father wasn't a coward either; I was. I made both him and Mama go to Switzerland because I was afraid for their lives.

"Maybe he'll just hide away till they lose his track?" Heinrich suggested. "Wait out for several weeks and then go back to his work if he wants to."

"But why do you want to help him anyway? Why do you care so much what happens to him?"

I felt my heart skip a beat when she asked us that. Another pinch of shame made me lower my eyes to the floor. My husband, however, was a much better liar than I.

"If the Gestapo gets Josef, the Resistance will be basically beheaded. You understand that he is the only one who ties all those different people into one big net, and without him we'll all be no better than just a bunch of stranded blind kittens." He was not just a good liar, but a great psychologist. "We want to help him help the others to stay in this fight. That's why we care. We care for the sake of Germany."

Rebekah finally nodded.

"Do you know the old church around the corner from the market?"

"Yes," we both answered at the same time.

"Go over there and tell the priest who's hiding him that you are Gunter's sister's caretakers. She said that she's feeling better, but he still can't come visit her yet because the measles are still contagious. However, you can take him to the house nearby where he'll be absolutely safe. That's the code. He'll know that I sent you and that he should go with you."

"Thank you, Rebekah." Heinrich shook hers and then her father's hand. "We'll try our best to help him out."

"Please, do."

As soon as we got back to our car, I covered my face with my hands and moaned.

"Heinrich, this is so wrong, what we're going to do! We really, really shouldn't! What if we just leave everything as it is?"

"I'll tell you exactly what will happen if we leave everything as it is. Josef, he'll still die. The Gestapo won't sentence him to hard labor in one of the camps as a minor criminal, they'll most definitely execute him, just to put the picture of his hanging body on the front pages. Adam they will execute too for giving false information, and also they'll most definitely send a message to their undercover agents in Switzerland to get your parents as well. But before that not only they will get from Josef the names of all his closest connections, they will get the names of the ones who work with us as well. And those people in their turn under torture will most likely testify that a certain SD officer and his lovely wife have been doing very shady business lately. And even if we'll be lucky enough to die an easy death from cyanide, they'll start checking all of our friends and close acquaintances, which will lead them to Ingrid and Rudolf. They will prefer committing suicide to talking of course, but the two best American counterintelligence agents will still be dead. Now think about it, isn't saving all those lives justified by taking one man's life who won't get to live anyway?"

Heinrich was right. He was right through and through. I sighed and finally nodded at him.

We were driving outside Berlin for quite some time already. Well, actually it was Josef who was driving, because Heinrich told him that that's the way it should be. Josef hesitated for a moment but agreed, as my husband and I got in the back seat. Even I wasn't sure why Heinrich made such a request, hoping deep inside that he at least wouldn't shoot Josef right in our car.

"I thought the hideout was in Berlin?" The leader of the Resistance looked at us in the rearview mirror. The further we were getting from the German capital, the more suspicious he was getting, even though just half an hour ago he so willingly followed us to the car, right after he recognized me and even asked me how my father was doing.

"No, it's actually not," Heinrich replied. "It's a hut in the woods, the best place for you to wait out, because it's exactly in Berlin where they're looking for you."

"How are we going to find it now? The night is pitch black and they don't have any lampposts in the forest, you know."

"Don't worry about it, we have a flashlight."

"So what exactly shall I be looking out for along the road? I mean, how do you know where to enter the forest to get to the hut?"

I noticed how Heinrich frowned. Josef started to get nervous and was asking more and more questions.

"Just stop where I tell you to stop, alright?"

"No, it's not alright." Josef suddenly hit the brakes and turned around to face us. "I'm not going anywhere until you tell me where the hell you're taking me."

I saw how he put his hand in the right pocket as he was saying that. Heinrich saw it too. I pulled to a side a little, just in case.

"Josef, listen to me." Heinrich reassuringly put his gloved hand to Josef's left shoulder, slightly pulling him back to his seat. "You know us. Well, at least you know my wife. We're your friends, and you have to trust us. Just drive a little further until you see a road sign and the big tree sticking out to the road, that's where we should enter. We can't do this if we don't trust each other, right?"

Josef shifted his eyes from my husband to me, and I forced myself to smile at him. Finally he nodded, however his hand remained in his pocket.

"Alright. But you drive this time, and I'll sit in the back."

Heinrich wasn't moving for several seconds, and I could sense the tension growing between the two men. Suddenly, Heinrich smiled and patted Josef's other shoulder with his right hand.

"Deal. But don't flirt with my wife too much!"

The Resistance leader chuckled and turned away for a moment to open the driver's door, when all of a sudden Heinrich reached both hands across the man's throat and pulled him backwards with a thin cord that I had no idea he was holding this whole time. I yelped and jumped to the opposite side of the back seat, pressing my legs to my chest. Josef was struggling with the cord with his hands, trying to somehow release the grip on his neck, but Heinrich kept tightening it more and more, with a deadly determination on his stern face. I never saw him like that before and that frightened me even more than what he was doing to his victim.

Realizing that he was going to die very soon if he didn't do anything, Josef did something that only a desperate man can think of: he pressed the accelerator hard with his foot and the car started quickly gaining speed, swaying all over the road. If he was going to die, he had decided to definitely take us with him.

"Annalise, grab the wheel!!!" Heinrich yelled at me.

"What?!" There was no way I was getting in the front next to the man who was struggling against the cord around his neck. The car was going even faster now, getting dangerously close to the woods.

"Do it, now!!! We'll crash!!!"

I don't know how, but I found the strength to leave my corner and reached for the wheel, just in time to turn it all the way to the left, straightening out the car. Miraculously we escaped crashing into a tree, but now I found myself hanging over the front seat, trying to control the wheel with both hands. The hand of the speedometer was getting closer and closer to the furthest point and the loud grunting of the motor mixed with Josef's death-rattle.

"Get in the front seat and stop the goddamn car!" Heinrich yelled at me again. I don't think he understood that I was so terrified with everything going on right next to me that I could hardly move my half-paralyzed limbs, leave alone trying to operate any machinery. The panic made me feel so lightheaded that I honestly started to feel that I might lose consciousness any second now.

"I can't!" I cried out back at him.

"Yes, you can! You're doing great, baby, come on, just crawl into the passenger's seat!"

Still holding the wheel with one hand, I grabbed the front seat and climbed into it.

"Now what?"

"Now put your leg on top of his, then move his away from the accelerator and then slow down the car!"

"Heinrich, I'm not touching him!!!"

I didn't have to touch him. With his last breath, Josef jerked for the last time in convulsion, straightened out completely, and pressed both feet to the floor simultaneously hitting the breaks as well. The last thing I remembered was slamming my head into the dashboard; then everything went dark.

I woke up for the second time already in our bed at home, my head still fuzzy from the morphine the doctor shot into my vein despite all my protests. I was incredibly thirsty and there was no water in sight.

When I opened my eyes for the first time, it was from my husband slightly slapping me on both cheeks. Josef's body was already gone from the driver's seat, and I didn't even want to know where. I hardly remember how we made it back home because I kept losing consciousness again and again. At dawn, before our housekeeper Magda would come to work, Heinrich carried me to bed and changed my clothes into the night gown and told me to say that I fell off the stairs when the doctor comes. The pounding in my head was unbearable, but I somehow managed to nod.

"Just a slight concussion. You hit your temple area right here," the doctor concluded after checking my eye reflexes and asking me several questions to which I mumbled something in reply. "You're very lucky you didn't break your neck!"

"It's our dog, he's grown to be so massive, constantly throws himself under the feet whenever we go up or down the stairs." I heard Heinrich say. "She was sleepy and didn't see him."

The doctor clicked his tongue several times and shook his head. I closed my eyes again. I just wanted those horrible twenty four hours to be over and all of them to leave me in peace. The doctor spoke to Heinrich about the medicine he was leaving for my headache and the regiment I should stick to within the next week at least, pricked me with morphine and finally left. Heinrich had to leave to work as well, and I couldn't help but feel relief when he kissed me on my forehead and closed the door behind him.

Morphine put me out to at least a somewhat pain-free sleep without dreams, but made me wake up craving water as if I hadn't been drinking in days. And now it seemed like I had to get it myself. Magda was most likely downstairs cleaning or making lunch (I didn't even know what time it was), so the chance that she would hear me call her was very slim.

Struggling both with dizziness and nausea – the doctor warned me that I might be vomiting within the next few days because of the concussion, I put on the robe that Heinrich left for me on the bed and opened the bedroom door. To my big surprise I heard my housekeeper's voice coming from the hallway, far louder than usual.

"Sir, I assure you, Frau Friedmann is fine, her life is not in danger, she just needs a lot of rest. Doctor would have taken her to the hospital if it was serious."

"Well, maybe that doctor doesn't know any better! Let me have my doctor see her!"

I clenched my hand around the door knob. I could recognize that voice out of a million. Even though I still didn't feel too steady on my feet, I swung the door open and walked to the top of the stairs.

"What the hell are you doing in my house?" I couldn't speak too loud because of the immense pounding in my head, but it was more than enough for Gruppenführer Kaltenbrunner to hear me. He lifted his head to me and made a step towards the stairs, but I stretched my hand in front of me. "Stay where you are or I'll call the police."

Good argument I made, I thought to myself – *threatening the Chief of the Gestapo with the police.* But I think it was the tone of my voice than stopped him.

"I just came to apologize." He was looking at me with an almost pleading expression on his face. It was very unusual to hear him talk in such a soft voice. I

70

didn't say anything, so he turned to Magda. "Could you leave us for a minute, please?"

The girl looked at me as if asking what she should do. I motioned my head to the direction of the kitchen dismissing her and regretted it right away: I lost coordination and had to grab the railing not to fall. Dr. Kaltenbrunner noticed it and made a quick motion towards me, but I extended my hand in front of me again.

"I told you to stay where you are."

"I just wanted to help you."

"Get out of my house. I don't want to see you."

I guess that the doctor's advice to stay in bed was more than reasonable, because I started to get lightheaded again. I decided to sit down on the top step just in case. He was still watching me from the bottom but didn't move this time. My lungs were already burning from the morphine, and I thought that if I didn't drink right now I would definitely pass out.

"Are you alright?" Dr. Kaltenbrunner asked me with a concerned look on his face. "You look very pale. Do you want some water maybe?"

Yes, I do want the damn water, that's why I got up from my bed!!!

I hated to ask him for anything but right now it felt like a question of death or life.

"Yes. Ice cold."

He quickly disappeared, came back in less than a minute and ran up the stairs holding a glass of water that Magda made for him. *That bastard found the way to come close to me after all,* I thought, taking the glass from him very carefully so I wouldn't accidentally touch his hand. It was lucky that I was as thirsty as a dying man in a desert, otherwise I would definitely spill that water right into his face. But I finished the glass at once and pressed it to my forehead in the hope that it would alleviate my terrible headache. It felt good. I closed my eyes, too tired to fight with the man still standing next to me.

"Annalise."

He called me by my name for the first time. It bothered me for some reason. It sounded too unofficial, too intimate. Only my husband could call me by my name, but he wasn't my husband. He had no right to call me 'Annalise,' he had no right to kiss me and touch me all over, he had no right to come to my house and get into my personal space.

"Go away."

"I will. I just wanted to tell you how deeply sorry I am for everything that happened yesterday. That case they had against you, and the radio with your fingerprints, it all got me so angry that I wasn't acting in my right mind. I thought that you really were connected to those criminals, and that you were lying to me the whole time. I thought that you betrayed me, betrayed my trust, and it hurt me very much. So I wanted to hurt you too, so you would feel the way I felt. Of course it absolutely doesn't justify any of the things I did, but I thought I needed to explain myself to you."

"Well, what is your explanation about how you almost raped me in front of another man after all the charges had been already dropped?!"

I was so mad at him that the only thing that was stopping me from throwing the empty glass to his head was my terrible weakness. Gruppenführer Kaltenbrunner remained silent for a moment, probably thinking of the right words to say.

"I was still very angry with you. And besides you kissed me before. It was… a combination of both things."

"I kissed you because you were holding the goddamn dagger to my neck! It was the only way to snap you out of your torturing mood! Or did you really think that all the inmates dream of making out with their interrogators?!"

"No. I thought that you liked me, that's all."

I finally turned my head to him. He was sitting a couple of steps lower than me and looking at me with the most naïve doe eyes I'd ever seen. Was that really the same man who was pointing a gun to my head several hours earlier? I should have told him that I never liked him and never would, that he was a sick perverted person, and that he should leave me alone and never bother me again. I already opened my mouth, but somehow said the following, "Even if I did, you went and ruined it all."

Maybe it was the water that woke me up, but all of a sudden I felt enough energy to let the leader of the Austrian SS really have it. "And how could I be so stupid? I've been told so many times about so many things that you did, and I never believed any of it. I always spoke so highly of you, protected you before the others, blindly denied all the allegations, and for what?! So you would do something like that to me?"

"Annalise…"

"Don't call me by my name, I'm not one of your girlfriends!"

"You're right. I apologize, Frau Friedmann." He obediently lowered his head. "I just want you to know that I am terribly sorry about everything that happened. I've never been so ashamed of myself the way I am now. Of all the women that I've ever known you deserve the most respect, and I should have never treated you the way I did. There is absolutely no forgiveness or excuse to any of my actions. I understand how much you despise me, and you have every right to feel this way."

He paused for a moment, waiting for me to say something, but I had nothing to tell him. He sighed, looked at the floor and then at me again.

"I know that you probably don't want to ever see me again, and I will respect your wish and will never bother you again. But if there was the slightest chance to have your friendship back, I would do anything."

Anything, he said? For a second I realized that I had an upper hand with the leader of the Austrian SS, and such a chance happens once in a million years. I put the glass down next to me and crossed my hands on my chest.

"There is one thing you can do. I'm not saying that I'll forgive you if you do it, but at least I'll pretend to act nice and polite with you if we happen to meet in the future."

A hopeful smile touched the corners of his lips.

"Just name it. Whatever it is, I promise you I will do it."

I paused for a second, contemplating if I should really ask him that. Now that I knew by my own experience how quickly his personality can switch from the charming and courteous officer to the amoral and sadistic monster, I wasn't sure that my request wouldn't provoke such a change once again. However, I decided to try.

"Release Adam from jail. He's not some violent criminal, just a confused young man who got caught up in things. And I'll make sure personally that he'll board the first train to Switzerland, goes back to New York and never comes back."

Gruppenführer Kaltenbrunner frowned for a moment.

"Usually I have no mercy for the enemies of the Reich, no matter how big or small their deeds are. But I would do this just because you asked me to, if I could. However, I'm afraid, it's not in my jurisdiction. I have authority over the Austrian Gestapo, not the German one. It's Müller's personal playground, and I have no say in it."

I knew that he wasn't lying, but there should be a way he could help Adam get out.

"Well, what about if he gets transferred to the territory of Austria? He's a political prisoner, right? So he'll be sent to the camp for the political prisoners, which is directly under your supervision."

"Mauthausen?"

"Yes. Can you get him out of there?"

He was watching me with a pensive look on his face.

"I suppose I could," he finally said, and then added. "Why do you care about that Jew so much anyway?"

"I care about all my friends. Until they go and do something stupid. But even then I still do."

I gave him a stern look, but he still smiled at me. He knew that I was talking not just about Adam, but about him as well.

"If Müller decides to send him to Mauthausen, I'll have him released right away. Of course he'll have to leave the territory of the Reich immediately."

"Of course."

"Are we friends again?" he asked me after a pause.

"No, but I hate you a little less now."

"That'll do." He was smiling at me. "Can I have a handshake before I go?"

I thought about it for a moment and then extended my hand to him.

"Don't get too excited about it, that's the most touching you will ever get from me in the future."

"How about a hug for my birthday?"

"You're pushing it. Get out of my house!"

He laughed.

"Consider me gone." He got up from the steps he was sitting on and then, seeing me standing up not too steadily on my feet, asked, "Do you want me to help you into your bed?"

"No!"

"I didn't mean it in any bad sense…"

"I know, Jesus Christ!" I couldn't help but start laughing. "Just go already!"

"Goodbye, Frau Friedmann."

"Goodbye."

He finally went down the stairs and, still smiling, saluted me. As soon as he closed the door behind himself, Magda emerged from the kitchen and looked at me in confusion.

"Who was that, Frau Friedmann?"

I shrugged and shook my head.

"The biggest mystery I've ever met."

Chapter 6

Berlin, May 27, 1942

I was listening to Beethoven while trying to concentrate on the book I was reading. A week had passed since the terrible events of probably the scariest day (and night) of my life, and classical music and reading were helping me to somehow distract myself from constantly replaying them in my mind. I helped my husband kill a man. I was right next to him when he died. His blood was also on my hands, despite all Heinrich's arguments about how we didn't have a choice. I suddenly thought about my dead brother, and how he killed himself because he also didn't have a choice. It looked like no one in the whole Reich had a choice anymore. We all lived by the jungle law: kill or be killed.

Magda's polite knocking on the door interrupted my thoughts.

"Excuse me, Frau Friedmann, lunch is ready."

Both my dogs who kept me company all these days, my loyal German shepherd Rolf and grey-faced Milo – our old family dog, right away lifted their heads at the word 'lunch.'

"Thank you, Magda. Has Hanz come yet to pick up lunch for Herr Friedmann?"

"Not yet."

"You know what? I feel better today and I just can't take staying home anymore. Wrap up my lunch as well and I'll eat it by Herr Friedmann's office. Let me know when Hanz is here, will you?"

"Of course, Frau Friedmann."

"Thank you."

Heinrich's driver Hanz knocked on the front door precisely at eleven thirty; punctuality was one of his great qualities, and I knew how much my husband appreciated it about him. He was a little concerned about me leaving the house without the permission of the doctor, but knowing how stubborn I was, just sighed and helped me into the car. However, when we pulled up by the RSHA main entrance, a very unusual commotion surprised us both greatly.

"What's going on? Why is everybody running around like they're insane? Have the Russians signed the capitulation or has Reichsführer Himmler married a Jewish girl?" I asked Hanz, but he just shrugged, as confused as I was.

Even the guards at the entrance hardly looked at my papers and immediately got back to the black phones behind their backs; while I was walking through the hallways the noise of those constantly ringing phones was overwhelming, and I almost started to get my headache back. Something was happening, and judging by the serious and sometimes frightened faces of the workers of the RSHA, that something wasn't good.

When I finally made it to Heinrich's anteroom, I was surprised to see that even his adjutant Mark was not at his regular place. I opened the door to my husband's office to find him on the phone with someone, the expression of his face grave. He nodded at me acknowledging my presence but didn't even smile. As I sat on the chair across the table from him, he kept repeating *'Jawohl'* and obviously putting down someone's orders on the sheet of paper in front of him. When he finally hung up, he turned to me, looking very distressed.

"Have you heard already?"

"What? What happened?"

He looked at me a little longer and then said, "Obergruppenführer Heydrich has been assassinated today."

For a second I forgot how to breathe, and was just staring at him with my eyes wide open, afraid to ask the next question.

"Is he dead?"

"No, just injured. He's in the hospital in Prague. Reichsführer's personal physician flew out to take care of him."

I covered my face with both hands and rested my elbows on the table, bitter disappointment filling my eyes with tears. So Marek's friends failed after all, and the man who's responsible for the deaths of hundreds of thousands of innocent people every day exterminated in different camps will get to live. The heartless animal who provoked *Kristallnacht* and ordered to burn down synagogues with people in them all over the country will get to live. The monster who refused my brother's plea to transfer him from Auschwitz to the Eastern front and made my poor Norbert take his own life, will get to live. The Hangman. The Butcher of Prague. The Blond Beast. Himmler's Evil Genius. Reinhard Heydrich will get to live.

"Oh God!" I whispered thinking of how all the efforts to end his life had been in vain. "No!"

Heinrich leaned over me and hugged me by the shoulders in an effort to console me, but there was nothing he could do this time. I swore on Norbert's and my unborn baby's grave that Heydrich would die and I broke my word. I felt absolutely terrible.

"Sweetheart, why don't you just go home and lay down?"

Heinrich was stroking my hair, deep concern in his voice. He still remembered the way I was right after Norbert's death and my miscarriage, and was afraid that the failed assassination on Heydrich would bring me back into that half depressed, half angry vengeful state, and I'd go and do something stupid again, like last time when

I went all the way to the Austrian capital to ask Gruppenführer Kaltenbrunner for help. I wondered how he took the news about Heydrich, and what he was going to do to poor Marek now.

"Sweetheart?"

"Yes, I think you're right. I'd better go home."

Heinrich was surprised that I agreed so easily, but also seemed to be relieved by it. I left him the bag with lunch, gave him a quick kiss goodbye and went outside to find Hanz. He had already found out the news, and on the way home kept shaking his head and saying what a stupid thing the Czech Resistance members did.

"Why stupid? He's been terrorizing the population of the country for how long now? Of course they wanted to kill him," I said.

"I understand that, but just think of the retaliation that will follow now. Obergruppenführer Heydrich's terrors will be nothing compared to the massacre that the Führer will definitely order, if he hasn't already. They will level Prague to the ground."

I sighed and looked out of the window. *More people will die now, and Heydrich will still live.* The rest of the way back home we spent in silence mostly because I didn't want to talk. *What good will talking do now?*

As I entered the house and hardly had time to make both dogs stop jumping on me, the phone rang. I answered, wondering if it was Heinrich making sure that I made it home safe.

"Yes?"

"Hello, Frau Friedmann. Have you heard the news?"

"Yes I... How did you get my number?"

"I'm the Chief of the Gestapo, aren't I?" I could almost hear how Gruppenführer Kaltenbrunner was grinning on the other end. "I only regret that I'm in Vienna and couldn't see a happy smile on your face when you found out."

"What are you talking about?" I quickly glanced in the direction of the kitchen, making sure that Magda couldn't overhear our conversation. "He survived!"

"He survived the attack, yes. Those goddamn British machine guns always jam when you need them to shoot the most. They had to throw a grenade under his car, the pieces of which wounded him. But he will most certainly die within the next few days."

"Why are you so sure?"

"Because Marek and his friends did soak all the parts of the ammunition in that highly toxic stuff I gave him, the name of which I can't even pronounce. Right now, even though his condition may be considered stable, it's slowly poisoning him from the inside. His days are numbered, Frau Friedmann, believe me."

"I hope you're not giving me false hope, Herr Gruppenführer."

"Oh no, I would never." He paused for a moment and asked, "How's your headache? Still bothering you?"

"It's much better now, thank you."

"Will you come to the funeral then?"

"I wouldn't miss it for anything."

"Great. I'll see you there then."

Dr. Kaltenbrunner hung up, and I silently prayed to God that he was right.

June 9, 1942

The day outside was warm and beautiful. Inside the Reich Chancellery it was dark and cold, despite many urns with burning fire. Looking around I thought that they killed half of Berlin orangeries to bring all those wreaths here. I actually felt like I was sitting in one big greenhouse, only with standards and swastika banners on every wall. Another huge banner with SS runes on it was covering the wall right above SS Obergruppenführer Reinhard Heydrich's coffin, at which I was staring through my black veil since the SS soldiers brought it inside. I wished that it was open so I could see his face, to look closely at the dead body just to make sure myself that it was indeed true: Reinhard Heydrich was dead.

When Heinrich broke the news to me several days ago, I didn't feel anything. I thought that I would feel happy, satisfied, victorious, but there was nothing. I was disappointed, disappointed with myself because I so naively believed that killing the man who caused me so much pain would make it go away, but it didn't. Norbert was still dead.

I kept staring at the coffin while Reichsführer Himmler was giving a eulogy. I tried to force some kind of emotions into myself. There was nothing. I kept staring at the coffin while the Führer Adolf Hitler placed Heydrich's posthumous decorations on his funeral pillow. Still nothing. *Another death doesn't bring the dead people back. Revenge is pointless.*

I looked at Heinrich in despair. *Help me, tell me what to do now,* I silently pleaded him with my eyes; but he just took my hand in his and slightly squeezed it. He didn't know how to help me. I sighed and looked away.

After the same SS soldiers took the coffin outside to transport it to the cemetery, we were left amongst the high ranking officers who didn't follow the procession. They were talking quietly among themselves, mostly about Heydrich and the consequences of his assassination for Czechoslovakia. Everybody was agreeing on one point: that very soon the Gestapo under Himmler's immediate control would bring its wrath on the Resistance members and anyone in any way

78

connected to them. I didn't want to listen to it and went all the way to the front, where Heydrich's coffin used to stand. *Was it really worth it?* I asked myself, and found no answer.

"He's gone." A familiar voice behind my back. Gruppenführer Kaltenbrunner found me.

"Yes, he is," I replied quietly without turning around.

"You seem upset though."

I was silent for some time and then said, "It doesn't feel the way I expected it to feel."

"Why not?"

"My brother is still dead. Nothing has changed. I thought it would, but it hasn't."

"You're wrong, Frau Friedmann. Something has changed. He's gone."

"And?"

"And it means that you don't have to hate him anymore. You can just let go now. Stop torturing yourself about the past and look into the future. He's gone. It's over with. Everything is over with. You're free."

The simplicity of his words stunned me like a sudden revelation. *He's gone. It's over. I don't have to hate him anymore. I can go back to my old happy self. I'm free.*

It sounded so unreal in my mind, but so straightforward at the same time that I hardly suppressed a little laugh and quickly covered my mouth with a gloved hand. *I'm free. I don't have to think about it anymore. He's gone from my life, once and for all. I will never see him again. He won't be a constant reminder of the painful memories, which seemed to be forever imprinted in my mind. I don't have to keep mourning the two ghosts from my past over and over again. They're free now. And so am I. Free.*

I laughed again, still covering my face with a shaking hand. And then I started crying, crying so hard that I could hardly breathe in between hysterical sobs. I needed somebody to hold me, and that somebody was standing right beside me, not touching me when I needed it most. I turned around to Gruppenführer Kaltenbrunner and pressed my head to his shoulder, and then he tightly wrapped his arms around me and I cried even harder.

"Shhh, it's alright, everything will be alright now." He was gently stroking my hair and back, as if comforting a little child. "It's over. I want these tears to be the last tears I see on your pretty face. Only happy smiles from now on, deal?"

I nodded several times, and gratefully accepted a handkerchief he gave me. I wiped my face, and the part of it where my running mascara touched it became black. I stared at it for a moment and smiled; I was glad those tears I cried were black, all that poison that I had inside was finally leaving my body.

Someone came over to ask if I was alright, and Dr. Kaltenbrunner answered without letting me go. "The poor thing was working with Obergruppenführer Heydrich, she's absolutely devastated! It's very sad. What an untimely loss."

"Absolutely, absolutely," the man replied. I didn't even turn my head to him, finally feeling safe and in peace in the strong arms of the leader of the Austrian SS. "Frightful times, frightful!"

The man left, and I wiped my face once again, noticing that the handkerchief was almost clear this time. Everything inside was clear too, no more pain, no more hatred, no more poison. I was finally free, and he made it possible. I lifted my face to him and whispered so no one else would hear us, "thank you."

"It's nothing. I'm just glad that you feel better now."

Dr. Kaltenbrunner softly touched my wet cheek, wiping the last few tears from it, and then he was just looking at me, very seriously, his hand still on top of my arm, his fingers still gently caressing my skin. I was standing so close to him, and I knew that if we were alone now he would have kissed me. I would have let him do it.

Then I suddenly felt very ashamed of myself and stepped away, thinking how I could even allow such thoughts with Heinrich in the same hall with me. Gruppenführer Kaltenbrunner let go of me right away, as if understanding my feelings.

"I should probably be going," I said. "My husband is waiting for me."

"Yes, of course," he nodded.

I looked at him a little longer.

"Well... goodbye then, Herr Gruppenführer."

"Goodbye, Frau Friedmann."

I extended my hand to him and he gently shook it.

"Thank you for your handkerchief. I'm afraid it's ruined though."

Gruppenführer Kaltenbrunner finally smiled.

"I'm pretty sure I can afford a new one."

I smiled back at him and had already started walking away, when he suddenly called my name.

"Frau Friedmann!"

"Yes?" I turned around.

"I forgot to give you this."

With those words he put his hand in his pocket and produced my Catholic cross which he took from me in the Gestapo jail, and also a little golden chain with little pointe shoes pendant on it, my husband's present, the one that he took several years ago in the same interrogation room. I couldn't believe that he still had it after all these years. I carefully took them both and raised my eyes to him once again.

"You kept it?"

"Of course I did. I just kept forgetting to give it back to you."

I didn't know what to say.

Berlin, June 1942

Himmler arrived. He walked all the way to the podium in a big conference hall where all the employees of the Berlin office of Amt VI or *SD-Ausland* were ordered to gather the day before. Well, technically probably only half of the employees, because of the nature of our department: we were the external intelligence office and many agents were working outside the country or travelling for different missions. Heinrich was sitting among the other high ranking officers in the first row, but still turned around and gave me a reassuring nod as Reichsführer Himmler was going through the papers he brought with him. I was sitting all the way in the back with the other *SS-Helferinnen* staff, which included all female secretaries, stenographers and radio operators. I nodded back at my husband and smiled.

Reichsführer made quite a long speech on what a tragic loss the death of our former Chief SS Obergruppenführer Heydrich was, and I couldn't help but wonder at the double nature of Himmler. Everybody knew that after Heydrich overstepped him in rank and became a Minister before Himmler, the latter couldn't stand his former colleague and protégé. I was personally convinced that on the day when Heydrich died, Reichsführer Himmler opened a bottle of champagne and quite possibly even had a piece of cake.

Then Reichsführer went on saying that before the Führer would find a suitable candidate to replace the 'irreplaceable' Heydrich, the RSHA would now fall under his immediate control, and our Amt will be supervised by SS Standartenführer Walther Schellenberg. I'd met Schellenberg before and was very surprised that Reichsführer decided to make such a young man our Chief, but rumors had it that Schellenberg was Himmler's eyes and ears, so I figured that Himmler appointed him to this position not just because of Walther's high intelligence, but also to basically spy on his own subordinates.

Reichsführer also made quite serious changes in the internal organization of the RSHA, and made a special accent on what an important part in the 'emotional health of the nation' Amt IV or the infamous Gestapo was playing, and stressed that all the information concerning the enemies of the Reich such as Jews, Bolsheviks, Communists, Sectarians and the traitors of the Reich – the Resistance members in all the occupied territories must be immediately transferred to Amt IV and its Chief – Heinrich Müller.

I frowned; such a shift in powers was almost giving Müller authority over our branch, and if before such information had been handled by our agents without the intervention of the Gestapo, now the failure to provide it would be subject to administrative punishment. Himmler was definitely happy that Heydrich was no longer his competition and decided to gain as much power in his hands as he possibly could, using the Gestapo as a means of achieving his goal. That decision of his was making mine and Heinrich's underground work extremely difficult. Himmler would most likely infiltrate some acting Gestapo agents into our office too, I thought and sighed again. Reichsführer was tightening up the screws not only on the nation, but on his own subordinates now. That man didn't trust anyone.

After some minor changes in positions amongst the top agents, Reichsführer told us to get back to work and proceed with our daily tasks as we would have been with Heydrich still in office, only now all the reports were to be delivered to Standartenführer Schellenberg. Then Himmler wished us a great day and left the conference hall, dismissing us.

Later that day Heinrich and I decided to go by our American Secret Service 'colleagues' to share the news with them. Ingrid was still mad at me for dragging them into my recent interrogation process with the Gestapo, and kept shooting menacing looks at me from the moment we had walked through the door. Rudolf, on the contrary, was as hospitable as always, and after hearing the news about Himmler taking over the RSHA, advised us to halt all of our activities except for gathering information and delivering it to them.

"If Himmler decided to put the Gestapo in some kind of control over *SD-Ausland*, even though not on paper, I consider laying low for quite some time the wisest thing to do, until at least we find out what's really going on in the office. Therefore I strongly recommend you to stop any kind of interaction with any incriminating elements including Resistance members and even our own agents, who might want to try to come into contact with you for whatever reason. Most likely after taking over the executive power on the RSHA, Himmler will start a thorough screening of all the members, especially those who occupy office positions and have access to the most important information, and this includes both of you. So just keep it quiet for a while, work like you used to, and as soon as we feel that we're safe to proceed, we'll get back to work. Sounds good?"

"Not really, but I guess we don't have a choice, do we?" Heinrich asked him.

"No, we don't. Besides, we still need time to get a new radio operator. So sad that they got Adam. He was an outstanding young man, so efficient and intelligent! It really is a shame." Rudolf shook his head. "Nothing is known of his fate, right?"

"Unfortunately." Heinrich lowered his eyes.

"Well, they will most likely send him to Mauthausen, and then they will either execute him upon arrival or sentence him to working in quarries, and truly speaking I don't know which is worse," Ingrid said bitterly. "They call that place 'bone-grinder' for a good reason."

"Well, actually if they decide to put him in Mauthausen, he'll be able to get out," I said, and regretted it right away after three pairs of eyes turned to me in surprise.

"I'm sorry?" Ingrid tilted her head to one side. "How exactly he'll be able to get out?"

Already thinking that I should have kept my mouth shut and now would have to explain things that were very difficult to explain, I answered, "He'll get an amnesty."

"Why would he get an amnesty?" This time it was my husband who asked the question.

"Because... because someone promised me that he will."

"Who could possibly promise you that? Himmler?" Ingrid with her interrogation was worse than the Gestapo.

"No. SS Gruppenführer Kaltenbrunner."

"How did you... What? You know Kaltenbrunner?" Ingrid was quite obviously surprised.

"Yes. It's a long story, but he promised me that as soon as Adam gets transferred under his jurisdiction he'll get him released, on the condition that Adam will have to leave the territory of the Reich and never come back."

Ingrid was staring at me for some time without blinking and then finally asked, "I'm sorry, what kind of relationship are you in with him?"

"What kind of question is that?" I answered coldly, genuinely offended by Ingrid's hardly veiled insinuation. "We met several times on several different occasions, that's all."

"So you're telling me that you, hardly his acquaintance, came up to him and said, 'Excuse me, Herr Gruppenführer, you arrested a friend of mine for high treason, could you please have him released?' And Kaltenbrunner, the man who they call 'little Himmler of Austria' for his sadistic nature, said, 'Yes, why not, I do that on a daily basis, let out political enemies who I swore under my oath of an officer to prosecute and exterminate.' You understand how hard it is to believe in, right?" Ingrid crossed her arms on her chest.

Heinrich suddenly laughed, making both agents turn to him now.

"He's in love with her, that's all," he finally said in answer to the Americans' inquisitive looks. "And Annalise uses it in her advantage."

"What?" Ingrid raised her eyebrows. "Is it true?"

"No, of course not." I gave my still smiling husband a stern look. "He's not in love with me, he's just being nice."

"Kaltenbrunner being nice, that's something you don't hear every day, or shall I better say, never." Heinrich laughed again. "He's clearly in love with you, and is trying to make you like him by pretending to be good."

"Wait, do you really think Kaltenbrunner is in love with Annalise?" Ingrid asked again.

"Absolutely. I can bet any money on it. He was looking at her with big interest the very first time he met her, on our wedding day. And since then he's been trying to get her attention in any possible way. Once he even offered her, even though he didn't say it openly, a vacant position of his mistress in Vienna. Maybe I shouldn't say 'vacant' though, because he's quite a pathological ladies man, and in addition to the official spouse has another couple of girlfriends on the side. But I'm quite sure that for Annalise he would get rid of them all in a split second. It looks like she really got to him."

"And you're very happy about it," I concluded sarcastically.

"He's in love with you, but I'm the one who's married to you, so yes, it makes me very happy." Heinrich chuckled.

"You're a very evil man, you know that, Heinrich?"

"Stop arguing, you two! Let's be serious now." Ingrid clapped her hands to attract our attention. "If he's really in love with her, we can use it in our advantage. He's a very powerful man, even though his main sphere of influence is Austria, but we still can work something out."

"Excuse me, I guess I hit my head so hard recently that I forgot how I changed my legal name to Mata Hari." This time it was me who crossed my hands on my chest.

"But it's a brilliant idea, if you think about it," Rudolf interfered. "Right now, when we can't do anything in the office, Kaltenbrunner would be not only a perfect source of information for you, but also can help with some action. If he agreed to let out one inmate, he might agree to let out twenty. Why not try it?"

"How stupid do you think he is?" I asked him.

"Stupid, or shall I say, in love enough to let you out of jail twice, the last time after an accusation of espionage. And don't forget catching you one time with the suspicious suitcase and not even looking inside." My husband was clearly enjoying this. I shook my head at him.

"Well, perfect then!" Ingrid smiled for the first time in the evening. "I say it would be simply irresponsible not to use such an opportunity!"

"What do you suggest I do, start sleeping with him for the sake of your, not even my, government?!" I almost yelled at her in indignation.

"No, of course not," she answered. "Just keep being very friendly with him, borderline flirty. Let him think that he might have a chance with you if he keeps being nice. And play that card for as long as you can."

"And what do I do when he starts asking something in return?" I raised an eyebrow at the American agent. She shrugged.

"Nothing. Remind him that you're married and walk away."

I turned to Heinrich.

"Are you going to just stand here, listen to all this and consider it fine?! Your wife flirting with another man, you don't see anything wrong with it?"

"To me the more you torture the guy, the better, I think it's very funny actually. He deserved it."

For a second I was very tempted to tell my smirking husband how exactly Dr. Kaltenbrunner made Adam talk in the interrogation room, and see how funny he'd find it after my story, and how close after that he'd let the leader of the Austrian SS get to me in the future.

"All of you clearly have no idea what you're even talking about and what kind of a man you're talking about. I'm done with all this."

With those words I picked up my purse from the table, turned around and left.

Chapter 7

Zurich, August 1942

My mother wouldn't stop wiping her tears while holding my hands, as my father was driving us home from the train station where they picked me and Heinrich up just half an hour ago. We hadn't seen each other for over three years, and I couldn't help but notice what a toll Norbert's death and the life in hiding took on them: Papa was even thinner and was almost all grey, and Mama's pretty face was crossed with prominent lines right above her nose and on the sides of her mouth. I was terribly upset to see them like that; they both were only in their mid-forties.

Mother kept repeating how happy she was that Heinrich and I could finally visit them, and how lonely they felt in Zurich living all by themselves. They were so used to living as a big happy family with relatives visiting on weekends, with friends stopping by for dinners quite often, with neighbors knowing each other, and now they had to become almost hermits, with one child living in a different country and another one dead, with no means of communication with other relatives in order not to accidentally incriminate them if it comes to that, making no new friends just because there was a chance that they could sell them out to the undercover agents of the Gestapo.

Moreover, they were basically living off the money that Heinrich systematically sent to them, even though my father tried making a living working from the house and helping a local law office by organizing and writing up paperwork for the lawyers, and Mama typing official letters for the same office and a couple of others. It wasn't that they were struggling thank God, but deep inside I knew that it was my father's self-esteem that was hurting him the most. From being a successful lawyer in the heart of Berlin with a personal law firm and quite an impressive income, he now had to rely on his son-in-law to pay his bills. All of his assets were still in the bank of Berlin, since the official version of my parents' departure was Papa's poor health; if he'd taken all of the money out of the account, an investigation would follow right away.

Their apartment was very nice, even though terribly small compared to our old family house with several bedrooms, a vast library, study, dining room, enormous kitchen where old Gryselda, our loyal housekeeper, was always making something incredibly delicious. In the haste of their departure my parents had to let her go with a lot of tears and emotions from both sides, recommending her services to my father's old partner, Dr. Kauffmann. But Gryselda just shook her head and explained to my parents that they were her family, and she wouldn't be able to work for anyone else. She'd saved a lot of money from the generous salary my father had been paying her, and she could live the rest of her days without thinking of taking up a new job. I wanted to visit her on Christmas later that year, but her landlord informed me that the sweet old lady died just a month prior to that.

During the dinner that Mama cooked all by herself, she was asking us about all the people she knew, about Grandma, about the government and the war. After I told her that I had quit ballet a long time ago and started working for the RSHA, both my parents went suddenly very quiet. I felt guilty that I had to lie about it for so long, but it was definitely not a telephone conversation and I didn't want to bring it up that way.

"Honey, we read the newspapers here, the international ones," my father started carefully. "They're writing absolutely terrifying things about those kinds of government organizations. They say that they're responsible for the extermination of over one million Jews already. Is it true?"

I looked away and didn't want to reply at first; after all it was indeed the RSHA that was responsible for the extermination program, but my parents still deserved to know the truth.

"Yes, it is."

They both were looking at me in hardly masked shock. I could almost read an unspoken question in their eyes: *'And you're working for those people?'*

"It's not our office though who's dealing with the deportations and the extermination program. It's the Gestapo," Heinrich hurriedly clarified. "We mostly deal with international affairs. And Annalise is just an office worker anyway, all she does is sends teletypes and makes coffee, that's about it."

I gratefully smiled at my husband for that. At least he spared them and didn't say anything about my radio operator functions, which were far from harmless for the Allies. But it was a part of my job and a price that I had to pay to continue with my counterspy activities, of which I still unfortunately couldn't inform my parents.

"But it is absolutely horrible! Goebbels and Himmler themselves promised that the German Jews would be merely resettled to a certain territory chosen for them, and won't be harmed in any way. And now they're putting them all in camps and killing them?" My mother couldn't believe the horrific fact.

"Well, they lied, Mama. Just like Hitler lied about his pacifistic politics in the late 30's, and then started the most blood-shedding war the world has ever seen. They all lie. About everything."

"Why did you start working for them then? You're Jewish yourself and now you're technically helping them put other Jews to death. You know how it's called in legal terms, daughter? An accessory to the murder," my father concluded with a stern face.

I sighed. I shouldn't have brought up the whole topic at all, should have just kept lying that I was still dancing. Now my own parents think that I adopted the Nazi doctrine and walk around with a swastika on my left shoulder.

"Richart, I've already told you that our office doesn't have anything to do with the camps, and especially *SS-Helferinnen* staff. They are merely secretaries, that's all." Heinrich tried to pacify my father, but got a completely opposite reaction.

"SS? My daughter is a member of SS too?!"

"It's a women's SS, Papa, it's quite different from the main one. And I had to join it, it was an order from the former RSHA Chief, Heydrich."

"Oh God, I'm going to lose both of my children to this war! My Norbert, my only son has already died, and now they want my daughter!"

My father covered his face with both hands in desperation. I had no idea how stricken by my brother's death he was, and how hard he would take the news of me belonging to the SS, even though *SS-Helferinnen* was in no way near the regular SS.

"Papa, please stop killing yourself. Nobody's going to take me, they won't send me to the front or anything, it's just mandatory for all the secretaries who work in high security offices to become a member of SS, that's all. A pure formality, that's all it is. And the good news is that I'm working right next to Heinrich."

I tried to smile at least at my mother, who looked very worried as well.

"Mama, I promise, I'm not doing anything dangerous. Or horrible, Papa. Just sending teletypes and making coffee, as Heinrich told you. So please, let's change the subject and talk about something else. How are the theatres here in Zurich, any good?"

We had to be in the office in Berlin the next day, so we could only stay for a couple of hours, during which we spoke about everything except the Nazis or SS. Already on the way home Heinrich shook his head at me and smiled.

"You became such a good liar, you're starting to scare me."

"I had the best teacher." I grinned at him, and then looked out of the window. I started to scare myself too, because even Heinrich had no idea what was going on inside of my head. I had become a terrific liar.

———————

That Friday Heinrich and I were going to the opera with Max and Ursula. Even though we lived quite close to each other and even worked in the same office (at least with Max), we often had lunches and dinners together, but it was a long time since we all dressed up and made, as Ursula called it, 'a social appearance.'

She was right in a sense, putting on a long silk dress and wrapping my neck in several layers of pearls certainly felt nice compared to my official uniform I was obliged to wear every day. I even let my hair down, and, hardly tying it in a low tail, let it lay on one side of my shoulder. I had always considered my waist long hair one of my main assets and proudly displayed it despite the envious looks from the other female opera house patrons, who in majority had short hair according to the fashion.

We had already taken our seats when I suddenly remembered that I left my purse in the car, and to my 'luck' Heinrich had just left our balcony to bring both Ursula and me champagne. I excused myself and went outside, making sure to be quick not to miss the third bell. I grabbed my purse from under the passenger seat where I left it, closed the door and was just going to turn around when someone suddenly grabbed my elbow. I instinctively yanked my hand out, trying to see the face of a poorly dressed young man standing in front of me.

"Shhh, it's me, Adam."

Even in the light of the lampposts I couldn't see him clearly, but his voice left me no doubts. It looked like Dr. Kaltenbrunner did keep his promise after all. I hugged him and smiled.

"Adam? What are you doing here? Are you alright?"

I had to ask the last question because he looked anything but alright, with a thick beard covering his face, uncut hair and worn out clothes. It looked like he'd lost a lot of weight too.

"I'm fine, I was living in slums, trying to find you for the past month, but you were out of the country I guess."

"Yes, I was in Paris with Heinrich, gathering some intelligence for Standartenführer Schellenberg. Are you coming from the camp?"

"Mauthausen, yes. What a terrible place, I have to tell you. If I hadn't seen it with my own eyes, I wouldn't have believed it. I was sent to Dachau first, but then they transferred me to that one, I don't know why."

"I asked Gruppenführer Kaltenbrunner to let you out. It's thanks to him that you're free now." I smiled at him again. "But I promised him that you'll leave the territory of the Reich and will never come back, so come tomorrow night by my house, I'll prepare clothes, money and papers for you so you can leave immediately."

Adam frowned at me.

"I'll go only if you go."

"What? Adam, I can't go anywhere, I have a husband and work to do. And why would I go anyway? They dropped all the charges against me, my resume is perfectly clean."

"I'm not talking about your resume, I'm talking about that bastard and what he did to you. Don't you understand that he's not going to leave you alone?"

"Adam, he wasn't acting in his right mind, he already apologized a million times and would never do such a thing again."

"Did he tell you that?"

"Of course he did."

"And you believe him."

"He let you out as a gesture of good will, didn't he now? Yes, I believe him."

"That's interesting. He told me the completely opposite."

Adam was looking at me with his hands crossed on his chest.

"What did he tell you?"

"The night when he ordered the camp Kommandant to release me, they were having a party at the Kommandant's villa. So when I was brought from my barrack to the back entrance of the villa, Kaltenbrunner went outside to say a few words to me. He let the guard go, and I was left alone with him. He was very drunk, he lit a cigarette and laughed when he looked at me.

'Here you are, Jew-boy,' he said. 'Or shall I call you lover-boy? Still in love with my girl, aren't you? You're lucky that she's so good and asked for you, otherwise you would have long been dead, you Jewish piece of trash.'

He then came up very close to me and blew the smoke into my face. 'I'm letting you out on one condition, Jew. You board the first train and get your sorry ass out of the Reich immediately. Understood? And don't even think about going back to Berlin, and especially, let me emphasize it so it imprints into your tiny mind,' he tapped my forehead with his index finger several times. 'To never even think about getting close to her, do you get it? If I see you near her ever again, and the whole Nazi Germany territory I consider still too near, I'll break your dirty neck personally with these very hands. Are we clear on this matter?'

I nodded, because he seemed to get more and more aggressive as he spoke. 'Remember, Jew, she's mine. Mine! And only the thought that you're nursing some kind of romantic feelings for her is insulting to me. So do yourself a favor if you want to live to your twenty-fifth birthday, get out of the country and never come back, especially for her. She belongs to me and to me only.'

He then stared at me a little longer and then whistled to a guard. Kaltenbrunner gave him my release papers and told him to let me outside and that I'd have to walk to the nearest town to board the train. I almost hadn't eaten anything in two months, and I think that he found it very funny."

Adam paused for a moment and then asked me again, "Well, do you believe me now? He won't leave you alone, Annalise. You have to come with me, we can go to New York and stay there till at least the war ends. My father will take care of us, and I'll start working too, you won't have to worry about anything."

"Have you forgotten that I'm married?"

"No, I haven't, but Kaltenbrunner clearly did," Adam replied angrily. "And if you stay here, he'll get to you in no time."

"He won't get to me, Adam, at least not against my will."

"Oh really?" Adam sarcastically raised his eyebrow. "So what he was doing to you in the interrogation room was consensual?"

I had to admit, he had a point there, but after Dr. Kaltenbrunner came to my house begging for my forgiveness, I was more than sure that he had learned his lesson and the situation would not repeat itself.

"No, of course it wasn't, but trust me, he won't do it again. And he's right, you do have to leave the country, Adam, because if the Gestapo agents see you walking freely on the streets of Berlin, they'll throw you back into the camp in a split second, and then neither me, nor Gruppenführer Kaltenbrunner will be able to help you. Please, come by my house tomorrow and I'll help you with the money and clothes."

"No."

"Adam, you have to leave!" I almost screamed at him. "You can't stay here anyway, you can't even talk to me right now, if someone sees you, we'll both get arrested again and then that's it, end of story. You can't work for Rudolf and Ingrid anymore either, you got compromised, there's no point for you to stay!"

"Yes, there is." The stubborn boy shook his head and looked at me. "I know that I can't help the American intelligence anymore, but I'm going to join the Resistance then and look after you from a distance. Don't worry, I won't bother you so as to not incriminate you or your friends, I'll just make sure that that Nazi bastard keeps his hands away from you, that's all."

"Adam…"

"Goodbye, Annalise." He quickly turned away and left before I could say something else.

I stood motionless for some time, but then remembered that the first act was supposed to start any time now, and walked back inside the opera house. I took my seat next to Heinrich who kissed me on my cheek and told me once again how beautiful I looked tonight, sipped a little bit of champagne he gave me, but inside my head I kept hearing *his* voice: 'She's mine. Mine!'

I was doing paperwork at my desk, when Standartenführer Schellenberg's adjutant walked in, looked at all five *SS-Helferinnen* who I was sharing the room with, and asked who Annalise Friedmann was. After I rose from my place and indicated that it was me, he ordered me to follow him. When we reached Standartenführer's office, I was already sure that I was in some kind of trouble, even though I couldn't understand why. Meanwhile, the adjutant announced my presence, and after Schellenberg dismissed him, disappeared behind the door.

"*Heil Hitler!*" I raised my hand out of habit just like Heydrich demanded from all of his subordinates.

The young Chief of *SD-Ausland* just smiled at me.

"You don't have to do this with me, Frau Friedmann. Can I call you Annalise, perhaps? I think it shall be easier."

"Whatever you find suitable, Herr Standartenführer, is fine by me."

"Good. Sit down, please." He pointed to the chair across the table from him.

I sat and straightened out my skirt. He didn't seem upset or angry, so I guessed I wasn't there because I did something wrong; neither was I asked to bring any documentation with me, so it wasn't a business matter as well. What did he want from me then?

"Annalise, I have a big problem, and I hope you're the person who can help me."

"If it is in my powers, I'll be more than glad to assist you with whatever it is you need help with."

"Oh, I'm pretty sure it is." He flipped the file laying in front of him open, and I saw that it was my personal file, the one that every office worker of the RSHA had, with personal characteristic, vital accomplishments, fingerprints and basically everything else that Amt I or Personnel and Organization office wanted to know about the Reich Main Security Office staff. "It says here that you're a very good wireless radio operator, isn't it so?"

"I'm afraid I can't make such judgements about my own work, but if it says so in my file, I believe that my superiors consider it true."

"You don't have to be modest about your work, Annalise, I need you to be truthful with me. How fast do you make transcripts from the radiograms?"

I smiled. "Very fast, Herr Standartenführer. As a matter of fact I'm the fastest in my department."

"Very good. Next question is this: it says here that you know how to operate teletype quick and without mistakes, and that you're also a very quick stenographer?"

"Yes, it is true, Herr Standartenführer."

"Excellent. And this brings us to question number three: it says in your file that you speak two foreign languages, English and French, is it true? And if it is, to what level?"

That information was put into my file recently, after I spent almost two years practicing with Rudolf in English, and with Heinrich in French, since the latter used to live in Paris for quite a long time and spoke it almost flawlessly. Surprisingly, both languages came to me very easily, and I was now able to read, write and communicate in both almost freely.

"I speak both, Herr Standartenführer. Most of the time I understand almost everything that is being said."

"Really? Let's try your English first then." Schellenberg gave me another smile and asked me several questions in English concerning different spheres, mainly political and military. It seemed like he was very satisfied with my replies, because he kept nodding and smiling wider and wider. "Fantastic. And where, if I may ask, did you acquire such an excellent Harvard accent? You see, I'm speaking Oxford English, but your American pronunciation is really fascinating."

Crap. Now I understood why Himmler appointed Schellenberg to the position of the Chief of the Intelligence – no detail would pass him unnoticed. And how was I supposed to explain the origin of my 'excellent Harvard accent?' By the fact that my teacher was an American Secret Service agent and a Harvard graduate? *That'll work well.*

"My husband taught me both languages. I was simply imitating his speech, that's all. I think his tutor, when Heinrich had just started his career in SD, was from the United States."

Standartenführer Schellenberg seemed to be satisfied with my reply, because he just nodded and skipped right to asking me some other questions in French. After I passed that little test as well, he closed my file and put both hands on top of it.

"Last question, Annalise. Can you make coffee?"

"I suppose I can, Herr Standartenführer."

"Wonderful! You see, the reason why we were just having this conversation is that I'm in desperate need of a good secretary, who can do a better job than my lousy adjutant." By the way Schellenberg rolled his eyes I realized that he wasn't too happy about his immediate subordinate. "I need someone fast, efficient, smart and preferably bilingual. In the course of my work I've noticed that women are much better than men when it comes to multitasking, so after going through many files of *SD-Ausland SS-Helferinnen* staff I came to the conclusion that you would make a perfect candidate. You'll be working under my immediate command and basically just help me out with all the files and documentation, teletype, radiograms, translations, everything. The best part of course is that it'll be reflected in your salary as well."

Schellenberg smiled again and so did I, but for another reason: the best part was that such an appointment was giving me unlimited access to every single top secret document going through the hands of the Chief of the Intelligence, and it was as good as finding treasure in your backyard.

"So what do you say? Think you can manage that?"

"I would be honored, Herr Standartenführer."

"Great. You'll start tomorrow then, I'll have a table set for you in my anteroom by then with everything you need. Today try to finish all the work that you still have left and spread the rest between the girls. Sounds good?"

"Yes, Herr Standartenführer."

"Fine then. I'll see you tomorrow."

I left Schellenberg's office still smiling as if I won a lottery. I couldn't wait to share the great news with Heinrich. The Americans were supposed to send us a new radio operator any day now, and the timing couldn't be more perfect.

They say that with great power comes great responsibility. In my case with my new promotion came great responsibility, and I hardly had time to take care of all the papers and radiograms, which were continuously dumped on my table by different employees and my boss himself. For the first couple of weeks I had to stay overtime to finish the day's work, just to find double amount of paperwork the next morning. But little by little I started to organize my working time more efficiently, invented a new filing system allowing me to get and process the needed papers faster, and finally after a very stressful month with a lot of coffee, very little sleep and fingers hurting from typing all the time, I was able to leave office at five, like all my less busy colleagues.

Standartenführer Schellenberg was very happy with my work and never missed a chance to praise me every time I would do something even before he would ask me to do it. I'd already learned his working habits and principles, and knew which correspondence needed to be handed to him immediately, which orders needed to be copied and re-sent to which organizations and their supervisors, which radiograms deserved his immediate attention and which could be put aside for him to go through on the way home.

The only person who at first had some doubts about my new appointment was Reichsführer Himmler, who would stop talking immediately as soon as I would enter Standartenführer Schellenberg's office and throw suspicious looks at me. However, when the Chief of *SD-Ausland* told him that I was worth three adjutants put together and that he trusted me like he trusted himself, Reichsführer seemed to relax a little and at least tolerate a woman in such an important position.

Very soon Herr Schellenberg started taking me with him on different trips, sometimes using my services as a radio or teletype operator whenever he needed something top secret to be transmitted directly to Reichsführer's office, sometimes I was helping him with stenography or just organizing his papers. It turned out that a lot of people who Walther Schellenberg was dealing with were quite hesitant about a woman being present at their conversations, but my boss didn't seem to leave them much of a choice.

He was actually the best chief anyone could ask for: demanding but just, highly intelligent and always respectful, very professional and always attentive to details. He was a great judge of character and already after ten minutes of talking to someone would give me a complete characteristic on that person later in the car, pointing out their strong and weak sides and how we can use each to our advantage.

The only flaw in working with Schellenberg for me personally was that I couldn't figure out what he was thinking at all. With Heydrich it was always very simple: everyone knew that he was a careerist always hungry for power, cruel, inconsiderate to others and ready to step over yesterday's colleagues to reach for a new level of power. Heydrich was purely evil.

Schellenberg on the contrary was always in good spirits, smiling, joking, but at the same time I could swear that he was thinking twenty steps ahead of everything. It was impossible to get inside his mind and understand what was going on in there. I personally witnessed how he could say one thing and do the complete opposite if it was in his interests, not due to an evil nature, but just because he needed such a thing to be done as an intelligence agent. It seemed to me that he was always playing a game of chess, but with people instead of wooden figures on a board.

Rudolf and Ingrid couldn't be happier about me timely delivering them one piece of information after another, but were always sure that their superiors on the other side were carefully handling it and double checking everything in order not to get compromised because of the falsified information; with Schellenberg I could expect anything.

Chapter 8

Berlin, February 1943

I was almost done with typing an order for Standartenführer Schellenberg, when my former colleague from *SS-Helferinnen* staff Barbara walked into the anteroom, looking very anxious.

"Annalise, stop whatever it is you're doing, and let's go to the conference hall. The new Chief of the RSHA is here, and he ordered everyone to be present at the meeting."

The news was more than surprising: after the power struggle with Heydrich, I was more than sure that Himmler would leave the management of the RSHA to himself and wouldn't appoint anyone to this position. Everybody was probably thinking the same because no rumors were spreading about any candidates even being considered to such a position.

"They appointed somebody?"

"Oh yes, and from what I heard, he's even worse than Heydrich. Already fired a third of the staff from the other offices!"

"Really? Worse than Heydrich? Is it possible?" I raised my eyebrow at her, smiling.

"We are about to see." Barbara sighed.

I left the order in the typing machine and followed my friend to the conference hall, where most of the *SD-Ausland* staff were already nervously awaiting the arrival of our new Chief. It was a smaller conference hall, and this time *SS-Helferinnen* staff were sitting on a side by the wall, and I noticed right away that no one dared to take the seats in the first row, obviously intimidated by the rumors of the new RSHA Chief's temper. Standartenführer Schellenberg saw me and motioned me to sit in the front; Barbara tried to sneak out in the back too, but I grabbed her arm and made her take a place next to me, whispering to her that there was no way I was going to sit there alone. Thank God our boss made several other girls join us, and now they were sitting clinging to each other like sheep expecting to be slaughtered.

In less than a minute the new Chief of the Reich Main Security Office arrived as I understood, because everybody suddenly stood up from their seats and froze in attention. I was very interested to see who Himmler had delegated the office to after all, but since I couldn't turn my head to take a look, I stood there with my colleagues listening to his firm steps on the wooden floor as he was making his way to the podium in the front. However, as soon as he turned around and loudly dumped a pile of papers on the table in front of him, I almost laughed. The new Chief of the RSHA was SS Gruppenführer Dr. Ernst Kaltenbrunner.

Already wearing a new green uniform with insignias of SD on it instead of his always black *SS-Totenkopf*, he looked at the hall full of his new subordinates from Amt VI and grinned.

"Good afternoon, ladies and gentlemen. As you already know, I'm your new Chief now, so let's get two things straight right away: number one, I don't want to hear 'This is not the way we did things with Obergruppenführer Heydrich, we did it differently.' Since now on you do things my way, you do them fast and no questions asked. Number two, I don't care how much your former boss loved Amt IV and allowed its staff to stick their noses into every other offices' business, I demand absolute and unquestionable following of subordination in your own sphere of work. In other words, you're the external intelligence, you do your intelligence work, and therefore no files are allowed to be shared with the Gestapo under no circumstances unless approved by me personally."

Someone from the first row seemed to have an objection to this new order.

"Excuse me, Herr Gruppenführer, but Herr Reichsführer said—"

"Get out."

The officer clearly didn't expect such an answer and was standing and looking at his new boss not knowing if he was serious or not.

"I said, get the hell out." The officer quickly left before causing any more trouble for himself. "Rule number three, do not interrupt me when I talk, I don't like it."

I heard how Barbara quietly whispered "Oh, God!" under her breath. I tried not to smile too obviously. Most of my colleagues were already petrified of Gruppenführer Kaltenbrunner.

"Reichsführer delegated this office to me on one condition from my side: that I can reorganize the mess that Heydrich left after himself the way I want it. So Reichsführer clearly approves of the way I'll be doing thigs here, and if some other 'smart' guys still have doubts on this matter, the door is right there, close it behind you, because I don't want you in my office." *SD-Ausland* staff exchanged looks but everybody stayed in their places. The Austrian smirked. "No one? Good. I'm glad we clarified that. Let's get to some staff reorganization then."

Everybody started shifting in their seats, since they had already heard the rumors of how a third of their colleagues from other departments were fired or replaced by Gruppenführer Kaltenbrunner. Nobody wanted to become a part of this statistic. Meanwhile the new Chief of the RSHA took a paper out of a file in front of him and started reading the new appointments.

"Chiefs of the departments will be the following. Department A – Organization and Administration: remains the same. Department B – Espionage in the West: Standartenführer Erich Geisler. Department C – Espionage in the Soviet Union and Japan: remains the same. Department D – Espionage in the American sphere: Oberführer Heinrich Friedmann. Department E – Espionage in Eastern Europe: Obersturmbannführer Paul Meinhardt. Department F – Technical Matters: remains the same."

I glanced at my husband sitting in the front row, who was looking as surprised as I was by his sudden promotion both in job title and rank. I wondered what was behind such a generous gesture though, because Dr. Kaltenbrunner definitely didn't belong to the type of people who were doing good right and left just because they were so kind. Just like Standartenführer Schellenberg, he always had a hidden motive.

After making more changes in the commanding staff positions, Gruppenführer Kaltenbrunner read the list of people who were to be transferred to other offices or fired from their positions because 'they didn't meet the requirements necessary for the excellent service.' Barbara whispered another 'Oh, God' when he proceeded with *SS-Helferinnen* staff. Surprisingly, he didn't start firing every second girl, but turned to Standartenführer Schellenberg instead.

"Standartenführer, I don't really care for the *Helferinnen* staff as long as their immediate bosses are satisfied with their work, but I still need a secretary to take care of the correspondence. Just tell me which one of them has the most brains, types fast, pretty to look at and can make decent coffee?"

Schellenberg smiled and looked at where all of us were sitting, not making any eye contact with me though.

"Well… they are all fine workers with excellent characteristics, I don't really know how to single someone out…"

"They've been working under your supervision for more than half a year already, and you don't know which one is the best?" The Austrian raised an eyebrow at Schellenberg.

"Well… the best would be Annalise Friedmann, but she's *my* personal secretary and—"

"Not anymore, she's not." Gruppenführer Kaltenbrunner looked at me for the first time since he started the meeting and grinned. "She'll be working for me now."

"But Herr Gruppenführer, I need her." Schellenberg was obviously not happy about such a move. "She really is an irreplaceable worker for me, I can't find anyone else to do her job."

"Are you arguing with me?"

"No, of course not, Herr Gruppenführer, I'm only saying that she has proven to be invaluable as my work assistant."

"Well, too bad, Herr Schellenberg. Now she'll become invaluable as *my* work assistant." Dr. Kaltenbrunner gave the Chief of *SD-Ausland* a charming smile, and I knew right away that there would be war between the two of them from now on. "That about sums it up, ladies and gentleman. Any questions?"

Even if there were any, no one dared to raise a hand.

"Good. Dismissed."

"Son of a bitch!" Standartenführer Schellenberg cursed out very rarely and only when he was really angry. "He did it on purpose! Any girl from the department has enough brains and ten fingers to print orders, and that's all he needs her for. I shouldn't have said that you were so good."

I had almost finished packing my office supplies in a small box and shrugged.

"It's not your fault, Herr Standartenführer. He would have picked me anyway, even if I wasn't good at all."

"Why do you think so?"

"Trust me, he would have." I picked up the box from the table and extended my hand to my former boss. "I'm very sorry that I have to leave. It's been a wonderful opportunity working with you, Herr Standartenführer. Thank you for everything. And please, let me know if I can do something for you in the future, I can take some paperwork home and do it for you if you need me to."

He shook my hand and nodded.

"Thank you for the excellent work, Annalise. I'll make sure it'll be reflected in your personal file. And… good luck with your new boss."

I chuckled at the expression of his face.

"Thank you, sir."

I felt really sad leaving Walther Schellenberg's office since I really enjoyed working under his command. But regarding my counterspy activity, my new appointment was even better than the previous one: all of Gruppenführer Kaltenbrunner's paperwork would be going through my hands now, and his position was of much greater importance than Standartenführer Schellenberg's. Rudolf and Ingrid's superiors would be very happy with that.

When I walked in Gruppenführer Kaltenbrunner's anteroom, his adjutant just nodded to me from the table in the corner without moving the phone from his ear. I just started organizing my working place when he put the phone down and headed to the exit. Already at the door he turned around and said, "He wants coffee. Go make him coffee."

Great. From the position of the SD-Ausland's Chief's personal assistant I am degraded to an ordinary coffee maker. I opened my mouth to ask Gruppenführer's adjutant how our new boss preferred his coffee, but he had already disappeared. It seemed like I had to go and ask it myself. I knocked on the door, and after getting a 'yes' from inside, I opened it to find the new Chief of the RSHA on the phone as well. Dr. Kaltenbrunner was more polite than his immediate subordinate though; he covered the phone with his hand and smiled at me.

"Yes, Frau Friedmann?"

"How do you want it, Herr Gruppenführer?"

"How do I want it? Hot and on my table," he replied with a grin.

I squinted my eyes at him trying really hard not to start laughing. He was incorrigible.

"I'm talking about your coffee."

He grinned even wider. "Me too."

"Well, if you're such a big joker, you're going to have it the way I like it."

Only after saying it aloud I realized the double meaning of it, but Dr. Kaltenbrunner noticed it first of course.

"Oh really? That's fine, that's even interesting when the girl is in charge."

"Oh, God!" I closed the door behind myself before he would say something even dirtier, and heard him laugh on the other side. It seemed like working in my new office would be a lot of fun to say the least.

If I thought that dirty jokes about coffee was as far as it would go with my new boss, I was very mistaken. The very next day, when the new Chief of the RSHA entered the anteroom, he looked me up and down and noticed with his infamous arrogant grin, "You know, it's a shame that you have to wear this uniform."

I naively thought that maybe he'd allow me to wear regular dresses to work and even smiled back.

"What would you prefer to see me in?"

"I'd prefer to see you naked."

Right. What else did I expect to hear?

"Go away with your dirty insinuations, Herr Gruppenführer. I thought you were serious."

"Oh, I very much am!"

I don't even want to think where that conversation would go if Georg didn't come in and handed Dr. Kaltenbrunner the morning correspondence.

The next day Gruppenführer Kaltenbrunner was leaving his office and motioned me to follow him.

"I want to see if you're really that good of a stenographer as Schellenberg was saying. I have a meeting with Reichsführer and will need you to put down every word."

"Of course, Herr Gruppenführer."

I had just gladly assumed that we were finally back to a professional relationship, when he started his tricks again. First of all, he told me to sit right next to him so he could 'see if I'm writing everything down correctly.' Then, as soon as

Reichsführer Himmler turned to a map on the wall and therefore couldn't see what was going on behind his back, Dr. Kaltenbrunner put his hand on the back of my chair and slightly moved my left hand towards himself, so he could 'have a better look at my report.'

I gave him my best murderous look and mouthed, 'What are you doing?' so Reichsführer wouldn't hear me. But the mischievous Chief of the RSHA just tapped his finger on the paper in front of me and mouthed back, 'Keep writing.' Of course he moved away from me only when Reichsführer turned around.

On the way back to our office, when we finally could speak again, I squinted my eyes at him and said, "If you don't stop it with your behavior, I swear I am going to take you down to the Gestapo basement one day and will be killing you slowly and painfully."

But as it turned out, nothing could impress the Austrian and his dirty mind.

"Mm, sounds promising. Personally I didn't know that you were into *that* kind of stuff, but I'm open to experiments."

Trying very hard not to start laughing or blushing, I quickly looked around and making sure that we were alone in the hallway, I smacked him hard on his shoulder with the report I was carrying.

"Are we starting right now?" He playfully raised his eyebrow.

"We're not starting anything! Here, take your report and I'm going to check if the transcriptions Herr Müller promised you are ready."

"What do you mean, take your report? I need a transcription for it."

"You said you knew stenography! Just an hour ago!"

"I lied."

"Why would you watch so closely what I was writing then?"

"I wasn't looking at the paper."

Gruppenführer Kaltenbrunner lowered his eyes to the level of my chest. I shook my head.

"You are absolutely disgusting."

"It sounds like a complement coming from you."

"I feel like I need a shower after everything I heard from you in the past few minutes."

"Let's take it together, I can scrub your back."

I tried my best to keep a stern face, but failed, burst out laughing and went to see Gruppenführer Müller, thinking what a difference from the always professional Schellenberg Dr. Kaltenbrunner was. Surprisingly, but I couldn't get mad at him no matter how hard I tried.

Compared to my multiple duties in Standartenführer Schellenberg's office, being Gruppenführer Kaltenbrunner's secretary was a vacation. All I did that day was basically type the orders that needed to be signed and sent out (but Georg already took care of that, as it was technically the responsibility of Gruppenführer's adjutant), make coffee and take care of the calls if Georg was running errands around the building. Georg even let me go earlier that day, saying that Herr Gruppenführer and he had to go to the Reich Chancellery for a meeting. I picked up my bag and went by Heinrich's new office, which he occupied now instead of the old Chief of Department D.

My poor husband was buried under the pile of reports and orders, which he had to become familiar with in a matter of a few days, and accepted my help with filing them with gratitude. When the working day was officially over, we decided to take the rest of the files home, and went down to the garage, where Hanz was already waiting for us. However in the car Heinrich threw the file that he was trying to concentrate on for quite some time on the seat, and said, "How about to hell with work and let's go celebrate our promotion tonight?"

"Sounds fine by me!"

"Great! Let's go home, change and then I'll take my beautiful wife to the best restaurant in the city. Did I tell you that I got a very impressive raise as well?"

"Really? Does it make me a trophy wife now?"

"Absolutely. I'll buy you all the French dresses that you like and will be showing you off right and left. After all, I'm a very important *Oberführer* now, aren't I?"

He straightened out in his seat with a very pompous playful look and I couldn't help but laugh.

"Yes, darling, you look very important. You have to change the insignia on your uniform now, don't you? I'll have Magda take care of that, she's a great seamstress, she'll fix it in five minutes for you."

"Thank you, sweetheart."

I smiled and asked him after a pause, "Do you remember when you came over by my house for the first time and I couldn't fix you a proper lunch without my housekeeper? You laughed at me and said that you feel bad for my future husband because—"

"…because you'll starve the poor fella to death, yes, I remember it very well," Heinrich finished for me and smiled. "And you said that I shouldn't be feeling bad for him because he'll marry a girl, not a chef and will have to afford a housekeeper. And I said, what if you marry a military man, and the war will start and you'll have to take care of him?"

"And I did marry a military man, and the war did start," I concluded with a smile. "But thank God you're not in the *Waffen-SS* in the Eastern front, but here with me. And thank God we still can afford a housekeeper."

Heinrich chuckled, but then got serious again.

"I'm going to be away a lot now, you know that, right? That new position requires a lot of travelling. It's not my former steady office post."

I frowned. "Really?"

Heinrich nodded, and then it suddenly hit me. *He* did it on purpose. Gruppenführer Kaltenbrunner knew perfectly well what he was doing by delegating the office to my husband, to be able to send him away whenever he wanted. It all came together now, Heinrich's promotion, my new appointment and more than anything Adam's story about what Dr. Kaltenbrunner had told him in Mauthausen. *She's mine.* I didn't give Adam's words too much meaning because he clearly said that Gruppenführer was very drunk, and people say a lot of things when they get drunk. But this move was calculated and done on purpose, definitely not under the influence of alcohol. Did he really have some sinister plans on my account, and was pretending to be nice just to make me drop my guards?

"God dammit."

"What happened?" Heinrich turned to me.

"Oh… nothing. I just remembered that I didn't type one of the orders he asked me, that's all," I lied. "I'll do it tomorrow morning. Tonight we celebrate."

———————

It was almost eleven, and I was drunk. Heinrich kept telling me stories about the former Chief of Department D and what he got fired for (think prostitutes and alcohol, sometimes even on duty), and I tried not to laugh too loud. The other patrons of the restaurant were paying us too much unwanted attention anyway, but mostly thanks to Heinrich's SD uniform, the organization that regular people tried to stay away from the further the better, and me, 'half-naked' (as Heinrich called it) in my black dress, which I brought from Paris a couple of years ago. I wasn't 'half-naked' of course, but the back of the dress was completely open, and it was way against the modest fashion that the Führer approved of.

"Well, I'm not dressing up for the Führer, I'm dressing up for you." I raised my eyebrow at Heinrich, and he laughed. The dress stayed.

I didn't want to think of the Führer that night, of the Party, of the war and everything else, I wanted just to go back to the way it was when Heinrich and I just started dating, when I didn't have to wake up every single day thinking if I'd get caught today or not, if Heinrich might get compromised, if we'd survive another week. I wanted to be that carefree young girl again, to get drunk with my husband, to roll in the snow outside and not to think of tomorrow.

"Heinrich, let's go by that park again, remember where you took me after I got drunk on Christmas party for the SD staff where you took me as your date?"

"Of course I remember. I kissed you there for the first time." He grinned at me.

"Yes, you did." I giggled. "And then we almost got arrested by the Gestapo."

"Let's go do it again!"

Heinrich finished his drink, threw the money on the table and helped me get up.

In twenty minutes we parked our car next to the park, and I was happy to see that it was snowing outside, just like it was four years ago. I was wearing the fur coat that Heinrich gave me for my eighteenth Birthday, after I left my old one in the hands of Ulrich Reinhard, who tried to assault me in my own theatre. He was working in the same building with me now, but I didn't want to think about it tonight.

We slowly strolled down the white alley, reminiscing about the first time we met, the first time we kissed, of our wedding day and how happy we were back then. We still were, and we still loved each other the same, but that air of the pre-war innocence was long gone. We both got caught in the current of events that we couldn't really control, and were forced to make choices that we would never make if it wasn't for that damn war. But we didn't want to talk about it either. It was our night, and ours only.

Heinrich pulled me close and kissed me. He always knew how to kiss me the way to make me forget about everything in the world, how to hold me so close that I couldn't breathe, how to make my head light and my legs weak. He put his hands inside my coat, and I liked how the leather of his gloves felt against the thin material of my dress.

"Come here," he said, taking my hand in his and pulling me towards the car parked nearby. "I want to show you something important."

"What would that be, Herr Oberführer?"

"My backseat."

I was still giggling like a little girl when my own husband pushed me inside the car and laid on top of me, stripping off my coat and pulling up the skirt over my thighs. I took his overcoat off him and it fell on the floor next to us; we didn't care at that point. Heinrich pulled his gloves off with his teeth just to feel my body with his bare hands, to cup my face when he covered my mouth with his again and to undo his pants faster, because he didn't want to waste any time.

He didn't even bother to take my underwear off me, so he just moved it to one side and entered me in one strong move, making me gasp and dig my fingers into his shoulders. I didn't want to close my eyes this time, I wanted to see his face, wanted to see his eyes while he was watching me, wanted him to see how good he could make me feel.

"Annalise…" he whispered my name next to my ear and kissed my neck, then my lips again, slightly biting me as he started moving faster. I pressed my legs closer to his body and stretched my arms over my head, grabbing onto the handle of the door. The backseat was definitely not designed for the purpose that we were using it for, so Heinrich put my left leg on top of his shoulder to make more room for us. In this new position he all of a sudden was so deep inside that I yelped and grabbed his arm, overwhelmed by the new sensations.

"Am I hurting you?" Heinrich stopped moving and looked at me; I shook my head and slowly lifted my other leg on top of his other shoulder.

"No... no, it feels so good... please, don't stop."

He grinned at me and started picking up the tempo again, looking me straight in the eye. Very soon I couldn't take it anymore and started moaning loudly, biting my lip in order not to scream. I had already ripped my stockings on his medals and crosses and probably bruised my skin too, but as long as he was moving so fast and strong inside of me, nothing else mattered. Heinrich was licking and biting my legs right through the silk of the stockings, grabbing my ankles, leaning even more on top of me and thrusting even harder, until I had to press both palms into the door not to bang my head on it. I shut my eyes and started screaming his name, begging him to never stop; he put his fingers on top of my mouth to keep me quiet and I started biting on them hard, which excited my husband even more.

Heinrich straightened out and pulled my legs even higher onto his shoulders, lifting up my hips with his hands and pushing himself in as deep as it was possible. I pressed as hard as I could against the door and arched my back, my whole body shivering in ecstasy. He loved seeing me like that, it only made him do it more and more, until I would start begging him to stop and to never stop at the same time. He was holding me by my waist now, digging his fingers into my skin and slamming his heavy body against mine.

"Heinrich, please!" I cried out, grabbing him by the neck and pulling him closer. He didn't let me go though, and didn't slow down either. He would only stop when he wanted it, even if it would mean that I would be half-conscious by that point. That's exactly what he did this time: after he finally satisfied his insatiable appetite, he crashed on top of me, burying his face in my hair, his arms still wrapped tightly around my waist. I moved my leg to the floor, but found no strength to move the other one. I just wished that the time would stop and we could stay like this forever, just him and I, just the two of us in the whole world.

It was a beautiful Monday morning, and I just laid out all the marked and filed correspondence on Gruppenführer Kaltenbrunner's table, when he walked in and stopped in the middle of the room, looking past by my shoulder.

"Good morning, Herr Gruppenführer." I smiled at my new boss.

"What's that?" He nodded at something behind my back.

I turned around and saw several potted flowers on the windowsill that I brought here last Friday while he was at the Reich Chancellery at the meeting with Reichsführer, after I had seen firsthand how much the new Chief of the RSHA was smoking. I thought that opening the window every time he would leave the room was a subject that needed no discussion, but while the windows would be closed, the flowers would at least somehow filter the air.

"*That* is called flowers, Herr Gruppenführer. Orchids, to be exact."

His brow slightly furrowed.

"And what are they doing in my office?"

"I brought them."

He looked even more confused now.

"Why?"

"Well, you smoke too much, and the plants are known for consuming carbon monoxide and producing oxygen from it. So this is mostly a health issue."

He finally smiled at me.

"So you brought me flowers so I wouldn't die of lung cancer in the next five years?"

"Basically... yes. You can say that."

"Well, that's very sweet of you, Frau Friedmann. Thank you."

"You're welcome, Herr Gruppenführer." He was still standing in the middle of the room looking at me, so I decided to ask for the further instructions. "Would you like me to make you coffee first, or you prefer to start with the mail?"

"Coffee would be nice."

"Coming right up."

I made him coffee just the way he liked it, with cream, a lot of sugar and not too hot, because Dr. Kaltenbrunner liked drinking it fast and in one shot. He was looking through his correspondence when I placed on the table a little tray with coffee and several biscuits which Magda had made. By now I figured that whatever he would put in his mouth instead of another cigarette was a good thing, so I started sneaking in different snacks for him in the course of the day. Busy with work, he wouldn't normally even notice my little tricks.

I was already leaving back to my working place, when Dr. Kaltenbrunner called out my name.

"Frau Friedmann!"

"Yes, Herr Gruppenführer?"

"You didn't sort these letters."

He lifted up one with the marking 'Top Secret' on the envelope.

"I'm not allowed to touch those."

"Who told you?"

"Georg did."

"Is he the Chief of the RSHA?"

"No, but... I thought it was your order."

Dr. Kaltenbrunner shook his head.

"You're my personal secretary, and I don't have secrets from you. From now on, sort them out for me, please. You won't believe how much nonsense there is amongst those letters, and I don't have time to deal with it."

"Could you be more specific about what you consider nonsense, Herr Gruppenführer, so in the future I know how to sort them out?"

"Why don't we open them together so you know what I mean?"

He motioned me to come closer, and I walked up to him, taking a place behind his shoulder while he opened the first envelope.

"See, for example this one has several names on top, it means that it should be distributed through several offices including ours and contains general information. This one is concerning Auschwitz deportations, and I don't want to be bothered with all that Gestapo business. It's Müller's sphere, let him handle his Jews." Dr. Kaltenbrunner put the letter away and opened another one. "This one is for me personally from the mayor of Vienna asking for the working force for one of the factories, you'll type the answer to it later. Whatever is being sent to my name personally, put in a separate stack."

I nodded. Gruppenführer Kaltenbrunner handed me another letter and took a coffee cup in his hand.

"Why don't you open this one yourself now?"

I picked up his letter opener from the table and carefully opened an envelope while he was watching me closely.

"From Reichsführer, top secret, personally in your hands, concerning *Einsatzgruppen* on the territory of the Soviet Union." I heard from Heinrich what those *Einsatzgruppen* or death squads were formed for – to round up and exterminate the Jewish population of the occupied territories. The Slavic Jews were considered the main carriers of the 'Bolshevik threat' to the Reich and were subject to immediate execution. The fact that they were just ordinary people didn't concern anybody. I glanced at my boss. "Shall I continue reading it?"

"Yes."

"It says here that SS Brigadeführer Otto Ohlendorf was asking for instructions concerning the activity of *Einsatzgruppe D* in Southern Ukraine, specifically the village Grushevka the population of which is mostly Jewish. It's out of his group's way as they're moving south-west, so he was asking Reichsführer if he should send part of his people to liquidate the village. Reichsführer approved of it and now forwards this letter for your signature since it falls under your jurisdiction as the Chief of the RSHA."

Gruppenführer Kaltenbrunner looked at his coffee, drank it as if it was a shot of whiskey, put the cup back on the tray and reached for his cigarette case.

"Whatever requires my signature put on a side of the table, right here."

I slowly put the letter where he told me to and kept looking at him, but he turned away from me and just passed another letter to me, busy with his cigarette.

"Next one."

I didn't open it though and kept looking at him, until he finally turned his head to me.

"What is it, Frau Friedmann?"

"How many people live in that village?"

"I don't know. Why?"

"They're all going to die now?"

"If Reichsführer approved of it, yes."

"But *you* have to sign the actual order for their execution."

He turned in his chair to me and looked me straight in the eye.

"Where are you going with this, Frau Friedmann?"

I shrugged.

"This job is new to me, and I'm only making sure I understand everything correctly, that's all. So the orders of the mass executions have to be signed by the Chief of the RSHA, correct?"

Gruppenführer Kaltenbrunner frowned at me, but I didn't look away. I didn't care if I was making him upset; if he could send all those people to death simply by putting his signature on a piece of paper, I had all the right to make him upset by at least pointing it out to him.

"Correct, Frau Friedmann. That's called jurisdiction and subordination."

"I thought it was called mass extermination."

He rose up from his chair so fast that I unwillingly stepped back.

"What the hell do you want from me?! Do you want me not to sign it now because you feel bad for the poor people of whatever its name is, village?! Is that what you want me to do? Not to follow Reichsführer's order and go before the tribunal for treason maybe, to save a couple of hundred of goddamn Bolshevik Jews?!"

I'd already saw the effect his loud voice and angry face was producing at his subordinates, who would freeze in awe like rabbits in front of a cobra; I, however, wasn't scared of him one bit, especially now.

"No, of course not, Herr Gruppenführer," I replied in a cold voice. "I merely made an observation. I'm sorry if that upset you, I won't make any more observations in the future. I'll just follow the orders, like everybody else does."

"You do that." Gruppenführer Kaltenbrunner sat back on his chair, took a long drag on his cigarette and handed me the rest of the 'top secret' mail without looking at me.

"Take care of the rest of it. Dismissed."

"*Jawohl*, Herr Gruppenführer."

I left his office hardly restraining myself from slamming the door.

Chapter 9

Ursula gladly accepted my invitation for lunch on a Saturday afternoon since Greta, her little daughter, was now running and talking way too much for her to handle, so my best friend decided to take a long needed break from the infant. Our husbands were having lunch with some important man from the Reich Chancellery, and we were even glad it was only the two of us.

After telling me the latest gossip about our neighbors and our husbands' co-workers' wives, Ursula asked me what was new at my work. I just rolled my eyes in response.

"Ugh, don't even ask. I thought that my theatre was a pit with snakes, but the RSHA office definitely puts it to shame."

"Oh, please, tell me everything!" Ursula was almost shaking from excitement. The life of an ordinary housewife was way too boring for the always bubbly blonde, and she was always looking forward to get as much gossip and news from both her husband Max and me. Too bad I couldn't share most of the things with her.

"There's nothing to tell, really, it's just a continuous power struggle between the departments, intrigues, false accusations, arrests even amongst the employees, all of it is very… overwhelming. And my new boss is the icing on the cake."

"Why? Is he mean? Meaner than Heydrich was?"

"It's not that he's mean…" I caught myself thinking that I didn't know how to characterize Dr. Kaltenbrunner. "He's just… I don't know. Confusing."

"Confusing?" Ursula lifted her eyebrow at me. "That's an interesting description."

"Well, that's the way he is. One minute he's all smiles and jokes, and then something triggers him, and he turns into a completely different person. Did I tell you that one time he threw a glass at his adjutant?"

"No! He didn't!" Ursula opened her eyes wide in amazement. She was definitely going to tell this story to her neighbors. "Why?"

"I don't know. He got mad over something, and threw the glass right into poor Georg's head. Georg ducked of course, instinctually, so he didn't get hurt, thank God. But the fact remains."

"He's not mean to you, is he?"

"Well, let's just say, he didn't throw any glasses at me yet."

No, Gruppenführer Kaltenbrunner didn't throw glasses at me, but our working relationship remained very official and standoffish since that argument about *Einsatzgruppen*. I would bring him coffee every morning and sort out his mail. The letters that required his signature – most of them concerning concentration camps,

Einsatzgruppen, forced labor and other absolutely horrible things so pedantically put on paper as if the numbers on the orders were bank statements and not living people – I put separately on a side of his table, just like he told me to.

One day when I brought Dr. Kaltenbrunner his coffee, he was just taking the first letter from that stack I put for him. As I was pouring coffee into his cup, he signed the letter without looking and put it away, took another one, quickly signed it again and put it on top of the first one; the rest of the letters and orders were handled in the same manner in the matter of less than a minute. I stood still in my place watching him do it and not believing my eyes. He didn't even care about the contents of those orders.

"Don't you want to read them first?" I finally couldn't contain myself anymore; unlike him I knew too well what was inside those orders.

"Are you telling me how to do my job now?" Dr. Kaltenbrunner asked me harshly.

"No, but you might want to be curious what you're signing at least, Herr Gruppenführer."

"Maybe I don't want to know what I'm signing. Have you thought of that, Frau Friedmann?"

I didn't say anything and just frowned at him more. He got up from his place, lit up a cigarette, and started pacing around the office. I remained where I was, watching him from the side of my eye. Suddenly he walked up very close to me.

"Look at me." I lifted my head to him to meet his eyes. "Do you think I like that? Do you think I enjoy it, signing all this shit every single day?! Do you think I want all this Gestapo dirt going through my hands?! Do you think I wake up every morning thinking, oh great, I have a day filled with joy of signing orders for 'special treatment' ahead of me, let me get to work as soon as possible so Reichsführer Himmler can send another several thousands of people to death by my hands. Is that what you think?!"

"I don't think that my opinion matters, Herr Gruppenführer. I'm merely an ordinary secretary."

"No, you're not!" He almost screamed at me. "You're everything but an ordinary secretary. Ordinary secretaries don't walk around all day giving their chiefs those accusing looks. I know exactly what you think, Frau Friedmann. You think that I'm a murderer, that's what you think. And you think that I like what I'm doing."

"Maybe you don't like it, but you agree with it, and no matter how much you try to justify yourself, Herr Gruppenführer, the result is still the same."

"Maybe I don't agree with it. What choice do I have? Not to sign Reichsführer's orders?"

"If you didn't agree with Reichsführer's policy concerning the RSHA, you probably shouldn't have accepted the position of its Chief."

"I didn't accept it!!!" He shouted so loud that I held my breath for a moment. And only then I comprehended what he said. For a moment silence filled the room, and it was even louder than his words. I blinked several times trying to understand what he meant by it.

"If you didn't accept it, how come we're having this conversation right now?"

Dr. Kaltenbrunner made another step towards me and said very quietly but still with anger in his voice, "I refused to take over the office three times, Frau Friedmann. I refused to be a replacement for Heydrich. As a matter of fact, I asked Reichsführer Himmler for a position in the Eastern front instead. But he rejected my request, and sent me a military order to summon me to Berlin immediately. And you know what a military order is: you don't follow it, you get executed for treason, and your immediate family members get sent to the labor camps. Now you can go ahead and keep despising me, just don't forget to send out these signed by your terrible chief orders to whoever they're for. You can go now."

All of a sudden I felt extremely ashamed of myself and the way I acted around him this whole time. Naturally, I had no idea that Gruppenführer Kaltenbrunner was *ordered* to take over the position of the Chief of the RSHA, just like my late brother was ordered to transfer into *SS-Totenkopf* and become one of the guards in Auschwitz instead being sent to the Eastern front.

"I'm very sorry, Herr Gruppenführer," I finally said. "I didn't know that."

He remained silent, looking through his papers. Still feeling guilty, I asked, "Is there anything I can do for you?"

Dr. Kaltenbrunner rubbed his forehead and finally looked at me. All of a sudden he seemed very tired.

"Your job. That's what we're here for after all."

I nodded and picked up the signed orders from his table.

"I apologize again, Herr Gruppenführer."

"No need to, Frau Friedmann. You can go."

I nodded again, and left his office feeling absolutely terrible. I made a mistake by jumping to conclusions when in reality I had no idea what was going on. But at the same time for some reason I was extremely happy that Dr. Kaltenbrunner didn't turn out to be a heartless monster as I had already started to portray him in my mind. He didn't like all that police activity, he didn't want to be a part of it and was signing all those orders without looking not because he didn't care, but because he didn't want to know what's inside.

After another week Dr. Kaltenbrunner told me to hand all the orders concerning the Gestapo matters and coming from Reichsführer that required his, Chief of the RSHA's signature, to Georg so the latter would stamp them with the facsimile. It seemed that he didn't even want them on his table anymore. I didn't blame him; I loathed even reading those orders. But very soon, however, I had to face those orders way closer than I ever wanted to.

One afternoon, when Gruppenführer Kaltenbrunner and his adjutant left to the Reich Chancellery, Gruppenführer Müller walked in asking for the Chief.

"He's left for the meeting with Reichsführer, Herr Gruppenführer." I apologetically smiled at the Chief of the Gestapo. "Is there anything I can help you with?"

"Yes, as a matter of fact you can. I missed him by five minutes and this order needs to be signed immediately. Do you have the keys for his office?"

"Yes, I do."

"Great! Go stamp it for me quickly and I'll send it to the Kommandant of Mauthausen right away."

Gruppenführer Müller was holding a piece of paper in his outstretched hand and I took it from him.

"Well, go ahead and stamp it."

"Do you want me to…?"

"Yes, I need his signature on it. Do you know where he keeps his facsimile?"

"Yes."

I rose from my chair, took the keys to Dr. Kaltenbrunner's office from my pocket and opened the door. Gruppenführer Müller settled himself comfortably in Georg's chair behind my back. I walked up to Dr. Kaltenbrunner's table and unlocked the top drawer with another key he gave me. And then I glanced at the paper I was holding. It was an order for the 'special treatment' of the Soviet Commissars, prisoners of war, which Reichsführer wanted dead because they could spread 'communist propaganda' amongst the inmates of the camp they were confined in. Eighty seven people. And Müller needed a signature under it, a signature that would seal those eighty seven people's fate. And I was the one who had to put that signature under that order, condemning the Soviet Commissars to the gas chamber.

I dropped the order on the table and pulled both hands to my chest. There was no way I was doing it. No way. *You're going to incriminate yourself, Annalise. You have to do it.* No, I can't. *It's not your signature and not your facsimile. It's Dr. Kaltenbrunner's responsibility. The order will bear his name, not yours. You're not doing anything wrong.* It doesn't matter whose name is on the order. I'm the one who's putting it there. Without the signature those people won't die. *Yes, they will, in any case they will, and you know it. You're just following your superior's order, you aren't killing anyone.* Yes I am! Their blood will be on my hands, just like on everybody else who gives such orders. I'm an accomplice to the murder. *No, you're not. You're a counterintelligence spy and you have to pretend to be a faithful Nazi. So go ahead and play the part. Stamp it.* I can't.

"What's taking so long?" Müller's voice disrupted my inner dialogue I was having with myself. Too bad I still didn't know which voice to listen to.

"Just a second, Herr Gruppenführer. I can't find Dr. Kaltenbrunner's facsimile, his adjutant must have put it someplace else again."

Of course I lied. Dr. Kaltenbrunner's facsimile was right where it always was, in the top drawer in a little black box. I had already taken it out and was holding it in my hand.

Do it. I can't. *You did much worse things before, Annalise. If we're talking about being an accomplice to the murder, you helped to put already two people to grave.* Heydrich deserved it. *What about Josef then? Did he deserve it too?* No, he was just a victim of the circumstances. And I still feel terribly guilty about his death, every single day. *Fate of these eighty seven people has been decided already. If you don't stamp it, you'll just get yourself in trouble. You're playing a devoted Nazi, remember? Stamp it.*

"Have you found it yet?"

Both voices got quiet. Now I needed to make a decision on my own. I closed my eyes and swallowed hard.

"Yes, I have, Herr Gruppenführer."

The loud bang of the facsimile on the wooden table was like a gunshot. I felt as if I just put a bullet in every single one of those Commissars' head. I was no better than *them* now: Müller, Reichsführer Himmler and the Führer himself. And I suddenly realized how Dr. Kaltenbrunner must have felt signing all those orders every single morning. It was a disgusting feeling. I started to understand why he was smoking so much.

I put away the facsimile, picked up the stamped paper from the table, locked the office door behind, and handed the order to the smiling Chief of the Gestapo.

"Thank you very much, Frau Friedmann. It was very nice of you."

"You're welcome, Herr Gruppenführer."

Müller nodded at me and left the anteroom. I sat behind my table, put my elbows on top of it and rested my head in my hands. That's exactly how Dr. Kaltenbrunner saw me when he came back from the Reich Chancellery. He was joking about something with Georg as he walked in, and I quickly tried to regain my composure. I hoped that he wouldn't notice that I cried before.

"Good afternoon, Herr Gruppenführer. Would you like some coffee?" I tried not to look at him, reorganizing some papers on my table.

"No, I've had lunch with Reichsführer, thank you."

I nodded and kept my nose in my paperwork, but I could feel that he was watching me. Already in the doors of his office, Dr. Kaltenbrunner turned to me.

"Frau Friedmann, come in for a minute."

Less than anything I wanted to 'come in for a minute,' but I still had to inform him about Müller's request, so I had no choice but to follow my boss inside. He closed the door behind me and stood still next to it, next to me. I was still looking at the floor.

"What's going on?"

"Nothing." I shifted my gaze to the carpet, away from him.

"Look at me."

I lifted my eyes to meet his, but then looked away again.

"What is it with you? Are you upset over something?"

"Nothing, just a little tired, that's all."

"You're not feeling well? Do you want to go home?"

"No, I'm fine, Herr Gruppenführer. I'm sorry."

He was talking in such a half-concerned, half-comforting way that I felt tears building up in my throat again. I hated when my father used to talk like that to me when I'd already stopped crying over something, and that sympathetic tone would only trigger me again. I took a deep breath and dug my nails into the palm of the hand, putting myself together. I lifted my eyes to him again and this time even managed a smile.

"I just need coffee, that's all. I'm making it for you all day, and never for myself. I think it's time I start drinking it too."

Dr. Kaltenbrunner slowly smiled back at me, but his eyes remained serious; I knew he wasn't buying my lies.

"You can take coffee breaks whenever you need to, Frau Friedmann."

"Thank you, Herr Gruppenführer." I smiled again and added, "Oh, by the way, Gruppenführer Müller stopped by, he needed you to sign one of his orders about the Soviet POWs. He asked me to stamp it for him, and I used your facsimile. I hope it's alright with you? Herr Müller told me I was authorized to do that."

"Yes, you can stamp whatever he brings in my absence. Just read it first."

"Will do, Herr Gruppenführer."

I was waiting for him to dismiss me, but he kept looking at me.

"What about those POWs? What was the order for?"

Why did he have to ask me that?

"Order for the execution of eighty seven Soviet commissars."

Gruppenführer Kaltenbrunner nodded.

"Did you put a signature under it?"

I wasn't smiling anymore. The feeling I had was as if I fell on a glass, but instead of taking that glass out of my wound, he started slowly turning it inside.

"Yes, I did. He told me to."

"That's why you're so upset? Because you feel guilty about it?"

I remained silent.

"You don't have to blame yourself for it, Frau Friedmann. You just happen to be a part of this big bureaucratic machine, and your position in this machine requires you to do such things from time to time. That's how I look at it. But it requires me to do even worse things, even though I don't want to have anything to do with them. You see, when I was taking over the office, I made a deal with Reichsführer Himmler. I told him that all I want to be concerned with is the intelligence. I like it, and I enjoy doing it. All the secret police matters with the Gestapo and concentration camps, I don't want to even know what's going on there. I've been telling all of them from the very beginning that the extermination of the Jews and prisoners of war is hurting the image of Germany abroad. Himmler doesn't care about that, but he still promised me that he and Müller would keep the Gestapo under their direct control and will only send me some paperwork for signing, in order not to create confusion in subordination. But technically, it's still me who signs those people's death sentences, you understand now?"

"Like I did today?" I finished his thought.

Dr. Kaltenbrunner looked at something in the distance and then quickly walked to his table, looking for something in the bottom drawer.

"If you keep thinking about it that way, my dear Frau Friedmann, you'll give yourself a nervous breakdown, and later a severe depression. It's not our fault that the Reich works this way. It's them on top who are pulling the strings; we're merely mute dolls moving under their music. But you know what always helps me feel better?" Gruppenführer Kaltenbrunner put a bottle of champagne on his table and two glasses next to it. "Alcohol."

I watched him as he opened the champagne and poured both glasses full.

"Come here, Frau Friedmann. Take this glass, and let's toast to you."

"To me?"

"Yes. Welcome to the club of people who don't decide anything in this world."

The bitterness in his eyes reflected mine when I toasted my glass with him. We both drank it all the way, to the bottom. And then another one. And another, until we emptied the bottle and switched to brandy and soda, which he also kept in his bar. We kept drinking all day, until both of us forgot why we started drinking in the first place. When at the end of the working day Georg knocked on the door and said that my husband was waiting for me outside, I could hardly get back on my feet from the chair I was sitting in. Heinrich didn't say anything while I was following him unsteadily all the way to the garage, but in the car he turned to me and finally asked, "Is there any reason why you're leaving your Chief's office almost incoherent?"

"Yes, there is, Heinrich." I leaned back in my seat and closed my eyes. "Remember how you told me that you executed a hundred of Jews in your early *Waffen-SS* days? Well, I executed eighty seven Soviet Commissars today."

"What are you talking about?"

And then I told him everything.

"I always thought that I'm this good Jewish girl working for the sake of my people, Heinrich. But I'm no better than the last butcher of the Gestapo. I'm one of them now. I'm a murderer."

"No, you're not, Annalise. It's not your fault."

"Yes, it is, Heinrich. You know what my father always used to say? Standing next to a person who's committing the crime and not doing anything about it is the same thing as committing that crime with your own hands. And it's not just that I didn't do anything about it, I handed the gun to the killer. I'm a murderer."

"You're just drunk and upset. You're not thinking clearly."

He could say whatever he wanted to. Dr. Kaltenbrunner could say what he wanted to. But I still knew it inside myself that I would never be the same person again. I had innocent peoples' blood on my hands. I was a murderer.

"Annalise, we could really use that paperwork." Ingrid sat across the table from me and tried to catch my eyes. I was still looking at my tea cup. "Especially if you're saying that Kaltenbrunner doesn't even read it. He's never going to know where the leak is coming from."

The Americans wanted me to start copying the top secret orders I had access to, and my husband had the misfortune to brag to them about it.

"He'll know."

"How would he know?"

"He will. He always knows everything. He has a sixth sense when it comes to…" Me. When it comes to me. "When it comes to espionage. He always points out just the right people to Müller even in the most complicated cases. He's a very smart man."

Ingrid's gaze was almost accusing this time.

"You could try at least. You know that we're always very careful when it comes to handling the information. You're not risking anything, if you look at it closely."

"If you look at it closely, I'm risking everything. You're the ones who get pulled out right away if something goes down; I'll end up on the gallows, together with my husband. But you don't care about it, do you?"

"Of course we care about it."

"No, you don't. You only care because you're afraid to lose a good source of information, that's all. You don't care who that source is. People can be so easily replaced in this game, can't they, Ingrid?"

"Why are you talking to me like that, Annalise?"

"I know that you don't like me, Ingrid. But making me risk my life for you, I'm sorry, that's a little too much."

"You aren't risking your life for *me*, darling. You're risking it for the sake of your country. The future, better country. Free of that Nazi plague. I think it's a very noble goal to risk your life for."

I didn't say anything. She was right of course.

"I can get you something that's being distributed through several offices. This way it's not too incriminating."

"That'll do." Ingrid finally smiled. "And try to get back with your old boss Schellenberg, we could really use some information from his part too."

They all wanted something from me. I had no other choice but to comply.

It was a good morning for the Americans: a lot of letters came through concerning the situation in the Warsaw ghetto. I had just finished sorting them out, learning by heart all the numbers and names on the orders, when Dr. Kaltenbrunner walked into the anteroom.

"Good morning, Herr Gruppenführer."

"Good morning, Frau Friedmann. A lot of mail today?"

"Yes, the Warsaw ghetto uprising issue."

Gruppenführer Kaltenbrunner walked to the table where I was sitting and looked over my shoulder to the letters I was sorting out for him.

"Have Georg stamp them and send them out when he's done, will you?"

"Of course, Herr Gruppenführer."

"I also need you to type a letter for me, it's urgent. Müller just gave me a radio message in the hallway."

Müller was never good news. But I still pulled a typing machine closer to me, put a piece of paper in it and turned my head to my boss, waiting for his instructions.

Dr. Kaltenbrunner had a habit of walking around the room while dictating his orders, but this time he stood right by me. The order was for the immediate execution of any armed rebels who possessed an immediate threat to the *Waffen-SS*. The uprising started even before Dr. Kaltenbrunner took over the position of the Chief of the RSHA, and the Warsaw issue was his so-called field test, which was supposed to show the Führer if he had made the right choice appointing his fellow Austrian to such an important position. Therefore, Gruppenführer Kaltenbrunner was trying to resolve the issue the sooner the better.

The problem was that the rebels, who knew that their only fate would be the deportation to the labor camps and slow and agonizing death from starvation, hard work and diseases, decided to die fighting. I knew that if I happened to be amongst them, I would have probably done the same thing. And if my great-grandparents hadn't immigrated to Germany in the middle of the nineteenth century, I would have been amongst them. Deep inside I was very proud that they had courage to fight their oppressors for so long, and deep inside I kept saying prayers every morning for them to hold for another day.

"…by being shot on the spot." Gruppenführer Kaltenbrunner finished another sentence. He stood behind my back, and then put both hands by the sides of the typing machine, leaning over my shoulder and looking at the already typed text. I could feel the warmth of his body right against my back. "New paragraph."

I readjusted the typing machine and waited for him to speak.

"It is necessary to suppress any attempts of the rebels to escape the territory of the Ghetto. It is strongly advised to all the SS guards to reinforce the surveillance of the wall separating Jewish and Aryan sides, in order for the rebels not to get any more ammunition from their supporters on the outside. New paragraph. All the food supplies should also be put on hold."

I turned my head to him and immediately regretted it, because his face was now only inches away from mine. He looked at me with his dark eyes, and all of a sudden I was very aware that Georg was absent fetching some radiograms from Amt IV, and that it was only the two of us in the anteroom. I quickly turned back to the paper, blushing for some reason.

"They will die starving then," I almost whispered because Dr. Kaltenbrunner kept looking at me very closely.

"You feel bad for everybody, don't you?" he said softly. "You should step away from your religion a little, just like I did. It doesn't help with our work, you know. The guilt that they insert in you during every mass, it's not good."

He slightly touched my black Catholic cross and then the beads on my wrist, one by one, very slowly.

"Don't you feel bad for those people, Herr Gruppenführer? There aren't only rebels inside the Ghetto, there are mostly women and children. Why do they have to suffer?"

"If I could separate women and children and put them in a different place, I would have sent them food," he replied with a pensive look on his face, still playing with my cross. "But they all live together. Right now it's not me who's at fault that they'll starve, it's their men, who aren't too bright, obviously."

"What would you have done if you were Jewish, living in the Ghetto with your wife and children and knowing that the Germans are coming to kill all of you? Wouldn't you take a gun in your hands to protect them?"

"But I'm not Jewish."

"What if you were?"

"Probably you're right," Dr. Kaltenbrunner answered after a pause. "If I were, I would have. But I'm a German, and it's my duty to protect my German soldiers from their bullets."

I sighed. I knew that in his mind it made a lot of sense. But I was Jewish, and for me he was an aggressor, a representative of the nation who came up with the idea to exterminate the people I belonged to. We would never understand each other. Why then did I feel so strangely sensitive to his presence while he stood there, over me, almost touching my hands with his, far too close than a chief should stand next to his subordinate? I could swear that he smelled my hair as he took a deep breath straightening up behind my back. And then Georg walked in, and I was glad that he distracted me from the very controversial emotions I started to experience. I tried to concentrate on what I was going to report to Ingrid.

Chapter 10

I was helping Heinrich with his tie as we were both getting ready for work. He already had new insignia on his uniform jacket, and I thought once again what a handsome officer he was. After I finished fixing his tie, he smiled gratefully at me and kissed me on the lips.

"What would I do without you?"

"I don't know. Probably you'd have found yourself another pretty ballerina and married her."

"I wish you still were a ballerina and didn't have to do what you do now."

"You just miss seeing me dance on stage all dolled up." I pinched my husband on a cheek, trying to lighten up the serious subject with my little joke. "Now let's go over the plan of me becoming friends with Standartenführer Schellenberg again."

Last evening after Magda left and it was just the two of us in the dining room, we started working on me getting back at least a partial position as Walther Schellenberg's assistant. Our American friends from the Secret Service were more than happy with our reports, and especially Heinrich's, after his recent appointment to the position of the Chief of Department responsible for the American sector. My husband informed the Americans about every single possible threat discovered by his agents, and Ingrid once even told Heinrich that one of the 'very important' US generals announced *Mr. Friedmann* the most valuable counterintelligence agent.

Since Heinrich was reporting to Standartenführer Schellenberg on a regular basis and because the two were on very friendly terms, we decided that inviting the Chief of *SD-Ausland* to lunch to Heinrich's office (where I would happen to be by 'pure coincidence') would be a perfect plan for me to offer him my services of a part-time secretary. It would mean that I would take all the paperwork he needed help with to my house and bring it back the next day filed, decoded, translated or whatever he wanted me to do with it.

The main goal of that mini-operation was to regain access to all those reports of which Schellenberg wouldn't even inform his immediate boss Dr. Kaltenbrunner, bringing them right to Reichsführer Himmler with whom he was getting along far better than with the Chief of the RSHA. I had already proven myself to be an efficient and trustworthy assistant to Standartenführer, and no matter how hard we tried, neither my husband nor I could find any possible reasons why the Chief of *SD-Ausland* would reject my offer.

He didn't. On the contrary, it seemed like Herr Schellenberg was more than glad to hand me a part of his correspondence, on one condition from my side – that my helping him would be absolutely confidential and no one, especially my immediate boss, would know about it. He agreed with a smile.

However, in the following couple of weeks Standartenführer Schellenberg's daily visits to my table (normally at the end of the day, when he would discretely hand me a small portfolio containing top secret reports, with which he didn't trust anybody, even his own adjutant), started to irritate our very easily irritable superior – Gruppenführer Kaltenbrunner. One day, when he happened to be leaving his office earlier than usual and saw Walther Schellenberg leaning on my table and talking to me, it got him really mad.

"Don't you have anything better to do than bother my secretary all the time?"

Herr Schellenberg straightened out before his superior, but did it with visible reluctance.

"I wasn't bothering her, Herr Gruppenführer. We were discussing some matters concerning the reports I brought. I was instructing her on what to do with each one." He was a great liar.

"Herr Schellenberg, it seems to me that you forgot your position in this office." Gruppenführer Kaltenbrunner menacingly squinted his eyes at his subordinate. "I'm the Chief of the RSHA, not you. Therefore, you are not to discuss and definitely not to instruct *my* secretary about anything. It's my job to tell her how to handle the correspondence."

"I was just trying to make your job a little easier." Walther Schellenberg gave Dr. Kaltenbrunner the fakest charming smile I'd seen. The latter's jaw line hardened; he was definitely not in the mood for joking.

"I appreciate the effort, but don't bother next time. And if you need to bring anything to my office, send your adjutant. It's really not necessary to bring the paperwork to my secretary personally."

"What if I don't trust my adjutant? He always loses something."

"Well, he's a shitty adjutant then and needs to be fired. Get yourself another one and have him do the job. Understood?"

"Yes, Herr Gruppenführer. You've made yourself more than clear."

"I'm glad I did. I hope we won't be having this conversation again." With those words Dr. Kaltenbrunner turned to me and nodded at the papers I was working on for him for the following day. "Frau Friedmann, put the rest of my correspondence in the folder, please, and help me bring it to my car, will you?"

"Of course, Herr Gruppenführer."

He could have taken it himself of course, but he obviously didn't want me to stay in the company of my former boss, so I quickly put all the paperwork together and got up from my chair. As all three of us were leaving the office, I politely nodded at Standartenführer Schellenberg.

"Goodbye, Herr Standartenführer."

"Goodbye, Annalise. Herr Gruppenführer."

I knew that he called me by my first name on purpose, just to aggravate his superior even more, and he more than succeeded. If looks could kill, than the one that Dr. Kaltenbrunner threw at the Chief of *SD-Ausland* would leave from the latter only a tiny pile of ashes. I followed Dr. Kaltenbrunner all the way to the car in complete silence, and only when we were alone in the garage, he all of a sudden decided to interrogate me in a manner that even my lawful husband never did.

It turned out that Gruppenführer Kaltenbrunner was thinking that the friendship between the Chief of *SD-Ausland* and me was more than just a friendship, and almost accused me of having an affair with Standartenführer Schellenberg. I was standing in front of my very angry boss, holding the files next to my chest and blinking at him, not able to believe what he was saying.

It took me quite some time to persuade Dr. Kaltenbrunner that there was nothing going on between me and my former superior, and only the argument about such kind of relationship being physically impossible just because I was coming to and leaving the RSHA with my husband and the rest of the time spending in his, Gruppenführer Kaltenbrunner's, anteroom finally made him believe me.

"Well, despite the innocence from your side, I'm still convinced there's a reason that bastard is bothering you. Has he been saying anything suggestive to you? If he has, I'll immediately let Reichsführer know about his unprofessional behavior and make him take certain measures."

"It's not necessary, Herr Gruppenführer." *The only person who always says or does those kinds of things is you! Why don't you go make a report about your unprofessional behavior?* "He hasn't been saying or doing anything, I promise."

Even though he didn't seem to be satisfied with such an answer, Dr. Kaltenbrunner at last got over his jealousy fit and took the papers from my hands. His chauffeur had just came down to the garage and was hurriedly approaching us, but before getting in the back seat of his car, my boss turned to me again.

"If he does, let me know immediately. I won't tolerate anybody harassing *my* secretary."

"I will, Herr Gruppenführer. Have a good evening."

"You too, Frau Friedmann."

I waved to the leaving car and decided to walk out of the garage as well to get some air. I'd never had to deal with scenes of jealousy before and this one, which wasn't even coming from my own husband, left me speechless. The cold March air made me rub my shoulders with both hands, but at least freshened me up. And then, just before I turned back to the entrance, a woman standing on the opposite side of the street for some reason attracted my attention. Maybe because she was standing motionlessly unlike all the other people hurrying home from work, maybe because I felt as if she was staring at me hard, but I squinted my eyes at her trying to decide if

I knew her. The scarf covering the lower part of her face wasn't helping; however, as soon as I made a move towards the opposite side of the street, she quickly turned around and walked away.

"I'm going to be leaving at the end of this week," Heinrich announced at dinner.

I knew that something was not right because he was too quiet on the way home; after we got married he never had to leave me alone and took me with him on all his trips. But this time was different. I wasn't a housewife with more than a flexible schedule anymore, and couldn't leave my work at the Reich Main Security Office whenever I pleased.

"For how long?"

"Several days, a week maximum. I have to go to Italy, to set up some connections between ours and the Italian intelligence agents." He motioned Magda to pour him more wine and smiled at me. "Don't be upset, sweetheart, you won't even notice that I'm gone."

"Yes, I will." I knew that I shouldn't have, but I wasn't even trying to hide that I was upset and put away my fork. "And I always wanted to go to Italy! It's not fair!"

"Stop pouting like a little child." Heinrich smiled at me. "You know that I would have taken you with me if I could. But your boss enjoys your company way too much, I don't think he'll let you go so easy."

I chuckled at the very truthful joke, and rubbed Rolf's ears, as he sat on the floor next to me. I was glad that the huge German shepherd was going to keep me safe while my husband would be gone. I didn't know why but I didn't want to stay all by myself in our big house.

In two days Heinrich packed a small suitcase, kissed me goodbye and left to Italy. I started missing him as soon as he closed the door behind himself. The situation at work wasn't making it any better: the Warsaw ghetto uprising started to get on the Führer's nerves, and he demanded the immediate resolution of the problem as it was hurting the image of his Reich through all possible means. Needless to say, Gruppenführer Kaltenbrunner was the one to 'take care' of it and wasn't happy about it at all.

He dealt with the stress by his favorite stress relief means – alcohol – and would start pouring himself a healthy glass of brandy as early as ten in the morning. By some strange coincidence, it made him think much clearer than his non-drinking subordinates, who were running around like chickens with their heads chopped off, and soon he outlined the plan for taking the ghetto back under the *Waffen-SS's* control.

That day Dr. Kaltenbrunner was nursing his drink even while dictating to me the orders concerning the ghetto, and by the time that we finished (way past the regular five o'clock), he was already quite drunk. I wisely decided to keep my mouth shut and not to agitate him by any speeches concerning the fate of the poor habitants of the ghetto, or about him needing to slow down with brandy. The Austrian, just like most of them, had a very short fuse and bad temper as it is, and triggering him by my usual preaching would be pure suicide.

When Walther Schellenberg showed up later with a report though, I knew that a storm was coming. In the Chief of *SD-Ausland's* case getting his superior angry was more than easy – he just had to show his face in Gruppenführer Kaltenbrunner's office. I sighed as soon as I heard the latter raise his voice more and more, and even Georg decided to run for cover 'to fetch radiograms.' I shook my head: some men were such cowards.

In less than five minutes I heard my chief yelling even louder, but when the sound of glass breaking accompanied the yelling, I just silently prayed that he didn't kill Standartenführer Schellenberg: after all, he was a nice guy and I needed him to get the information for my American friends. The door to the office swung open, and the Chief of *SD-Ausland* quickly made an escape before the next glass could hit its target.

"If I were you, I would have gone home," he said to me walking through the anteroom and nodding at Gruppenführer Kaltenbrunner's office while making circles with his index finger by his temple, clearly implying that my boss wasn't in his right mind to put it mildly.

I considered such an option for about ten seconds, but then got up, took a deep breath and opened the door to Dr. Kaltenbrunner's office. He was smoking next to the window and didn't even turn around. The mess next to his table was impressive: I guess that he also threw papers at Herr Schellenberg prior to aiming a brandy bottle to his head. The bottle itself, broken in a million little pieces, was lying next to the opposite wall. I shook my head again and went into the Chief of the RSHA's personal bathroom to get a towel. I picked up the biggest pieces of glass and wiped the rest of the liquor with a wet cloth.

"Don't bother. They'll clean it later," Dr. Kaltenbrunner finally said.

"Before they do, you'll step on it and cut your foot," I replied without turning around. "And stop smoking for Christ's sake, it's impossible to breathe here."

Without asking for permission I walked up to the window behind his table and opened it, and then the second one, next to which he was standing, slightly swaying on his feet and looking at me closely.

"You should go home and get some rest, Herr Gruppenführer. I'll go wash this towel and after that I'll tell your driver to wait for you in the car."

He didn't say anything, so I took his silence as a 'yes' and went back to the bathroom to clean the towel and my hands. Because of the running water I didn't hear him come in, and he scared the living hell out of me by tightly wrapping his arms around my waist.

"What are you doing?!" I screamed and tried to worm myself out of Gruppenführer Kaltenbrunner's embrace, but he just pressed me hard against the sink with his body. "Let me go!"

"No. You look so pretty today. I want you."

He started kissing my neck and unbuttoning my uniform jacket at the same time. He distinctively smelled of alcohol, and only then I realized how much he must have really drank. I desperately tried to push his hands away, but he was far too strong for me, and it appeared that he had a lot of experience in relieving ladies of their clothing.

"Well, I don't want *you*, so get your hands off me this instant or I'll make a report to Reichsführer on you!"

"I couldn't care less about Reichsführer. I want you. I need to touch you again, I missed you."

He shoved his hand under my jacket and grabbed my breast, pressing me even closer to himself. His other hand he put on my throat, trying to make me turn my face towards him. I couldn't loosen his grip even with both of my hands.

"Let go of me!"

"No. You're mine now."

Gruppenführer Kaltenbrunner tried to kiss me, but I jerked my head to the opposite side, pressed both hands into the sink, and tried to push him off with my behind. It was a bad idea.

"Stop fighting with me, silly girl, it won't help you. It just makes me want to fuck you more."

He bit my neck and yanked the jacket off me. I was still trying to get his hand out of my chest, but he pushed my hands off and ripped my shirt open. I started panicking and screamed. The Chief of the RSHA laughed.

"Scream all you want, sugar. Nobody's going to help you here. As for me, I even prefer my girls screaming."

No matter how much I tried to stop him, he still pulled my bra up and started feeling up my bare breasts, pushing me against the sink. I frantically looked around trying to find something to hit him with, but there was nothing. I was absolutely helpless and alone there. Even if Georg came into the anteroom, he wouldn't get involved in his chief's business.

There was no way I could make Gruppenführer Kaltenbrunner stop either. He was too drunk to think what he was doing; right now he was thinking only about satisfying his instincts. He was petting my hip through the skirt, and rubbing himself on my behind, biting my neck and shoulder. I slapped his hand when he tried to pull up the hem of my skirt, but he caught my wrists together and, holding them in one hand, still pulled my skirt up.

"No!" I yelped once again, when Gruppenführer Kaltenbrunner pushed me down onto the sink with the weight of his body until I was almost laying chest down on it, while he was grabbing my butt and thighs with his free hand.

"I swear, you have the most perfect ass I've ever seen!" He pushed my legs apart with his knee and placed his foot next to mine so I couldn't put them back together. "Oh, sugar, I'll make you feel so good!"

He probably would have had such an opportunity, but Gruppenführer Kaltenbrunner was *really* drunk, and made one mistake: he couldn't open his pants with one hand and had to let me go for a couple of seconds, which was more than enough for me to turn around and smack him across the face with all the strength I had. My chief clearly didn't expect such a move, and froze in his place looking at me in surprise. I decided to use his astonishment in my favor, pushed him out of my way with my shoulder, quickly snatched my jacket up from the floor and ran out of there while I could.

In the anteroom, already by the door, I readjusted my clothes the best and fastest I could and, holding my jacket close with both hands, ran towards the garage, where Hanz was already waiting for me. He frowned seeing me in such disarray, and asked if something happened. I managed a smile, nodded and lied that I spilled coffee on my shirt and completely messed it up. He believed me and stopped further questioning.

First thing I did at home was change and call Ursula. She heard by the sound of my voice that something wasn't right and ten minutes later already knocked on my door. She had to bring little Greta with her, because her housekeeper was busy making dinner and couldn't watch the little girl at the same time. I immediately dragged Ursula to the library, further from Magda's ears.

"What's going on? You sounded so worried on the phone, is everything alright?" I was touched by the genuine concern on my best friend's face, but first I needed to make sure that I could rely on her.

"Not really. I'll tell you if you swear not to tell Heinrich or your husband."

She was looking at me with her big blue eyes wide open.

"I'll keep quiet if you want me to. But what happened that you don't want Heinrich to know?"

I sighed. It was more difficult to say than I thought it would be.

"It's Gruppenführer Kaltenbrunner. He got very drunk today, cornered me in the bathroom and tried to…"

Ursula's brow furrowed, but she still didn't grasp it. "Tried to… what?"

"Have sex with me!"

She forced me to say it, and it came out louder than it should. Ursula gasped. "No!!! Did he really?!"

"Oh yes. And if he wasn't that drunk and I didn't have a chance to escape, he most definitely would have. Now you understand why I asked you not to tell anyone? If my husband finds out, he'll shoot him. And if you tell Max, he'll tell Heinrich right away."

"Oh my God!" She covered her mouth with her hand, still not able to believe what I just told her. "Your secret is safe with me, I promise, dear. But don't you think you should tell someone? How are you going to go back to work?"

"I'm not going back to work. I'll bring the papers asking for my resignation tomorrow morning and make him sign it. And if he refuses, I'll tell him that I'll go to Reichsführer with the report."

"You think it'll scare him?"

"No. But that's the only option I have."

"How did he even… why?"

"I don't know. He had to move to Berlin a month and a half ago, his wife and all his mistresses stayed in Austria. So he got drunk, was feeling lonely and I happened to be around I guess."

"That is not an excuse!"

"Of course it's not."

"Did you tell him that you were not interested in taking up the position of his next mistress in Berlin? I mean, did you say it clear enough for him to understand? You know how they, men, are: they don't take hints."

She obviously underestimated the gravity of situation with Dr. Kaltenbrunner.

"Ursula, I was actually screaming while he was holding my hands and pulling up my skirt."

Now she finally understood, because she covered her mouth with both hands and was staring at me without even blinking.

"Oh God! You poor thing! How did you manage to get out?"

"He released my hands to undo his pants, so I turned around, slapped him as hard as I could and ran out of there."

"Good! Let it be a lesson to him!"

"He won't learn it anyway."

"What do you mean?"

I wasn't saying anything, but Ursula understood me without any words.

"He tried it already with you, didn't he? It wasn't a single occasion."

I slowly shook my head.

"Annalise, you should tell Heinrich! You can't take such a chance! I've heard so many stories from Max, that chief of yours, he's capable of anything! And if he already did it before, he'll most certainly do it again, until he gets what he wants from you."

"Don't you think I know it?"

"Talk to Heinrich!"

"No. He'll shoot him." I rubbed my forehead and closed my eyes. "Just do me a favor, keep quiet for now, will you? I'll figure out what to do tomorrow."

"Do you want me to stay with you tonight? We can tell Max that you're afraid to sleep alone, and we can both stay in your house so you feel safe."

"I have a gun in the drawer of my nightstand. I feel safe enough. But thank you for the offer anyway. I'm sorry I dragged you out of your house, I was just panicking. I'm fine now."

"Are you sure?"

"Yes. I really am. Go back to your husband, he must be looking for you already."

Ursula got up, carefully picked up sleeping Greta from the couch and looked me in the eye.

"Don't hesitate to call us, even in the middle of the night."

"Thank you, Ursula."

She gave me a slight hug in order not to wake Greta up, and followed me to the front door. Magda was already shifting from one leg to another next to the dining room waiting for me to tell her to serve dinner. I had no appetite at all, but didn't want to offend the girl, and nodded to her with a smile.

It was the first morning in a very long time that I walked inside the Reich Main Security Office wearing a regular dress and not my SS uniform. If I would still be working, I would have been two hours late, but I didn't care this time. I walked straight to Gruppenführer Kaltenbrunner's office, passed surprised Georg and opened the door to my chief's office without even knocking. He was talking on the phone, but froze in his place as soon as he saw me. I walked to his table and put the paper I brought with me in front of him.

"Sign it."

"I will have to call you back," he said into the receiver and quickly hung up the phone. I noticed with great pleasure that he was visibly embarrassed to see me. "Frau Friedmann…"

"I'm not here to talk to you. Sign it."

He picked up the request to immediately relieve me of my duties and looked at it.

"What is it?"

"Since when are you reading the orders that I put on your table? You're so good at signing them without even looking, what makes this one so different? Sign it fast, and I'll be going. I can't stand even being in the same room with you."

"Frau Friedmann, I'm really sorry about yesterday, I was too drunk to even think about what I was doing! I would never do something like that if I was sober…"

"You already did!!!" I yelled at him without a care in the world that his adjutant next door might hear me. I was too mad. "You are such a terrible, disgusting person, you don't care about anybody or anything except yourself and what you want at the moment! You're a controlling and despotic psychopath, that's what you are! Sign my resignation right now, because I don't want to see your face ever again!"

"Frau Friedmann…"

"No. We've had this conversation before. You know what, I don't even care if you sign this order or not, I'm not working here anymore, put me in jail for leaving my position in the time of war, because I would rather go there or even to a camp than spend another day in your company! Goodbye, Herr Gruppenführer!"

I turned around and walked out of the office even though he was calling my name. I didn't forget to slam the door on the way out. Georg looked at me with his mouth open, but didn't even find anything to say. I said goodbye to him as well and left the RSHA office.

Chapter 11

I was in the Gestapo jail where I'd already been before, in the basement of the same RSHA building where I used to work. This time I wasn't scared at all, and was sitting on the table instead of a chair waiting for my interrogator to come in. When he entered, I smiled at him. Dr. Kaltenbrunner, very handsome in his green SD uniform. He walked up to me and I opened my legs so he could stand between them right next to me.

He grinned at me, picked up my chin and kissed me, deeply and possessively, and I kissed him back with the same desire, pressing my chest next to his. Gruppenführer Kaltenbrunner was caressing my legs that I wrapped around him, until he picked up my skirt all the way up to my thighs and moved my hips closer to his. I was so aroused by the way he was touching me everywhere that I started to unbutton his uniform jacket and shirt, I wanted to feel his strong body under my fingers, I wanted to touch him everywhere as well. And then I lifted up my face to his and kissed him again.

Gruppenführer Kaltenbrunner put his hands under my skirt and pulled down my underwear, until he got it completely off me. I laid on the table in front of him and tugged on his shoulders, making him cover my body with his. I wanted him so badly that I could hardly wait for him to make love to me. I inhaled sharply when he entered me, and started moaning louder and louder as he was moving harder and faster inside. And when I couldn't take it no more, I arched my back and screamed his name.

"Ernst..."

I heard my own voice hardly whispering from a side. It sounded strange. And then I opened my eyes and found myself in my own bed, in the middle of wet sheets. I quickly sat up and rubbed my eyes, shaking off the rest of the most impossible dream I could ever have. My breathing was still very hectic and my whole body was covered in sweat. I slowly put my hand under the covers, between my legs; I was all wet there too, as if I was really making love to my former boss all night. That was the most disturbing part.

What the hell is wrong with me?! Why did I even dream that in the first place? I hate him. I absolutely hate him. He's a perverted sadist. After what he did to me two days ago I probably hate him as much as I hated Heydrich.

But deep inside I knew that it wasn't true. I didn't hate him like Heydrich. I didn't even hate him like Ulrich Reinhard, who also tried to get to me several years ago. Reinhard was disgusting to me, but Dr. Kaltenbrunner was anything but. As a matter of fact I was attracted to him, in some twisted and absolutely irrational way, but I was.

The sound of the phone ringing interrupted my thoughts. I stretched my hand to it and answered, "Yes?"

"How's my beautiful wife doing this morning?"

"Heinrich?"

"Do you have another husband?" He was laughing at me.

"No, of course not." I smiled into the receiver. "Your voice just sounds strange."

"The connection is not so great here, sorry about it. Is everything alright with you? Max told me you didn't come to work yesterday, I started to worry that something happened, but didn't want to call you too late. I thought that you might be sleeping already."

"Oh, no, I'm fine, just a little cold, that's all." I faked a little cough, and immediately felt ashamed for lying to my own husband. I still had no idea how I would explain my resignation to him. "Nothing to worry about."

"Are you sure? Do you want me to call our doctor so he could come and check on you?"

"No, don't bother him with this, it's nothing serious, I promise."

"Alright then. I have to run now, I just wanted to hear your voice to make sure you were fine."

"I am, sweetie. Thank you for calling. I missed hearing your voice."

"I miss you too, sweetheart. I'll try to call later today if I get a chance. I love you!"

"I love you too, dear."

I hung up the phone and went to the shower. I stood under the running water for a long time, shameful thoughts running through my mind after Heinrich's call and my more than unexpected dream. If I didn't want to confess to myself that the attraction between me and Dr. Kaltenbrunner was mutual, the sub consciousness in me just pointed the ugly truth out. I did feel different in his presence, I did like it when he would stand very close watching me type his letters, I did like the way he was looking at me, as if undressing me with his dark eyes. It excited me. I didn't like him drunk or rough, but what if he touched me gently? What if he would hold me like that night when we were dancing together? What if he approached me differently? Would I still say no? I was a terrible, terrible person, and an even more terrible wife, as I wasn't sure of what my answer would be.

Still preoccupied with my thoughts, I dried myself with a towel and put on a silk slip and a robe on top of it; I was going to spend all day home and didn't feel like dressing up just for Magda and my dogs. I had just sat down in front of my dresser and started to comb my hair, when I heard a horrible scream coming from my back yard. I immediately jumped to my feet and ran towards the window.

It was Magda screaming; she was standing on the steps leading to the back entrance of the kitchen. There was something laying in front of her, but I couldn't make out what it was. Even though the girl was there alone, I grabbed the gun from under my pillow where I'd kept it all night and ran downstairs. She met me halfway in the hallway, and by the look on her face I knew right away that something bad had happened.

"Frau Friedmann… It's Milo. It's so… horrible!" She was clenching to my arms all shivering and sobbing. "Don't go there… let's call the police, I'm begging you!"

"Milo?"

I pushed the crying, hysterical housekeeper away and rushed to the door, feeling the growing cold of fear inside my heart. But when I opened it, I had to cover my mouth with my hand not to scream myself. By all means I wasn't prepared to see what appeared before my eyes: the lifeless little body of my poor old Milo, his fur and the steps all covered in blood from the huge cut on his neck. And next to him, right there on a marble column, in blood: "You're next. R."

I stepped away not able to avert my eyes from the terrifying view, and slowly sat on the floor. Hot tears were streaming down my face, and I squeezed tightly my gun. I couldn't understand who would do such an appalling thing, who would hurt an innocent animal to send a horrifying, bloody message to… who? Heinrich? Me? Both of us?

I pulled my legs to my chest, wrapped my hands around them and started crying, loudly and inconsolably. I wished they killed me, and not my little Milo. He was such a kind hearted dog, a loyal and loving family member from the happier times, when I lived in my old house with my family, when my parents were so young and happy, and my brother was still alive, and now my last piece of that old carefree life was gone, ripped away from my heart forever, leaving an open hurting wound instead.

"Frau Friedmann… what if they're still here?" Magda was still trying to catch her breath in between the sobs. "What if… what if they come back? Let's call the police, please! I'm really scared!"

I wished that they'd come back, so I could put all the bullets I had in my gun in their worthless bodies. But Magda was right, we had to call the police anyway. After all, there was a most definite threat left for us, and besides I wanted more than anything to find the bastards who did it. And then all the Gestapo tortures would seem like a children's game next to what I'd do to them. I got up from the floor, pushed away Rolf who came running from upstairs and was howling quietly trying to get to his dead buddy. I told Magda to lock him in one of the rooms so he wouldn't be under our feet and went to the phone to call the police.

The Kripo – regular criminal police arrived together with the Gestapo, probably because I mentioned that both my husband and I were working for the RSHA, which transferred the case under the secret police jurisdiction. After quickly looking around, the 'black coats' completely dismissed the regular officers, taking the investigation under their control. I didn't mind, if it meant more efficiency in finding the scumbags who killed my dog.

They were asking me a lot of questions: if I heard anything suspicious, if my husband or I received any threatening calls or letters recently, if we had enemies or if someone had a motive to harm anyone of us. I kept shaking my head in reply, finding myself in the same confusion as the investigators. Apart from being counterintelligence agents working for the US, which would give a motive to kill us both to this very Gestapo, I really couldn't think of anyone capable of such a heinous crime. But the Gestapo wasn't leaving any warnings, they were executing people without any complicated tactics.

What did signature 'R.' mean? Someone's name? Last name? Nickname? Organization? Just a letter to complicate the investigation and throw it off track? The 'black coats' were very interested in that bloody 'R.' on the column. They asked me to make a list of people I knew whose name was starting with R and who could have a motive to kill Heinrich or me.

In about an hour during which they were busy taking pictures and dusting everything for fingerprints, an unexpected visitor arrived – the 'black coats'' chief, Gruppenführer Müller. He seemed genuinely upset by my tragic loss and kept shaking his head and pursing his lips looking at the crime scene.

"And they call us torturers and animals! We fight with the enemies of the Reich! My people would never hurt an innocent soul like that. What a shame! It must be that Resistance, goddamn sons of bitches!" He quickly remembered that I was standing next to him and immediately apologized for his outburst. "I'm sorry, Frau Friedmann, I didn't mean to offend you. I have two dogs myself, I can't imagine what you're going through right now. I would have killed that waste of life right on the spot if someone did it to my dog."

"I would have killed them too, Herr Gruppenführer. Trust me."

"Don't worry. We'll find them. No one threatens a family such as yours, so devoted to the Reich, without being severely punished." Gruppenführer Müller sympathetically patted my shoulder. "Your husband is still away, right?"

"Yes. He's still in Italy."

"I'll leave four of my agents to guard your house around the clock then. You'll be absolutely safe till he arrives."

"Thank you, Herr Gruppenführer. I appreciate it."

"Don't even mention it, Frau Friedmann. I'm just following my duty." He saluted me, but at the door he turned around and added, "And don't worry about your boss, I'll explain everything to him. I'm sure he won't mind giving you leave for a couple of days. Goodbye."

I was just going to say something in protest, but he had already left.

I was making coffee myself because Magda was too shaken up by the events earlier that morning, and I decided to let the poor girl go home. I looked out of the window once again, and saw one of Gruppenführer Müller's people in plain clothes smoking outside. Another one was patrolling the side where the library was, and two others the back yard. For the first time in my life I was welcoming the presence of the Gestapo in my house.

Now that the first shock and anger had passed, I settled down with my coffee in Heinrich's study and started thinking. *Who would want to hurt us? Or just me?* Because if they were watching our house in order to get inside unnoticed, they must have known that Heinrich was away for several days. *And they killed Milo, my old dog, not Rolf who Heinrich and I got together after we got married.* The more I was thinking about it, the more I was sure: that message was meant for me alone. Somebody wanted me dead. 'R.'

Who was that 'R.'? Gruppenführer Müller's opinion that the threat was related to someone from the Resistance I put aside right away. The Chief of the Gestapo suggested that the members of the Underground movement wanted Heinrich and me dead because we both worked for the RSHA. Little did Gruppenführer know that we both also worked with the Resistance as well, and they definitely wouldn't want to kill people who were fighting on their side.

The first name that came to my mind was Ulrich Reinhard. He had never hidden how much he hated me for 'hurting his career' after he'd attacked me in my theatre and I'd told my future husband about it. He even promised me that he wouldn't stop until he destroyed me, his exact words. But would he really sneak in my backyard to kill my dog? It seemed very improbable. I knew him too well: he would have sneaked in my bedroom and slit *my* throat instead.

After another ten minutes of staring at the blank piece of paper in front of me on which I was supposed to put all the people whose name started with R that I knew, I realized that I didn't know anyone too close who would fit the criteria. Unless Reinhard Heydrich came back from the dead and decided to revenge me for his assassination. I chuckled, but then suddenly got serious. *What if someone knew? Someone close to him who wanted revenge but for some reason couldn't do it openly? His wife? No, impossible. A woman wouldn't be able to hurt an animal so cold heartedly. A family member? Brother? No. How would they possibly know? Only Gruppenführer Kaltenbrunner and I knew. What if he told someone? Got drunk and bragged about it to one of his girlfriends? No, he wasn't stupid, he wouldn't risk his own life like that.*

Who else could it be then? A loud knock on the door made me jump in my seat, but I quickly regained my composure and went to open it. Killers never knock, and I had four armed Gestapo agents near my house, whose favorite pastime was shooting people in the head. If they let someone through, they were sure that it was safe. I was hoping that it was Max, who promised my worried sick husband to come by after work to check on me. Being alone in the huge house knowing that someone out there could be watching me was terrifying.

But it wasn't Max. It was Dr. Kaltenbrunner, and he let himself in without asking for my permission.

"I'm sorry I couldn't come earlier, I was at the Reich Chancellery all day, and Müller only told me about what happened when I stopped by the office to pick up the paperwork. Are you alright?"

"Someone killed my dog and wrote 'You're next' in blood next to it. Can I possibly be alright?"

"I'm sorry. That's not what I meant." He lowered his eyes to the floor. "I meant to ask if anybody hurt you."

"Still have some black and blues on both wrists, but apart from that, totally fine."

I was fighting the urge to slap him once again, but decided that my sarcastic tone should be enough for now. He seemed to be very concerned about my well-being after all.

"I am terribly sorry about that, Frau Friedmann." I saw him looking at my hands, crossed over my chest, but he decided against taking them in his to inspect the very superficial injuries he'd put there. "I never wanted to hurt you. You are too dear to me. I always wanted to protect you from everybody else."

I looked away. He actually did. First from the Gestapo who wanted to send me to the camp after my former colleague from the same dancing company saw me wearing a Star of David; then from the same Gestapo when they almost caught me with the radio in Poland, then from Ulrich Reinhard, who was threatening me in the dark hallway of the RSHA; he helped me to organize the assassination on Heydrich…

"But I can't protect you from myself." Dr. Kaltenbrunner put his hand in the inner pocket of his coat and handed me a folded piece of paper. "I signed your request for resignation, but you'll still be getting your salary for the excellent service as long as I'm in the office."

"You didn't have to do that."

"No, you deserve it. That's the least I can do for you after all you've done for me. Schellenberg was right about you, you really are an irreplaceable assistant. And I went and screwed it all up."

"Yes, you did."

"I'm sorry. About everything. Well, I won't be bothering you anymore, I know that you want to be left alone, and... I deserved it. I just stopped by to make sure you were guarded well, and that you have everything you need. I already told Gruppenführer Müller about the importance of this case, and I'll keep an eye on it personally. I promise you, I'll find the people who did it. And I'm very sorry about your little friend."

I was trying to stay firm, but his sad eyes and soft voice started to get to me again. It was not the cruel Chief of the sinister RSHA who was standing in front of me now, but the real Dr. Kaltenbrunner, the intelligent and respectful person he would have been if it wasn't for the war and his position in SS.

He nodded at me and went to the door.

"Wait." *Goddamn it, what am I doing?* "If you want to, you could stay for a couple of minutes so I can tell you my thoughts about... the investigation, and... who I think might have done it..."

He accepted my invitation with visible pleasure.

"I'd be happy to, Frau Friedmann."

A couple of minutes turned into a couple of hours, during which we both drank an amount of coffee that could kill a horse (I offered Gruppenführer Kaltenbrunner a drink, but he politely refused), and officially ran out of suspects. Max, who came by like he promised, was more than surprised to see my chief sitting in my living room, and wisely left us alone. He figured if the Chief of the RSHA himself was with me, I was more than safe.

When it was time for Dr. Kaltenbrunner to finally leave, he warmly thanked me for the coffee and my hospitality, and at the door said, "Don't get stuck on that 'R.', Frau Friedmann. It could be anyone. But don't worry about anything, you're safe here. And take this also." He took out a little notepad and a pencil he always carried with him and wrote something on it. "It's my home number. Don't hesitate to call me if you think you might be in danger."

I took the paper from his hand and nodded.

"Thank you, Herr Gruppenführer."

He smiled at me once again and left, the Gestapo agent freezing at attention as the Chief of the RSHA passed him by. Dr. Kaltenbrunner stopped for a second and said something to him, making the man click his heels and loudly answer *"Jawohl*, Herr Gruppenführer!" I closed the door.

"Poor old buddy Milo. I got so attached to him. But this one is just a ball of joy!" Heinrich picked up the little white Maltese puppy still wearing a pink bow on her neck. "It's a nice thing he did."

"Yes, it is."

A day before my husband's return Gruppenführer Kaltenbrunner stopped by to check on me and to tell me about how the investigation was going. It was pouring outside when I opened the front door to him, and noticed that he was holding something inside his coat.

"I thought that you must be grieving a lot about your old friend. So I brought you a new one." He smiled at me and produced a little white pup with a little pink bow around its neck from under his wet coat.

"Oh!" She seemed so tiny in his hands, and I carefully took her in mine. "She's absolutely adorable! What's her name?"

"She doesn't have a name yet. You'll have to name her yourself."

I pressed the little shivering ball of fur to my chest and rubbed her behind the ear.

"You are just too sweet, aren't you? Such a sweet little girl should have a sweet name. How about Sugar? Do you like it?" The puppy licked my hand. "I think you do! And what does nice Herr Gruppenführer, who brought you, think?"

"I think it's a great name." Gruppenführer Kaltenbrunner smiled at me.

The next day when Hanz and I were picking up Heinrich from the military airport, I brought Sugar with me. My husband immediately fell in love with her, and the two became almost inseparable. Sugar was even allowed to sleep in our bed, because according to Heinrich 'it was only April, and the poor girl would freeze to death in her bed.'

Heinrich never found out neither about what happened between me and Dr. Kaltenbrunner, nor of my resignation request, which I burned after giving it a thorough thought. I was working for the counterintelligence after all, and my position allowed me to have access to top secret information. I didn't want to take it away from the people who were counting on me. As for my boss, I was hoping that the situation wouldn't repeat itself. Even though Ursula kept shaking her head disapprovingly, hoping was all I could do.

"Why do you keep forgiving him?" Ursula scorned me after I informed her of my decision to keep my position. "He'll start thinking that he can get away with anything and will keep doing it more."

I would shrug and look away. Even if I had tried to explain to her my thoughts on the matter, she possibly wouldn't be able to understand. The problem with Dr. Kaltenbrunner was that he was too used to women falling at his feet during the first ten minutes of meeting him, and when the first one – me – rejected his advances, he didn't really know how to react to it. He simply lost his patience and decided to use force when nothing else seemed to work.

"I know it's hard to believe, but there was nothing malicious about his behavior." I gave Ursula a guilty smile. "He's just like one of those 'tough' boys we used to have in our class, who would start yanking your braids and pulling up your skirt when they want to attract your attention but don't know how to."

"Are you seriously trying to justify that evil man's behavior?"

"I am not, I'm just saying that he's not evil. He's stubborn, impatient and very, very spoiled by women's attention, but not evil."

"You're justifying him."

"He was drunk. He apologized."

"Justifying even more now."

"He brought me a puppy. He feels guilty. Evil people don't feel guilty about anything."

"That attitude of yours is not going to take you anywhere good."

Heinrich clearing his throat distracted me from my thoughts.

"We have to go to bed early tonight. Our plane leaves at 7 am sharp. I don't think your boss will be happy if we are late." Heinrich fed another piece of biscuit to Sugar while Rolf, sitting beside him, let out a little cry pointing out that he was still a member of the family and liked biscuits too. "You're a big boy, big boys don't eat sweets."

I smiled at the sight of him talking to the dogs, and thought about what a wonderful father he would make one day. What a wonderful father he would have been if we hadn't lost our baby. It didn't hurt as much as it did a year ago, but I knew that such wounds never completely heal. I decided to change the course my thoughts were taking.

"I don't even know how my boss will get up this early. Judging by the time he comes to work every morning, he's not an early riser."

"I still don't understand why he decided to delegate this to me. It's far from my department's usual sphere of activity."

I shrugged as if I didn't know why Dr. Kaltenbrunner was taking my husband with us to Poland to assist him in taking the situation with the Warsaw ghetto under control. It was a part of our new deal: I go back to work and even accompany Dr. Kaltenbrunner on his trips just like I did with Standartenführer Schellenberg. In return he keeps his hands to himself, and lets my husband come with us when it wouldn't interfere with his duties in his department. This way I would at least feel safe in Gruppenführer Kaltenbrunner's company. The next morning we were leaving on our first trip.

"He thinks that of the whole *SD-Ausland* you're one of the most intelligent agents with a cold, analytical mind. Exactly the person he needs for such a job: to evaluate the situation, to consider all the options and to help him come to the best decision."

"Best decision? With the way everything goes, there's only one decision left: completely clean the ghetto out. Those damn rebels won't give up."

Heinrich looked at me and shook his head, silently condemning the way his office would most likely handle the uprising. For a couple of years already we haven't spoken openly about anything compromising within the walls of our house, since the Gestapo would sometimes randomly install listening devices in the residences of even the Party's most trusted members. Goering himself hadn't escaped such a fate, and was spitting fire at Himmler and Heydrich's direction for more than a month after finding a microphone in his study. Therefore whispering into each other's ear and writing notes were our means of communication for quite a long time now. Otherwise, we spoke of matters just like two devoted Nazis.

"Yes, I know." I looked at the floor thinking of the rebels' fate and the ways we maybe could get at least some people out. "You're right, let's go to bed early. We have a big day tomorrow."

Chapter 12

Warsaw, April 1943

I was sending radiograms to Reichsführer's and Gruppenführer Müller's offices, previously dictated to me by Dr. Kaltenbrunner in his car. I was alone in his temporary office here in Warsaw: neither he, nor Heinrich hadn't come back up yet, after a Gestapo agent rushed to my chief in the hallway and in a quiet voice reported something to him. Gruppenführer Kaltenbrunner frowned and followed him, leaving me, Heinrich and Georg alone without any explanation. The latter two shrugged and comfortably positioned themselves in two chairs, still discussing the inspection of the ghetto. I decided not to waste time and send radiograms. Georg handed me the keys from Dr. Kaltenbrunner's office and returned to the conversation.

I was done with the radiograms in ten minutes. Another thirty passed, and I started to think that the men must have gone to lunch and forgotten about me, even though Heinrich said they'd call me if they were going to leave. I could have gone downstairs and sat with them, but conversations about what weapons and machinery to better use to take over the ghetto weren't something I wanted to hear. I didn't know how Heinrich was holding so well, but again, he'd been doing it for years and was a great actor.

I was resting my head on one hand and playing with a pencil with another, when I heard Dr. Kaltenbrunner's steps in the anteroom. I immediately straightened out and put Reichsführer's and Gruppenführer Müller's replies neatly together, waiting for my boss to come in and give me further instructions. However, when he opened the door, I hardly contained myself from a yelp; the Chief of the RSHA was covered in blood, which stained his grey field SD uniform, collar of his shirt and even left several dots and streaks on his face. But the worst part of this frightful picture was his hands, which were all covered in red, the blood soaking the cuffs of his shirt completely. He froze in the doorway, looking at me like a criminal caught on the spot.

"What happened to you?" I jumped from my chair and rushed to him, but he stopped me halfway stretching his hand in front of him.

"Nothing. What are you doing here? Go downstairs."

Dr. Kaltenbrunner quickly turned his back to me and opened the door to the bathroom. I followed him inside.

"Did you cut yourself?"

"No. I told you to go downstairs. Go away."

I ignored his order and stayed. He was washing his hands, making a mess out of the perfectly white porcelain sink. I squeezed myself between the sink and the wall, trying to find the injury that was making him bleed so badly, but aside from several little scratches on his knuckles couldn't see nothing. I tried to take his hands in mine to look closer, but he yanked them away from me.

"Go away, I said!!!"

"Let me see what happened, I've learnt first aid at *SS-Helferinnen* courses, I can put on a perfect bandage or even stitches."

"Annalise, it's not my blood," he finally said through the gritted teeth.

I lifted my eyes to his, and saw that they'd changed their color from regular golden-brown to almost black. They were not human's eyes, they were predator's eyes; an animal that had just killed its prey. I felt the shivers going down my spine, and terror, uncontrollable instinctual terror as if I was standing inches away not from a man, but a wild forest wolf, baring its sharp long fangs at me.

He was watching me as I made a step back, then another one until I backed out of the bathroom, and only then he turned back to the sink and proceeded with washing his hands. I almost ran out of the office.

———————————

As soon as I entered the hallway, the familiar group of men consisting of Heinrich, Georg and the Gestapo agent immediately stopped talking and turned to me.

"What the hell happened to him?" I addressed them, pointing to the direction from where I came from.

The men exchanged looks as if deciding whether they should tell me or not. Finally the Gestapo agent spoke.

"We arrested one of the rebels from the ghetto, but before we were able to take him in, he shot two of our *Waffen-SS* officers. Herr Gruppenführer… got upset about it."

Georg looked at the agent. "I thought that he beat him up because the Jew refused to give any information, no?"

"Who the hell knows?" The Gestapo agent shrugged indifferently. "You know how Kaltenbrunner is, one minute he's talking calmly, the next moment he shoots the guy's brains out."

Georg suddenly laughed. "No, that was one time only, and he had a reason to do that. That asshole American told him to go fuck himself, what did he expect in return? A decent treatment? It's not the United States where you can say whatever you want to the General, it's the Reich. We do things a little differently here."

The men laughed while I just stood there listening to them.

"Are we going back to the ghetto now?" Heinrich asked the agent.

"No, to the Poles who were supplying them with weapons. My men are already waiting outside. As soon as Herr Gruppenführer comes back, we're good to go."

"The Jew told him everything after all, didn't he?" Georg smirked.

"He didn't have much of a choice. You can try to be tough all you want, but when someone starts breaking your fingers one by one with bare hands, you'll start singing like a bird." The Gestapo agent chuckled.

"But Herr Gruppenführer still killed him."

"The Jew shot two of our good men. Herr Gruppenführer doesn't forgive such things."

"How did he kill him?" I asked my first question.

"It's difficult to say, because he kept beating him for a good twenty minutes." The Gestapo agent took out a cigarette case and lit one up. "My guess would be the massive head trauma after he banged the guy's head on the concrete wall. That's what most likely finished him. But again, I'm not a doctor."

He eyed me for another moment, took another drag from his cigarette and smiled.

"You're taking it all pretty well for a woman. Most of the ones I know would be throwing up outside by now. And you saw his hands and didn't even flinch."

"We're not supposed to have mercy for the enemies of the Reich." I answered indifferently, even though everything was twisting inside. "Besides, I've seen worse things in my life."

The agent nodded in satisfaction several times.

"Now I see why he brought you here."

We were driving in the car in silence, Heinrich sitting between me and Gruppenführer Kaltenbrunner. I turned my head all the way to the right, trying to look only at the city outside and not to think of anything.

"Frau Friedman?" Dr. Kaltenbrunner finally broke the silence.

I turned my head to him. "Yes, Herr Gruppenführer?"

"Is there any chance you can get me a new uniform here in Poland?"

"I'll see what I can do."

"Thank you."

"You're welcome."

I turned away again.

The next morning, back in the house where we were staying, I was sewing on the insignia from his old uniform jacket to the new one, perfectly clean and neat, just delivered by an SS man. When my chief appeared in the doorway and stood there indecisively, watching me work, I said without taking my eyes off the jacket, "Almost done. Two more minutes."

"Take your time and don't mind me, I'll wait here."

He went to the mirror and started struggling with his tie, from time to time quietly cursing at it and the people who invented it. I bit off the last thread and walked up to my boss.

"You have no idea what you're doing, do you?" I shook my head at what was supposed to look like a tie, undid it completely and then started to put it back in order.

"Not really." Dr. Kaltenbrunner gave me an apologetic smile as I was tying a perfectly neat knot on his neck.

"Here, all done. Take your jacket and please, don't mess this one up, it's very difficult to find it in your size."

I handed him the jacket and went to the sofa to put the sewing set back in order.

"Thank you."

"You're welcome."

Gruppenführer Kaltenbrunner paused for a moment and then asked, "Are you mad at me?"

"Why would I be mad at you?"

"For yesterday."

I shrugged. I wasn't mad, I was disappointed, terribly disappointed, but didn't want him to know it.

"You're not my husband, you're not a member of my family, you're not even my friend. You're my boss. I don't care what you do. You feel like splitting someone's head in two, it's your business, not mine."

"I'm sorry you had to see that. I didn't do it on purpose, it just… got out of control."

"It always does with you."

"He shot two of our *Waffen-SS* officers! The Jew! It's the war after all!"

"No, it's not the war, Herr Gruppenführer. You're at war with the French, with the British, with the Russians. With Jews, it's not a war. It's an extermination."

"But… he killed two Aryans… the Jew." He sounded like he was trying to explain to me the reason behind his actions. I almost laughed.

"And how many Jews have you killed so far? Two million? One finally stood up for himself, and he deserves to die a terrible death. That's your logic."

"He's a Jew…"

"And?"

"We're Aryans."

144

"And how are we different now?"

"Of course we're different. We even look different."

"If we look so different what is the reason behind making them wear stars on their chest or sleeves? Have you thought of that? Why make such a law if it's so easy to differentiate an Aryan from a Jew?"

His brow furrowed. He didn't know the answer to that question and obviously never asked himself that.

"We're going back to the ghetto, aren't we?" I said. "Good. I'm going to show you something that you'll find very interesting."

Waffen-SS soldiers were keeping their hands on their machine guns the whole time, even though the people they rounded up today were mostly women and children, scared to death, some of them keeping their hands up just in case, not to provoke *the Germans*. Right after we got out of the car, I wandered off further and further from Dr. Kaltenbrunner and my husband, until I turned to a quiet and half destroyed street, with several dead bodies still laying right there on the ground.

I had to cover my nose and mouth with a handkerchief because the smell was absolutely unbearable. Another reason was the typhus epidemic still widely spread amongst the habitants of the ghetto. I walked inside one of the buildings, its walls covered with bullet marks everywhere. A lot of rebels died here fighting for their right to live. No bodies were inside, however; the SS had already taken them out to search if they had any valuables on them or golden teeth they could pull out. Then they probably burned them. I knew the protocol, I was working for the RSHA after all.

I walked inside one of the former apartments and looked around. Broken furniture and peeling walls only emphasized the impression of desperation and death. Someone's coat was still lying on the bed, probably left in the haste of running away. I picked it up, shook the dust off it and put it on. It still had a Star of David band around the right arm. Good. I took off my *SS-Helferin* cap and hid it in my pocket. I buttoned the first two buttons of the baggy coat so no one would be able to see my uniform.

On my way out I looked at the piece of the broken mirror on the wall. I smirked in satisfaction: I almost looked like one of them. To make the resemblance perfect, I put a handkerchief over my head and tied its ends under my hair, covering my braid in a neat bun with a white cloth.

I descended the steps and cautiously looked out. I could see the rounded up people at the end of the street. Now all I had to do was to approach them unnoticed. Luckily for me, the SS were too busy staring at the big and scary Chief of the RSHA to later write home about meeting the Gruppenführer personally, and I snuck right into the crowd of Jewish women without anyone paying any attention to me.

Slowly I made my way to the front, and was standing now within twenty steps from Gruppenführer Kaltenbrunner and Heinrich, who kept frowning and looking around. They had probably noticed my absence and were wondering where I was. Georg was standing even closer to me, holding the map in front of his chief, while the latter was giving him orders. I smiled; in my disguise I was absolutely invisible to all of them.

"Keep moving in the circle like I outlined for you earlier. It seems to be working perfectly well," I heard Gruppenführer Kaltenbrunner say to the *Waffen-SS* leader standing next to him.

"*Jawohl*, Herr Gruppenführer." The officer clicked his heels and nodded to our, Jews, direction. "What about them? Shall we execute them right here?"

The group of women gasped as they heard the German speak of their fate and pressed their children closer to themselves, exchanging panicked looks. The soldiers shifted their machine guns ready for the command of their superiors.

"No, why would you do that?" Gruppenführer Kaltenbrunner frowned. "We promised them that if they surrender, we'll let them live."

"Shall I send them to Treblinka then?"

"Treblinka or Majdanek, depending on who needs fresh people at the moment. Coordinate it with the Kommandants directly."

"*Jawohl*." The *Waffen-SS* leader clicked his heels again. "Shall we sort them out maybe? There are a lot of elderly and sick among them. Some of them are barely standing, there's no point in wasting time and effort in transporting them, they'll die anyway."

"Yes, that you can do."

"What about the children? Them too? To the left?"

It was a camp code, unknown to the Jews next to me. To the left meant immediate execution; to the right – a chance to live a little longer, but still slowly working yourself to death.

"Let the Kommandant deal with the children."

The officer nodded, turned to us and started barking out the commands in a loud voice.

"Form a line by the sidewalk, stand close to each other, put your children next to you, do not hold them in your hands. Put your belongings in front of you. Go, *schnell, schnell, schnell!*"

In about ten seconds we were all standing shoulder to shoulder, while the *Waffen-SS* leader started walking along the line, making a fast selection with his baton, right, left, right, right, left, right, left, left, left, left, right... Finally he reached me and barked after a short glance, "Right."

"What if I want to go to the left?" I asked loudly, immediately turning all the heads into my direction.

"What did you say, Jew?" The officer squinted his eyes at me, clearly not expecting any of us to speak at all, especially in such an insolent manner. But I wasn't looking at him, I was looking at Gruppenführer Kaltenbrunner, who was staring at me with his mouth open, just like my husband and Georg next to him.

"I said, what if I want to go to the left?" I repeated again.

"I'll show you 'left!'" The officer put away his baton and took his gun out of the holster.

"Don't!!!" Two voices in unison behind the officer's back made him turn to his superiors in confusion. Both Heinrich and Gruppenführer Kaltenbrunner were already next to him, the latter quickly disarming the man.

"What? What did I do? That Jew talked back to me!"

"She's not a Jew!" Heinrich yanked the handkerchief from my head.

"What the hell are you doing?!" My chief joined him. "Do you realize that you almost got yourself shot?!"

Under the confused stares of the *Waffen-SS* leader, his soldiers and the former ghetto habitants standing next to me, I stepped forward.

"And that brings us to the point I was trying to prove to you this morning, Herr Gruppenführer." Then I turned to the *Waffen-SS* leader again. "So I'm a Jew, right?"

He shifted his eyes from me to Dr. Kaltenbrunner and back to me, not knowing what was going on.

"How about now?" I unbuttoned the coat and took it off, now standing in front of him in my SS uniform. "Still a Jew? Not so much, right?"

I put the coat back on and closed it. "Oh, look, I'm a Jew again."

"That's enough!" Gruppenführer Kaltenbrunner yanked the coat off me, threw it on the ground and wiped his gloved hands with a handkerchief in disgust. "Why would you even put that on yourself? It must have typhus all over it!"

"Don't change the subject, Herr Gruppenführer. All this time you were standing steps away from me and never even saw my face. What if I didn't say anything? I would have long been on my way to the camp now." He was frowning at me and not saying anything.

"Herr Officer." I turned back to his very confused subordinate again. "How do you differentiate Aryans from Jews?"

"Well, according to the official doctrine, the representatives of the Aryan race possess a certain set of features…"

"Like what?"

"Like… they're tall, lean, mostly with blue eyes and blond hair, they have elongated skulls with high cheekbones, straight thin noses and a strong jaw line."

I nodded.

"Which of the enumerated qualities do I not have?"

He opened his mouth and closed it again, not able to answer my question. I fit perfectly under the description of a typical Aryan.

"So let me get this straight. I look absolutely Aryan, but you still called me a Jew and almost shot me. Why? That little arm band with a Star of David confused you? What if I put it on you? Will it make you a Jew?"

"What's your point, Frau Friedmann?" Gruppenführer Kaltenbrunner asked me impatiently.

"My point, Herr Gruppenführer, is that half of these women look just like me. What if they were adopted when they were still babies? What if their German parents died during the Great War, or couldn't take care of them anymore after it because they had no money, and the Polish Jews adopted them? There were a lot of cases of such adoptions back then, and you should know it better than anyone else. Now their real parents are dead, and there's no way to ask them. But you'll still kill perfect Aryan women just because they wear these arm bands?"

"There's a very slim possibility that all of these women were adopted."

"What does your doctrine say though? That every single Aryan's life is precious. What if you're unknowingly sending some of these Aryans to death?"

"There's no way to tell."

"So *there is no* way to tell, is there?" I smiled at the frowning Austrian.

"What do you suggest then? Release them all just because they look Germanic?"

"No, not release, send them for re-education to Germany. I'm sure that they'd rather live as Catholics or Protestants and follow the Nazi doctrine than die as Jews."

Some of the women clinging to each other indecisively nodded.

"See? They're more than willing to come back to their Fatherland."

"I'm not sure that Reichsführer will be too happy about such an idea," Gruppenführer Kaltenbrunner said.

"Reichsführer himself, during one of the executions he was supervising, pulled out an Aryan looking boy out of the line. I think he'll more than approve of such an initiative of yours. You can send them to work as maids, together with Gentile Poles to the houses of German housewives. The latter will be able to spend more time with their husbands and children, and these women will take care of the houses."

"It actually makes a lot of sense, Herr Gruppenführer." Heinrich understood what I was trying to do and stepped up to help me persuade the Chief of the RSHA. "If you think about it, they'll make great maids. And German families won't have to pay them, just give them food rations. I think Reichsführer will love the idea. And in case if he doesn't, you can tell him it was mine."

Dr. Kaltenbrunner finally turned to the *Waffen-SS* leader and handed him back his weapon.

"Redo the selection. Pull out the ones who look Aryan and process them as the working force. Then send them for re-education back to Germany. Do it through the Amt IV, it's their business. Do the same with the rest who surrender themselves."

"*Jawohl*, Herr Gruppenführer."

Later that night, when I got under the blankets with Heinrich, he pulled me close and kissed me.

"That was a very brave thing to do. But please, don't do anything like that ever again, will you? I almost had a heart attack when he pointed his gun at you."

"I would have died among my people." I smiled. "It would have been a beautiful death."

He asked me if I was scared. No, I wasn't, not at all. But I didn't point out the other motive I had besides saving some more lives; I wanted to show Dr. Kaltenbrunner that despite the official and absolutely made up Nazi genetic laws, we were no different from each other, the Jews and the Aryans, I wanted him to actually start looking into things and ask questions that the Party strictly prohibited anyone from asking.

They taught him that the Nazi ideology was unquestionable, and he was killing people in their name. Yesterday I promised myself that I'd change him, I'd make him good again, because I knew that there was still hope for him. He wasn't evil like Heydrich; he was just confused and didn't know any better. He was like one of those kids who jump from a bridge to the middle of a river, taking the risk of breaking their neck or drowning: if you ask him why he's jumping, he wouldn't even know what to answer. Everybody jumped, so I had to jump too. For some reason I desperately wanted to take him away from those kids before they dragged him with them all the way to the bottom.

Chapter 13

Berlin, June 1943

"The war is lost for Germany. It's official now. There is nothing they can do to reverse it."

Ingrid sounded very pleased announcing the news to Heinrich and I; my heart skipped a beat, and all of a sudden my mouth was too dry to even swallow nervously. Heinrich frowned too. The Americans were standing in front of us, so tall and imposing, and I felt the irresistible urge to hold my husband's hand. As if guessing my thoughts, he put his hand on top of mine and squeezed it.

On our way home I looked at Heinrich and asked, "What have we done?"

"We did everything right." He didn't sound as sure as I hoped he would.

"It's going to be the same like it was after the Great War. They'll take half of our lands, our army and make us pay retributions. And then hunger, depression, inflation, like it was after the Versailles Treaty, a vicious cycle, all over again! And we helped to make it happen. We helped to destroy our own country."

I wished he said something to me, something reassuring, like he always did, because my husband always knew the right answer, always knew what to do, but this time he just sighed and kept looking at the road in front of him.

"Maybe it won't be as bad you think," Heinrich finally said.

That night we both couldn't sleep, so we just lay next to each other thinking about the same thing, but not saying a word. We hated our government, but we were still Germans and we loved our country. And now we both felt that we had betrayed it in the worst possible way.

"Good morning, Herr Gruppenführer." I smiled at my boss who just opened the door to the anteroom. "Would you like some coffee right away?"

"I would like some champagne, my dear, and from now on, please address me as Herr Obergruppenführer."

Even though he tried to conceal a smile, he seemed to be very proud of his recent promotion.

"Really? Congratulations!"

Five minutes later, when we were toasting champagne in Dr. Kaltenbrunner's office, he raised his glass to me.

"I wouldn't have done it without you and your help, Frau Friedmann. The Führer is very happy about how we handled the situation with the uprising. I know it was a very stressful time for all of us, and I wanted to thank you personally for putting up with me this whole time. You have the patience of an angel, and I couldn't wish for a better assistant. Even though sometimes your pro-Jewish propaganda and accusing looks can be very annoying."

"I'm glad it gets to you though." I touched his glass with mine and took a little sip.

"You're an impossible woman, you know that? I would have fired any other a long time ago for such speeches."

"Why aren't you firing me then?"

"No one ever dared to speak to me like you do. Even men didn't. Even Reichsführer himself. You aren't afraid of anybody or anything. I admire that in you."

Afraid? I was very much afraid of many things, and amongst the most recent ones was another anonymous letter, fourth already, with one short sentence on a white piece of paper: "You're dead. R." This one, however, was delivered to the RSHA office instead of my house. Dr. Kaltenbrunner was in Vienna for several days, so I immediately brought the letter right to Gruppenführer Müller. I knew that there wouldn't be any fingerprints found on it, just like on the rest of them, neatly put together in the case file, but I still brought it anyway. Müller was only shaking his bald head.

"Resistance, I'm telling you. One thing I can't get though, why do they want *you* so bad?"

He squinted his eyes at me.

"It's definitely not because of your job. You're just one of the secretaries. And this," the chief of the Gestapo waved his hand with the note in it. "This is personal. It's a vendetta. Only for what, that I can't figure out without your help."

"I wish I could help you, Herr Gruppenführer." I shrugged. "But I really don't know who and why someone would want to harm me."

"The sooner you think of something, Frau Friedmann, the better. It's in your own interests."

"So here's what the beautiful Annalise looks like."

I turned around from Dr. Kaltenbrunner's table on which I was arranging the paperwork, and saw a smiling officer standing in the doorway with his hands crossed on his chest. He was very tall, probably as tall as Heinrich and well-built. A long

151

horizontal scar was crossing the left side of his cheek, but apart from it he wasn't that bad looking.

"Excuse me?" I frowned at the intruder.

"I finally saw you with my own eyes. You're even prettier than I thought." I noticed that he was speaking with that purring Austrian accent, just like Dr. Kaltenbrunner.

"You can't be here. Please, wait for Herr Obergruppenführer in the anteroom."

"And as feisty as he was saying." The officer smiled even wider. "Don't worry, he won't be mad, we're good friends."

"I've never seen you here before." I walked up to him until he was forced to back away from Dr. Kaltenbrunner's office. Then I turned around and locked the door. "Please have a seat over there and wait till Herr Obergruppenführer comes back."

I was ready to kill Georg for leaving the anteroom unattended like that even though I was inside the office. Because that's what happens when you do – strange people wander in. The officer meanwhile obediently sat on a chair next to the wall and rested his head on his fist, still watching me closely and smiling. He remained in the same position till Georg came in and asked what time the visitor had his appointment with Herr Obergruppenführer.

"I don't have an appointment. He told me to come see him right after I come back to Berlin. My name is Otto Skorzeny."

I'd never heard Obergruppenführer Kaltenbrunner mention his name before, but I guess they knew each other from Austria: when my chief entered the anteroom, he welcomed his visitor with a warm hug and immediately invited him over to his office.

"Frau Friedmann, make us both coffee please, and cancel all further appointments," Dr. Kaltenbrunner said before closing the office door behind himself.

When I came inside with a little silver tray, the two Austrians immediately stopped their conversation and remained quiet while I was pouring the freshly brewed coffee into their cups. *The conspirators*, I chuckled in my mind and asked them if they needed anything else. After my boss negatively shook his head and thanked me for the coffee, I went back to my desk, wondering what the two men were talking about that was so secretive.

Surprisingly, I got the answer to my question sooner than I expected. The next morning Dr. Kaltenbrunner came to work earlier than usual and immediately called me to his office.

"Please, have a seat." He pointed to the chair across the table from his while organizing the papers he brought with him.

I was waiting patiently for instructions concerning those papers he was holding, but as it turned out he had a completely different thing in mind. Obergruppenführer Kaltenbrunner put the papers aside, put both hands on the table and looked me straight in the eye.

"Frau Friedmann, can I trust you with something very important?"

"Of course." I nodded, not sure where he was going with that.

"You see, I'm trying to reorganize the intelligence service in the RSHA the best I can after all that bureaucratic mess Heydrich left after himself. But I don't know people here in Berlin, I don't trust them and they – let's be honest – don't trust me. So when it comes to very important operations, I don't know who I can rely on. Otto, the man who was here yesterday, him I know very well. He's daring, fearless, and would rather die than fail me. He's currently working on something vital for the victory of the Reich. And I also know you, and trust you like I trust myself."

I had to put all my strength together not to look away after he pronounced those last words. I was an American counterintelligence spy who swore to destroy the Reich he'd swore to protect. Of all the people working in *SD-Ausland* he chose the one who was the traitor.

"I appreciate you saying that, Herr Obergruppenführer."

He nodded. "Will you help me?"

"What do I have to do?"

He smiled after I asked that.

"Otto is currently leading the operation, the main purpose of which is to bribe dissident Qashqai people in Iran to sabotage allied supplies for the Soviets. His SS battalion parachuted onto their land already and are working on bribing their leaders with gold. The problem is that… well, they're running out of that gold."

I smiled.

"Herr Obergruppenführer, what on Earth can I possibly do in this situation? Do you want me to get you gold from somewhere or do you want to send me to those rebel leaders instead of it?"

The Chief of the RSHA laughed.

"God forbid, Frau Friedmann! I would never do such thing even if the whole fate of the Reich would be depending on that. No, my dear, all you have to do is to take two suitcases with British Pounds to Switzerland, go to the bank and legitimately buy me some gold."

Now I was really confused.

"Excuse me, but… why do you want to buy gold abroad? And especially with British Pounds? And where did you get two suitcases of British Pounds?"

"Oh, Frau Friedmann, I have a whole depository full of stacks of British Pounds." Dr. Kaltenbrunner interlaced his fingers under his chin and was resting his head on them, looking at me with an enigmatic smile.

"Where did you get them?"

"I didn't *get* them. I *made* them."

I finally understood everything.

"They're counterfeit, aren't they?"

"Of course they are! Reichsführer and Heydrich got the idea of sabotaging the economies of the allied countries right after the war started. And now I have the best specialists in their sphere working for my office who can make any bill or any document if we happen to need one that will look absolutely identical to the real one. We've already bought gold worth millions of Reichsmarks and paid worthless paper for it!" All of a sudden he got serious. "You understand that you can't tell anyone about it, right? Not even your husband. This is a matter of utmost secrecy."

"I understand, Herr Obergruppenführer."

Dr. Kaltenbrunner smiled again.

"I knew I could rely on you. Tomorrow I'll have a fake passport ready for you, and the money. I'll give you the car with the driver, who'll also be your bodyguard, just in case. After you get the gold, he'll drive you to the hotel near the border where Otto will be waiting for you. You'll hand him the gold, and go back home. Quick and simple. What do you say? Will you do it for me?"

He didn't give me any time to think and therefore I couldn't even talk to Heinrich and decide if it was a risky thing to do. After all, if the bankers would notice that the money was counterfeit, I would get arrested. On the other hand I had to agree to later report to our American superiors Rudolf and Ingrid about how the RSHA was funding its operations, basically making the Allies pay for it.

"I'll do it."

Dr. Kaltenbrunner shook my hand.

I was sitting across the table from the director of the Zurich bank my chief instructed me to go to. The director was all smiles and courtesy, while I kept playing the role of a wealthy Bavarian countess, just like my new passport stated. To better fit the part, I decided to wear almost all the diamonds I owned and the most expensive silk dress I brought from Paris. It was a nice change after the *SS-Helferin* uniform I had to wear every day to work.

Despite all my inner nervousness my money caused no suspicion whatsoever, and after all of it was counted by the staff I signed the receipt for a suitcase full of gold bars. My huge driver/bodyguard, in reality one of the SS diversion team members, lifted the heavy suitcase as if it didn't weigh anything and carried it to the car.

Later that evening we were having dinner with Otto Skorzeny, after the gold was securely locked in his room upstairs. The Austrian couldn't contain his excitement about the new funds he just received, and kept thanking me for aiding him. He asked if we were staying a night in Switzerland, but my driver answered that he had clear instructions 'to deliver Frau Friedmann back to Germany the sooner the better.' The lack of sleep seemed to be irrelevant to this half-man half-bear. I smirked to myself as soon as I saw him back in Berlin waiting for me by the car: with that monster around no one would mess neither with my gold, nor with me.

At the end of the week, during our regular after mass meetings with the American intelligence agents, both of them were glad and upset to receive my latest report. Glad because the long-time suspicions of the Allies about the Reich Main Security Office making counterfeit money had finally been proven, and upset after they learned how much of this fake money was already circulating in world banks, while the Reich was getting pure gold to support its sinister goals.

"And they look absolutely real?" Ingrid asked me again.

"The bankers couldn't tell the difference even after a thorough inspection."

Rudolf and Heinrich were going over some new reports in Rudolf's office, so it was just me and her in the living room. I didn't like Ingrid and I knew that she didn't like me either, and I wished Heinrich would come back and stay with me while she was continuing her interrogation.

"Who makes them?"

"I don't know. Specialists, as Dr. Kaltenbrunner said."

"Is there any chance to find out their names or where they make the money?"

I almost laughed in response.

"I highly doubt that if I walk up to Herr Obergruppenführer and just ask him that he'll give me an answer."

"No, of course not, that's not what I meant."

Ingrid took a sip from her cup and looked at me hard.

"Annalise, you do realize that you could get any information out of him if you only wanted to, don't you?"

"Where are you going with this?" I squinted my eyes at the American.

"Let's not walk around the subject, you know perfectly well what I'm talking about."

"You are openly suggesting that I become his mistress?"

"Yes," she answered simply.

I couldn't believe my ears.

"My husband is in the next room, and you dare to suggest something like that?"

"It's the war, Annalise. The end justifies the means."

"No, it doesn't! Maybe that's how you do things at home, but this is a different country, and we have morals here."

"Allow me to remind you that your beloved German people with 'morals' already exterminated more than two and a half million people out of the European Jewish population. And I'm not even mentioning the millions of soldiers they killed at war so far."

"It's not the German people who did it, it's the Nazis. Two different things."

"It was the German people who elected the Nazi government."

"They were forced to! It was a different time, people had nothing to eat! You weren't even here back then, you don't understand what happened and why. My Jewish father had to become a member of the Party he hated! You're not a German, Ingrid, you will never understand. You can only judge us, and believe me, we know that we made a mistake and now we have to pay for it. But how could we know that something like this would happen?"

"I feel bad for you and your people, Annalise, I do. And if you do too, you know how to help them end all this the sooner the better. Right now the Minister of Interior Frick is using all his powers to bring as much working force from the occupied territories because in Germany there are no workers left. Almost all of them have been drafted into the army already, the casualties of the *Wehrmacht* are getting greater and greater day by day. The Soviets are already taking their lands back. Very soon we'll be able to open the second, Western front, and then the game will be over. The sooner we do it, the less people, your beloved German people, will die. We can have political and war polemics all we want, but it won't get us anywhere. You know my position in this matter, and whatever you decide for yourself, you'll have to live with."

"Exactly, Ingrid. Exactly."

I picked up my purse from the table and walked out of the room because I couldn't listen to her anymore. She was a good spy, yes, and a great psychologist too. And an even better manipulator. She knew all the pressure points she could use to make others do what she wanted them to do. And now she was attempting to make me feel ashamed that I was refusing to gather the top secret intelligence she wanted access to, even if it meant betraying my husband. I did want to help my people and my country more than anything, but not like that.

Chapter 14

Berlin, July 1943

I had just came back from lunch, but froze in the doors of the anteroom stunned by a woman's loud voice coming from behind the closed doors of Obergruppenführer Kaltenbrunner's office.

"What's going on?" I whispered loudly to Georg who seemed to be very amused by it.

"Family drama," he also whispered, hardly containing his laughter.

"What?"

"The *Frau* is here."

"His wife?"

"Yes. With children. And she's not happy."

"I can hear that."

Georg, silently giggling, pressed his finger to his mouth and then pointed to the office, inviting me to 'enjoy the show' with him. Saying that Frau Kaltenbrunner was not happy was an understatement. She sounded furious.

"Do you even remember what day is it today? It's your daughter's birthday. Do you remember that you have a daughter at all?! I think you might have forgotten about it, since you only stop by your house twice a year recently, and even then just to make a phone call to the office!"

"I've got work to do, Lisl!"

"Other people have work to do too, but nevertheless they come home after that work. And you moved away to Berlin and think that calling once a week to see if we're all still alive is enough!"

"What the hell do you want from me?!"

"I want you to remember what your children look like! You don't want to come home, I brought them to Berlin. Here, enjoy your time together, I'll pick them up in the evening."

"What do you think you're doing?! You can't leave them here! It's the RSHA office for Christ's sake! Take them with you, and I'll take them out for ice cream after work."

"I'm sorry but they need a little more than half an hour with their own father. Watch them at least till the evening. Goodbye!"

"Lisl! Come back here!"

I decided to hide behind Georg's back just in case, as the fuming woman yanked the door open and slammed it behind her back. She was in her mid-thirties I thought, and looked nothing like I'd imagined her to be. For some reason I always thought that out of all the women he had, Dr. Kaltenbrunner would choose the most beautiful one, but Frau Kaltenbrunner was more than ordinary looking, like many other German women you see every day on the street and won't even remember their face if you see them the next day. I was very much surprised by such a choice.

Meanwhile, she looked at me with all the hatred in the world and proceeded to the exit. Behind her back Obergruppenführer Kaltenbrunner opened the door, obviously trying to make her come back.

"Lisl! I'm not joking, take the children away this instant!!!"

"I'll see you in the evening," she answered loudly without even turning around and slammed the anteroom's door.

Dr. Kaltenbrunner quietly cursed under his breath, while Georg buried himself in paperwork on his table, by all means escaping his boss's look.

"Frau Friedmann, come here."

What did I do? I almost asked, but followed my chief to his office, keeping my eyes on the floor. Already in the doors, he suddenly nudged two kids, a boy and a girl, towards me.

"Frau Friedmann, this is Hansjorg, and this is Gerthrude. Watch them for me for the rest of the day."

After that he almost physically pushed all three of us out of his office and closed the door.

"Hey!" I opened it again and walked inside. "What do you think you're doing? I can't watch them! I don't know how!"

"Sure you do, you're a woman."

"I don't have any children! I have no idea what to do with them!"

"Well, neither do I, and I have a lot of papers to go through. Play with them, think of something." He positioned himself very comfortably in his chair with a cup of coffee and lifted one of the papers from the table, trying to look as busy as possible. "And close the door please."

I stood there absolutely stunned by such behavior for ten more seconds, and after I realized that there was no way to get out of the babysitting duties, I walked back to the anteroom, where Georg was almost red from hardly contained laughter.

"What are you laughing at?!" I barked at him.

He just shook his head and lifted both hands in the air.

"Nothing, absolutely nothing."

I turned my head to the children standing in front of me, looking as puzzled as I was. The boy looked older and taller than the girl, but both of them resembled their father greatly.

"So you're Hansjorg, and you're Gerthrude, right?"

They nodded.

"My name is Annalise. Nice to meet you."

"Nice to meet you," they echoed back after a moment's pause.

Now what do I do? Georg was ready to climb under the table to hide his laughing fit.

"So it's your birthday today, isn't it?" I asked the girl, remembering one of the things Frau Kaltenbrunner was yelling in her husband's office.

"Yes," she answered indecisively.

"Congratulations! And how old are you now?"

"I'm six."

"Six? So big!"

I smiled at her but she just pressed her doll closer to her chest, not smiling back at me. I turned to the boy.

"And how old are you, Hansjorg?"

"I'm eight."

"Eight? You're very tall for your age. You'll probably grow as tall as your father, right?" I smiled at both of them. "Are you excited to see your father?"

They looked at the closed door of his office and shrugged indifferently.

"You must be excited, you haven't seen him in a while!" I tried to put some enthusiasm in them, but in vain.

"He never talks to us anyway," Gerthrude finally said, petting her doll's hair.

"He just has a lot of very important work to do." I tried to explain, but then decided to switch the topic. "So, what do you like to do?"

A shrug again.

"I like to play with dolls, but I only have one with me."

"I play war with my friends."

I started to feel hopeless.

"Alright. But you must like the zoo, don't you? And I bet you've never seen lions in the Berlin zoo."

Finally some interest in children's eyes.

"And ice cream?"

Faint smiles. I was on the right path.

"I thought so. Good, let's go, we have a lot of things to see."

I picked up my purse from under the table and walked the children to the exit under Georg's surprised stare.

"Are you leaving?"

"Yes, I am. Mind the desk, please. And make Herr Obergruppenführer coffee."

"Wait! What if I have to... you know, go out for a minute?"

"And *that* you will discuss with your boss. You, men, are so good in sticking together, you decide how to solve that little problem!"

159

I closed the door behind me and smiled at his facial expression; he wasn't laughing anymore.

The children turned out to be perfectly well behaved, and I decided to spoil them rotten as much as I could during our short tour around the German capital. I bought them all the sweets they wanted in the zoo, which they absolutely loved, took them to the park where I knew the biggest playground was and climbed everything I could playing catch with them. I figured that they weren't used to a grown-up running around and playing with them, so they couldn't be happier to find such an unexpected play-mate in the face of their father's secretary.

I decided that if it was my duty to watch them at least for several hours, I wouldn't be yet another boring adult supervisor, and decided to let them do whatever they wanted. *Climbing the tree? No problem, let me just take my shoes off. Build the fort in the sand pit? I'll buy five bottles of mineral water just for that. Play pirates near the park fountain? You bet!* Only when our games started to seem too wild for the police officer who happened to patrol the park, he walked up to me while Gerthrude and I just captured 'pirate captain' Hansjorg and were tickling him to make him tell us where he and his invisible 'crew' were hiding the treasure.

"What are you doing, Frau? You're disrupting the order in the public place!"

I left Hansjorg to lay on the ground laughing, got up on my feet and straightened out, allowing the policeman to notice my uniform.

"I'm playing with my kids, do you mind?"

The policeman glanced at me once again, but turned around and walked away, demonstrating visible reluctance.

"Wow! You made him go away!" Hansjorg was looking at me as if I did something impossible. "How did you do that?"

"He's just a policeman." I winked at the boy and touched the runes sewn on the left side of my uniform jacket. "And I'm the SS."

"Are you in the army too?"

"Technically, yes, I am."

"But women can't be in the army, can they?"

"We don't participate in actual battles, but we do… other things."

"Like what?"

"We help other officers with work," I answered evasively.

"Are you helping Papa?"

"Yes."

"What do you do?"

"I'm a spy." I decided to go back to games. When they grow up, they'll have a lot of opportunities to know what both their father and I were really doing.

"For real?" The boy's eyes got even bigger. My authority was definitely growing more and more now.

160

"Yes, for real."

"And what does Papa do?"

"He supervises all the spies in the whole Reich. That's why he's always working. Did you see how many people work in the building with your father? They're all his subordinates, and without him they won't be able to do their job."

"Is he the main spy in the Reich?" asked Gerthrude, taking me by the hand as I was walking with them out of the park back to Heinrich's car I borrowed.

"You can say that." I smiled.

"And you help him spy on people?"

"Yes. We travel from place to place, track down the criminals, arrest them and put them in jail."

"Cool!" Hansjorg took me by the other hand. I smiled at this additional victory. "Did you ever shoot somebody?"

"I never had to," I smiled.

"Did Papa ever shoot somebody?"

What was I supposed to answer to his eight year old son?

"If he did, I never saw it."

He seemed a little disappointed. "Papa carries a gun all the time."

"Yes, I know."

"Did he ever let you shoot it?"

"No, never."

"Me neither." He sighed.

"I'm not promising you the shooting… but how do you feel about holding the real gun?"

Hansjorg was looking at me like at his new best friend. "Do you have one?"

"I don't. But my husband does. Do you want to go meet him?"

"Yes!"

Heinrich was more than surprised to see me walk the two children inside his office.

"Who're they?" He nodded at them with a puzzled smile.

"Our new children. Both their parents didn't want them, so I took them. This is Gerthrude, it's her sixth birthday today, and this is Hansjorg, and he can't wait for you to show him your gun."

"Seriously though, where did you get them from?"

"Obergruppenführer Kaltenbrunner's kids. His wife brought them for him to watch, but he's working."

"So he dumped them on you."

I shrugged. "I don't mind. I like them. I'm thinking to take them for good. Now let your new adopted son hold your gun."

Heinrich chuckled, but took his gun out of the holster under Hansjorg excited stare. After unloading it and making sure there was no bullet inside, my husband placed the heavy weapon into the hands of the mesmerized boy.

"Do you want me to teach you how to shoot it too?"

I just shook my head watching the two position themselves near the open window and taking aim at something outside. Gerthrude seemed to share my feelings.

"Boys are stupid. All they do is play war."

"Unfortunately it only gets worse as they grow up."

I sat on the carpet and petted the spot next to me, inviting the girl to join me.

"Will you introduce me to your friend?" I nodded at her doll. "She has a very pretty dress. She must be a princess."

By Gerthrude's smile I knew that I had found every girl's weak spot: princesses and fairytales.

"It's Rapunzel. Look how long her hair is!"

"Do you want to see the real Rapunzel?"

She nodded several times with an obvious desire. I started taking out all the hair pins out of the tight bun on the back of my head, and, in less than a minute, a cascade of my long golden hair fell all the way to the floor, making the little girl gasp in awe. To produce an ever bigger effect, I shook the hair with my hands, letting it fall all over my shoulders, covering me like a coat.

"Can I touch it?" Gerthrude hardly whispered.

"Go ahead."

She stretched her hand to the top of my head and carefully brushed her little fingers through my locks.

"You're so pretty!"

I leaned forward to the girl and whispered, "Can you keep a secret?"

She nodded, still stroking my hair with her mouth open.

"I'm a real princess. But you can't tell anybody because I'm hiding."

Gerthrude held her breath for a moment.

"If you're a princess… where's your princess dress?"

"I'll tell you if you promise not to tell anyone."

"I promise," the girl whispered.

I got up and walked to Heinrich's desk, on which he kept our wedding picture and the picture of me in my Swan Queen costume. I did look like a princess there, I even had a little crown in my hair. I thought that Gerthrude would love that. She opened her eyes even wider when she saw it.

"You really are a princess?"

I smiled and nodded.

"What happened to your dress? And the crown?"

"You see, a long time ago I lived in the Magic Forest with other forest habitants, the fairies, the gnomes, princes and princesses. And all of us lived in peace with each other, and the harmony was in the forest. All of us had different talents: I could dance, some other fairytale creatures could sing, play different instruments, some could write poems and books, and some write music. We had beautiful forest temples with stars all over them, where we gathered every week to praise our God for such a wonderful life he gave us. We had the best forest doctors who could heal any disease and the best professors who could teach you anything. All we wanted was for our life to be happy and peaceful. But one day an evil sorcerer came into the Kingdom, and he didn't like that we, the fairytale creatures, were living next to the people of that Kingdom. So he started telling the people that we were planning to start the war with them and take over their lands, because we were evil and not even humans like them. He started telling people that we had to be destroyed or taken into slavery."

The little girl gasped.

"At first the people of the Kingdom didn't listen to the sorcerer, so he cast a spell on them, and made them all believe all the lies that he and his minions were spreading. The sorcerer then created an army of the tallest and strongest men he could find and dressed them all in black, and put his symbol, the crossbones and skulls on their clothes. He armed them with swords, and ordered them to go inside the forest and capture any fairytale creature they could find, and then burn them in big ovens he built especially for it."

Gerthrude pressed her doll closer to her chest, listening to my story with her eyes wide open.

"We, the fairytale creatures, knew that the only way to escape the imminent death was to pretend to be the ordinary people living in the Dark Kingdom under the evil sorcerer rule, because he wouldn't stop until the last one of us was still breathing. So we took off our beautiful clothes and crowns, and dressed like them, and took their names, and started to act like them, so the evil army wouldn't find us among them. And that's why I have to wear this black uniform, so I would look like I belong to the black army, and no one would ever know that I'm really a princess from the Magic Forest."

Gerthrude, still under impression from my fairy tale, finally asked, "Can you kill the evil sorcerer?"

"It's very hard to do. He's always surrounded by his black army, and they will die protecting him."

"But why are they protecting him if he's evil?"

"Because he cast a spell on them, and they don't know what they're doing."

"How can you undo the spell?"

"You know how." I smiled at her. "Only love can undo the spell. See my husband over there? He was in the black army too. And then he fell in love with the princess, she kissed him and he became good again. But we still have to pretend that we're fighting on the evil sorcerer's side, so his other soldiers don't kill us both."

She looked at Heinrich, still supervising Hansjorg shooting an empty gun at something in the distance, and then at me again. Her brow furrowed and then, after thinking of something for another moment, she asked, "Is Papa in the black army?"

After a moment's thought I nodded.

"Is he under the evil spell too? That's why he's mean?"

"He's not mean, sunshine. It's all the sorcerer's fault. He made him like that."

"Well then… can you kiss him too to undo his spell so he can become good again?"

I couldn't contain myself from hugging the little girl tightly, kissed the top of her head and smiled.

"I'll try, baby. I'll try my best."

I had just left the familiar bank in Zurich, but this time I let my driver go back home alone, mentioning that I had sick relatives in the city who I wanted to pay a visit to. He was visibly hesitant to do so, and only when I lied that Obergruppenführer Kaltenbrunner allowed that, did he drive off with the gold in his trunk. It was Friday, and I had to be in the office Monday morning, so my boss wouldn't even notice my absence anyway.

Zurich was not a big city, so I decided to take a walk to my parents' house. The absence of flags and banners with swastikas still seemed very unusual to me, and I couldn't help but think what a wonderful city Berlin used to be a long time ago without all those bloody stamps on every window. Another reason why I wanted to stay in Zurich just for a day was that I could breathe freely here, walk around the streets and not hear the word 'Gestapo' on every corner, not see uniforms in every café and not wear one for a change.

I decided to make my happiness complete by getting myself a nice big piece of chocolate cake and coffee. A nearby café looked quiet and inviting, and I sat at a table outside. I was enjoying both my cake and the summer sun when suddenly a man in a dark suit sat right next to me without even asking for my permission. I opened my mouth to let the insolent intruder know that I was waiting for somebody, when he addressed me in English.

"Mrs. Friedmann?"

I instinctually moved away from the man who I saw for the first time in my life and who knew me by my real name, and not as a countess I was pretending to be. I nervously gulped, thinking of what to reply, but then he spoke again.

"No need to be nervous, nobody's going to hear us talk here. We've never met, you don't know me, but I know you, and I need to talk to you about something important."

"I'm sorry, I don't understand English…" I replied in German, just in case.

He leaned closer to me and looked me straight in the eye with his grey eyes.

"I'm from the same counterintelligence team you're working for, Mrs. Friedmann."

My thoughts reminded me of a beehive, in which someone just stuck a stick. *Is he from the Gestapo? Do they have agents who speak immaculate American English? How does he know me? What shall I answer? Shall I answer at all? Have I been compromised?*

"If you're thinking that I'm from your beloved Department IV, think why would they send me here to you and not arrest you right in Berlin?"

It did make sense. And I knew that he was an intelligence agent just because he guessed exactly what I was thinking about.

"What's your name and title then?" I asked in English, still expecting the familiar screeching of tires and 'leather coats' jumping out of a car to arrest me. The peaceful, almost pastoral street remained silent.

"I can't tell you my real name, but you can refer to me as Florin."

"It's a French name," I noticed.

"And yours is Italian, Juliette."

He knew my code name. Alright, I started to feel a little more comfortable, and moved closer to the American. He was in his late twenties – early thirties, a very clean cut man in thin, almost invisible glasses, with a strong jaw line. *Lawyers look like that,* I thought for some reason, *the ones who charge you an arm and a leg and never lose a case.*

He moved his hat a little from his face and continued.

"I know what you're doing here, Mrs. Friedmann, and I need you to tell me something: have you brought here British Pounds only or American dollars as well?"

"Only Pounds."

"Do you know how soon it may be when they are able to falsify our currency?"

I shook my head.

"I'm merely a courier, Florin. I'm sorry."

He was staring at me hard, and I started to feel more and more uncomfortable under his gaze.

"Really? What kind of a relationship is there between you and the Chief of the RSHA, General Kaltenbrunner?"

"I'm his secretary." I blushed and didn't even know why.

The American noticed that and squinted his eyes at me.

"And he trusts millions of British Pounds, and more than that, the secret of such an important operation to an ordinary secretary? You must understand how unbelievable it sounds."

I got genuinely offended.

"You can think whatever you want, but our relationship is purely one of a superior with his subordinate. I'm a married woman if you forgot."

He made a dismissive gesture with his hand as if my marital status was of no interest to him at all.

"I'll pretend that I believe you. Just tell me this now, who makes the money and where?"

"I wouldn't know."

"Well, ask him."

"He would never tell me that."

"I'm sure he would. Men tend to tell their mistresses the biggest secrets."

"I'm *not* his mistress!" I almost yelled back. A man reading a newspaper on the bench across the street lifted his head and looked at us.

The agent took something out of his pocket and put it in my bag which I held on my lap.

"It's a microphone, a very sensitive one, install it in his office and try your best to find out who makes them the money."

"Are you insane?!"

"Or better install it in his bedroom, get him drunk and make him talk. We need this information!"

"Forget about it!"

I tried to take the wrapped thing out of my purse as if it was a bottle of rat poison, and give it back to Florin. He caught me by the wrist, and stuffed the microphone back into my purse.

"Let me remind you, Mrs. Friedmann, that both you and your husband agreed to help our office with everything we need. Only on this condition our government agreed not to try you as war criminals after the war is over, and as you probably already know, you, Nazis, won't be the one who's going to win it."

"We aren't Nazis," I almost growled at him.

"I'm considering your refusal as a sabotage."

"He's going to find it right away, he's not an idiot! He'll know that I did it! And then he'll personally shoot me, is that what you want?"

The American paused for a moment as if thinking of something.

"Fine, forget the microphone then. Just get me that information, and try to do it as soon as possible. We can't afford for them to do the same with our economy what they're already doing to the British."

"I'll try, but you understand why I can't promise you anything."

"Try your best, Mrs. Friedmann," he said in a stern tone, and that last phrase of his sounded almost like a threat. I was sorry that I didn't go to Berlin with my driver.

Meanwhile the American got up, threw several dollars on the table as if picking up my tab, and walked away. I caught myself thinking that I didn't know which of my offices was worse, the RSHA or the American counterintelligence.

Chapter 15

Vienna, September 1943

I tried to look as invisible as it was possible in the middle of the wild party the Austrians were having with Obergruppenführer Kaltenbrunner as their leader and Otto Skorzeny as his right hand. The latter had just completed a flawless operation in saving the Italian dictator Benito Mussolini from captivity, and even received high praises from the Führer himself, who immediately promoted him to Sturmbannführer and proclaimed him 'the most dangerous man in Europe.'

I started to feel bad for our host's house, some banker who hoped to fix his financial situation by befriending high ranking officers and generously offering them his wine cellar, because when the northern Germans would get drunk and quietly nod off somewhere in a chair, our southern brothers would almost dance on the tables and break bottles off each other's heads, just for fun.

They're like a wild tribe, I thought to myself trying to hide in the corner of a big banquet room. *And look at their leader, the respectful lawyer Dr. Kaltenbrunner in his military jacket wide open, his tie long gone due to the alcohol, his bangs always neatly brushed back now falling on one eye, and he's hugging this monster Otto by the waist and lifts him up in the air as if the latter doesn't weigh over two hundred pounds.*

"Everybody raise a glass to my boy right here!" The obviously drunk Chief of the RSHA messed up his friend's hair and roughly patted him on the cheek. "Screw the glass, raise the whole bottle, he's the most dangerous diversionist in the Reich! In the whole of Europe! With him alone we'll win this war! To the victory!"

"To the victory!" An echoing roar like thunder shook the room. I walked out and tried to hide from the uncontrollable Austrians in the library. I figured that it would be the last room any of them would come in to, sat in one of the chairs and picked my legs up. I could have long gone back to the bedroom, which our host gave to Heinrich and I, but Heinrich was also among the celebrating crowd (not to cause any suspicions by staying sober during such a notable occasion), and I was afraid to go to bed alone.

It was long past two in the morning, I finally couldn't fight my own body anymore and fell asleep right in the chair. I woke up from somebody brushing my cheek. Still half asleep I smiled, thinking that it was Heinrich. But when I opened my eyes, it was Obergruppenführer Kaltenbrunner, barely standing on his feet and leaning over me.

"You're so beautiful when you sleep..." He brushed my cheek once again. "Like an angel."

Alright, we've been here before and it didn't end too well. I could have jumped from the chair and made it past him straight to my room and hopefully to my husband sleeping there, but my boss was blocking me from getting up by holding the back of my chair with one hand, probably the only thing that kept him from falling at this point.

"I was looking at your face while you were sleeping... no, it can't be."

What can't be? What is he talking about?

"Did you want something, Herr Obergruppenführer?"

He didn't answer anything, and suddenly grabbed me by my chin and lifted my head high, looking at me closely and frowning.

"Herr Obergruppenführer... what are you doing?" I whispered quietly, because he was staring at me with almost hatred in his eyes. The same eyes he had when he beat to death one of the Polish ghetto Resistance members; needless to say, I got scared.

"Do you believe in the victory of the Reich?" he finally asked, still holding my head like during the interrogation.

"Of course I do." I broke into sweat. He looked very menacing now.

"Are you ready to die for your country?"

"Yes..."

"Are you ready to die for your Führer?"

"Of course... why are you asking me that?"

He leaned closer.

"Are you lying to me?"

"What?"

"Are you lying to me?!"

He's getting angrier, that's not good. I have no idea what he's talking about, but I need to answer him what he wants to hear.

"No, of course not. Of course not. I would never."

I stretched my hands to his face, gently touched his cheeks and brushed away the hair from his forehead. I couldn't get rid of the feeling that I was stroking a wild animal, and didn't know what it was going to do next: lick my hand or bite it off. I was stroking Dr. Kaltenbrunner's evil twin. He finally slowly let go off my chin.

"If you're lying to me, I'll kill you," he said almost kindly; then in one swift move he suddenly grabbed my face, pressed his mouth to mine, kissed me loudly on the lips, turned around and walked away. I stayed in the same chair, thinking what the hell was all that about.

The next morning while we were making our way back to Berlin on our private plane, Dr. Kaltenbrunner wasn't even talking to anybody because of the terrible hangover he was nursing; he wrapped his head up in his uniform jacket covering himself from the light, and to all Georg's questions was mumbling the same reply, "Go to hell and leave me the fuck alone." Heinrich didn't look much better, and I kept shaking my head at both of them.

After getting off the plane the Chief of the RSHA right away declared that Reichsführer can execute him right there and then, but there's no way he was going to the office, got in the backseat of his car and fell asleep even before his driver started the engine. Heinrich, Georg and I exchanged looks deciding if we should follow his example, but then silently agreed that Reichsführer wouldn't be as forgiving to us as he was to the eccentric Austrian, and told Hanz to drive us to Prinz-Albrechtstrasse.

The next morning Heinrich left on yet another trip for his Department, and the already well-rested and smiling Dr. Kaltenbrunner was on his working place even earlier than usual. I kept throwing inquisitive looks at him waiting for the explanation of his more than odd behavior the day earlier, but then I realized that the looks didn't seem to do any good and decided to ask him straight forward. I waited till he asked me to bring him more coffee, and closed the door behind after I entered his office.

"What did you mean when you asked me if I was lying to you?" I inquired after handing Dr. Kaltenbrunner his cup.

"What?" He looked genuinely surprised by my question.

"That night in the library, you were asking me if I was lying to you." I reminded.

"What library? What are you talking about?" My boss looked even more confused now.

"Don't you remember anything?"

"Not really…" He shook his head negatively. "What did I do?"

"I was sleeping in the library, and then you woke me up and started asking all those strange questions: if I was ready to die for my country and my Führer, and if I was lying to you."

"Lying about what?"

"That was my initial question that I asked you just a minute ago," I answered with a smile. Obergruppenführer Kaltenbrunner burst into laughter.

"I'm sorry, Frau Friedmann, I was really drunk that night. I have no clue what I was talking about."

"I thought so." I smirked.

Dr. Kaltenbrunner stopped laughing and looked at me more seriously now.

"I wasn't… bothering you or anything, was I?"

I shook my head no; the scene with a very unexpected kiss I decided to omit. He wouldn't remember it anyway.

"That's a relief!" He laughed again and winked at me. I left his office thinking that there was something seriously wrong with him.

The working day was coming to an end, and my chief kindly offered me the services of his personal driver.

"I know that your husband is away, and I can't allow you to get home by yourself."

That was unexpectedly nice of him, but after all I had to admit that he was always nice when he wasn't drunk. We were leaving the Reich Main Security Office, and I was walking in front of Dr. Kaltenbrunner, who was reading a report just sent to him by somebody. I still don't know why I noticed the woman approaching us suspiciously and in a quick manner, but then everything happened as if in slow motion. She put her hand inside her pocket and took out a gun. She raised her arm and took aim. I didn't have time to think at that point, and acted only on instinct: I turned sideways and slammed my whole body weight into Obergruppenführer Kaltenbrunner, who was following me and, busy with the report, didn't notice the woman. Surprisingly, I managed to knock him off his feet just as we heard several gunshots piercing the air around us.

"Die, you murderer!!!" She screamed, still shooting at us. Her voice sounded very familiar.

Dr. Kaltenbrunner's reaction was incredibly fast; he grabbed me by the collar of my uniform, yanked me behind the car and completely covered me with his body. The SS guards opened fire at the assassin, while one of them rushed to see if the Chief of the RSHA was shot. Dr. Kaltenbrunner meanwhile got off me and was standing over me on his knees, looking for any possible injuries on my body with panic in his eyes.

"Annalise, are you alright? Are you hurt? You're bleeding!" He turned to the SS guard standing next to us and looking very lost. "Get a doctor here, now!"

"It's fine, I'm fine, I'm not hurt, I just scratched my hand while falling." I tried to calm Dr. Kaltenbrunner down before he began turning the whole of Berlin on its head.

He finally saw that my injury was very superficial, and then grabbed me in a bear hug that almost broke my ribs that luckily survived the fall.

"Herr Obergruppenführer... I can't breathe..."

He nervously laughed.

"I'm sorry, I'm sorry." He loosened his grip, and was still holding me now by my shoulders. "Are you sure you're alright?"

"Yes." I put my hands on his chest now and looked him all over. "What about you? Are you hurt?"

"Thanks to you, no." Dr. Kaltenbrunner gave me the warmest smile, and then helped me get up. "You saved my life."

We would have probably been still standing like that looking each other in the eye, if the workers of the RSHA didn't start pouring out of the building, half of them with their guns out, ready to execute any impudent attacker on the spot.

In less than five minutes the crime scene was total chaos, with Gruppenführer Müller giving orders to his agents right and left, and the rest of the RSHA agents just lingering around out of curiosity.

"Herr Obergruppenführer, order them to go home, they're interrupting my work!" Müller finally couldn't take it anymore, and turned to Dr. Kaltenbrunner. The latter's loud commanding voice immediately brought his subordinates to order, and they quickly dispersed, leaving only the agents of the Amt IV on the spot.

"Do you know her?" Müller turned from the dead body with multiple gunshot wounds on her to Obergruppenführer Kaltenbrunner.

"No. This is the first time I saw her."

"Well, she definitely knew you if she was screaming 'die, you murderer.'" The Chief of the Gestapo chuckled.

Only I wasn't laughing, standing over the dead girl. The very moment I first saw her frozen face with her eyes wide open, I knew that it wasn't Dr. Kaltenbrunner she was after, it was me. The dead girl's name was Rebekah, the former leader of the Resistance Josef's girlfriend. Josef, who Heinrich and I killed in order to save Adam's, my parents' and our own lives. And now I was more than sure that I wouldn't get any threatening notes signed 'R.' anymore.

"She looks Jewish," observed Müller. "I bet she's one of those, the Resistance or the Underground. Most likely we even have a file on her in our office. We'll take the body in and check her fingerprints. I'll let you know who she is by tomorrow."

I shifted uneasily from one foot to another. Less than anything I wanted the Gestapo to start their digging. All I could hope for was that Müller would open and close the case as an attempted political assassination and wouldn't try to find who the real target was, and why.

––––––––––––––––

We were sitting at the massive redwood dining table in Reichsführer Himmler's house, or better referred to as a castle perhaps. He certainly made a big step forward from a simple school teacher to the second most powerful man in Germany in just fifteen years. Only a few people had the honor to share a meal with privacy-loving Reichsführer, and Heinrich and I would never have been invited here, if it were not for Obergruppenführer Kaltenbrunner jokingly announcing that I was his personal bodyguard and that he refused to go anywhere without me.

"That's a very heroic thing to do." Heinrich Himmler gave me an approving nod after my boss once again told the story to the guests, who were ready to listen to it again and again. "I'll talk to the Führer about you. You should be awarded for your bravery. That's what a truly devoted member of the Reich SS should be ready to do, give their life for their commanders."

"I don't need anything," I answered quietly under the very proud look of my immediate boss, and a hard stare from my husband's side. "I was just doing my duty."

They were talking about the war a lot, but quietly. Our army wasn't doing too well on the Eastern front to say the least, but they were still hoping that Hitler's military 'genius' would somehow miraculously replenish the lack of ammunition, soldiers, and turn the course of war in our favor.

Dr. Kaltenbrunner, however, didn't participate in one of his favorite topics they were discussing. Instead he kept looking at me with an enigmatic smile on his face, while I tried my best to keep my eyes on my plate. And then, to attract my attention, the Austrian stretched his long leg under the table and slightly touched my ankle with his boot. I raised my eyes to him, and he smiled even wider.

"Erase that smug expression from your face, Herr Obergruppenführer, it used to be Heydrich's thing," I told him later when he came up to the window I was standing by, waiting for my husband who was still talking to Reichsführer.

"You can say whatever you want, but now I know your little secret." Dr. Kaltenbrunner almost purred the last word into my ear with his Austrian accent. "You would die for me."

His hand that he put on my back, too low to consider it a decent move, was burning through my dress like red hot steel.

"So what?" I turned to him. "You covered me with your body, you would die for me too."

I expected some indecent joke about how he would love to cover me with his body in a more intimate atmosphere, but Dr. Kaltenbrunner almost wasn't drinking tonight, so he simply answered after a pause, "Yes, I would." He brushed my cheek with his hand, and I quickly walked away before he would kiss me right there, in front of everybody, and I knew he was capable of something like that.

He still followed me around all evening, completely ignoring all norms of etiquette. He brought me an after-dinner drink and persuaded me to accept it saying that it was some special amaretto from Italy that nobody besides the Führer, Reichsführer and General Goering had. Pointing out that I was all by myself while Heinrich was talking to Himmler, he sat on the little sofa I was sitting on, and sat so close that he was touching my leg with his knee every time he needed to use an ashtray, which was on the little coffee table next to me.

"Stop doing that," I finally told him after noticing more and more inquisitive looks from Reichsführer's guests.

"Doing what?" he asked innocently, leaning over me again and this time openly pressing his body against mine, taking much longer to shake the ash off his cigarette than needed.

"This." I moved away a little under his very amused gaze; he was clearly enjoying his game. "People are watching."

"Is that what's bothering you? Or maybe this is bothering you more?" He put his hand between us and slightly brushed my hip with his fingers through the thin material of my dress.

"Stop it this instant!" I whisper-yelled at the insolent Chief of the RSHA, hardly restraining myself from smacking his hand.

"I can't. You saved my life and I want to express my gratitude to you. Would you do me an honor and follow me to the Reichsführer's guest bedroom?"

"You are something else!" I jumped from my seat straightening my dress. "I start thinking that I shouldn't have saved you at all!"

I heard Dr. Kaltenbrunner laughing out loud as I turned around and started walking away. He really was something else!

Later Heinrich would ask me why would I risk my life for *him*, and I wouldn't know what to say. *Because I wasn't thinking at that moment probably? Because I just did it... Because he meant something to me, and I didn't want him to die?*

"Weren't you scared?" Himmler's secretary, who was also his mistress, whispered to me after she finally caught me alone.

"No." I smiled at her. "Only after everything was already over."

Later Heinrich and I were standing on the balcony in Reichsführer's house, and pretending that we were kissing. In reality Heinrich just got back to Berlin, and I was filling him in about the latest events. I couldn't do it in the car because of Hanz, and obviously not during the dinner, so as soon he was done discussing something with Himmler, I motioned to him to follow me so we could talk.

"Do you think they have something on us?" Heinrich whispered in my ear, hugging me by the waist.

"No, not yet," I answered. "I don't think they would be able to connect us to her. They don't know about Josef."

"They might want to interrogate Rebekah's father. And under torture he'll definitely tell them that we paid them a visit before Josef went missing the next day."

"What do you suggest, kill Rebekah's father?" I frowned at Heinrich.

He didn't have time to reply because Reichsführer approached us with a glass of wine in his hand.

"What are you two whispering about like two conspirators?" he asked with a smile.

"Nothing. I haven't seen my wife in two days, and was telling her what I'm going to do to her as soon as we get home."

Heinrich didn't even flinch making up the most indecent lie he could. The trick worked, Reichsführer believed it and laughed.

"Well, then maybe you two should go home."

That night after he made love to me, Heinrich fell asleep with his hands wrapped tightly around me and even threw his leg over my legs. I tried to gently move away from his embrace, but he pulled me even closer.

"No, don't go anywhere. You're mine."

"Of course I'm yours, silly. I just can't breathe like that."

"No. You're mine," he mumbled again through sleep without releasing me. "I won't let him take you away."

"He won't take me away."

"He wants to. I saw how he's looking at you. But you're mine."

"Yes, I am."

I stayed in his arms and didn't try to release myself anymore for the rest of the night.

I made another trip to Zurich, but this time I made sure that my bodyguard was within five steps from me at all times. I still saw the American though, standing across the street from the bank. I got inside the car, and he, invisible to everyone else except me, tapped on his watch several times. *Tic-tock, Mrs. Friedmann, tic-tock.*

I had discussed with Rudolf all possible options of how to get the information the Americans so desperately wanted (our relationship with Ingrid wasn't so good lately, and I preferred to deal with her 'husband'), and we came to the conclusion that getting Obergruppenführer Kaltenbrunner drunk, and maybe even putting a small dose of sleeping pills into his drink so he definitely wouldn't remember anything the next day, was the best option.

"We're going away for inspection of some ammunition factory in Poland next week." I was rubbing my chin, thinking how to achieve two things: make my boss talk, but at the same time secure myself from his usual drunken harassment, which would most likely follow. "We'll be staying by some Polish businessman's house, and I'll try to do it over there."

"You understood how the pills work, right?" Rudolf put the little bottle on the table next to me. "Put three, maybe four in his drink… Yes, I think better put four, that giant will definitely need more than a normal person. And start asking him questions only when he starts falling asleep, got it? You'll have about three to five minutes before it'll knock him out."

I sighed and put the bottle in my pocket. I prayed that it would work.

Chapter 16

Poland, October 1943

It turned out that it was easier said than done. Dr. Kaltenbrunner was drinking, but he was drinking with my husband in absence of his usual Austrian drinking buddies like Otto Skorzeny, and for two days already I didn't get a chance to get close to the Chief of the RSHA.

It was long past midnight and Heinrich was still with Gruppenführer Kaltenbrunner. I knew very well about the mutual animosity the two had for each other, from Dr. Kaltenbrunner's side because Heinrich was married to the woman he wanted for himself, and from Heinrich's side because his superior was constantly sending hundreds of people to death, people who Heinrich tried to save. But somehow they still managed to have some sort of decent relationship, and even occasionally shared a bottle of brandy and a game of cards.

I had my own theory why they could tolerate each other for several hours so well: Dr. Kaltenbrunner loved rubbing his subordinate's nose into the fact that he was his boss and making jokes about how he's working on two very important documents – his divorce papers and the order of Heinrich's transfer to the Eastern front. Obergruppenführer knew how much the fact that I was friendly with him was bothering my husband and wouldn't miss a chance to make dirty insinuations.

Heinrich in his turn loved taking revenge by making his boss lose good money in cards, and sometimes even by getting some information when Dr. Kaltenbrunner would get really drunk. I didn't like them staying up all night, because Heinrich would come back to our room drunk and most of the time angry. But we were staying under the same roof, and they both silently agreed that they better spend the evening picking on each other than spend time in company of our intolerably dull host and his wife.

I got up from the bed and was pouring myself some water when my husband finally came back. He walked in unsteadily and right away filled the room with the smell of cigarettes and cognac. I knew that he sometimes smoked with Dr. Kaltenbrunner, even though he never confessed. I looked at his uniform, all in disorder, and sighed.

"Do you want some water too? You look like you might use some. Or better go shower, you stink of smoke through and through."

"It's not my fault that your boss is a chain smoker."

"He's your boss as well. Here."

I handed Heinrich a glass of water. He just looked at it and put it back on the table.

"I'm not that drunk."

"Right."

"I'm just upset."

"Well, maybe you shouldn't drink with people who upset you."

"You know I'm not doing it because I like him."

"Obviously."

"I'm trying to help people."

"I know." I took his uniform jacket off him and put it on the chair. "Sit down, I'll take your boots off."

Heinrich obediently complied and extended his legs to me.

"You're such a good wife, Annalise. I love you."

"I love you too, darling. But I don't like you drunk."

"I know. I'm sorry. He makes me drink. He knows that you don't like it and does it on purpose."

"No, he doesn't. You're being paranoid."

"Am I?"

I put away his boots under the table and started unbuttoning his shirt.

"I'm not being paranoid, sweetheart. Do you know what he told me tonight?"

"I'm not sure I want to know. You only say nasty things to each other."

"We were playing cards. He was already pretty drunk, and had lost a lot of money to me. But he didn't want to stop playing and asked if he can pay me later or if he can do me a favor or something. Right away I knew it was my chance. Remember that order for the transfer of three hundred Jews to Auschwitz?"

I remembered. Obergruppenführer Kaltenbrunner was supposed to sign it and send to the Kommandant of Auschwitz as soon as the latter would 'clear the space' for them. Which meant to send three hundred current Auschwitz inmates, who wouldn't pass the camp doctor's inspection, to gas and replace them with 'fresh' working force as they called it. Heinrich kept offering Dr. Kaltenbrunner to send them to the working factories in Germany instead, where both the conditions and the food portions were much better, but the more insistent he was getting, the more Obergruppenführer refused to listen to him.

"Yes."

"So I told him, why don't we play on people? You know, if I lose I'll pay you money, and if you lose you'll send the Jews to Germany instead of Auschwitz."

"What did he say?"

"And that's, my darling, where the most interesting part begins." Heinrich leaned back in his chair and crossed his arms. "He laughed and said, that's too easy. He said that this way he loses working force and I lose nothing, just money. He said,

'Let's make it interesting. If I lose, you get your Jews and do whatever you want to them. But if I win, I get your wife. Just for a night.'"

"What?"

"Are you still saying I'm paranoid?"

I couldn't believe that Obergruppenführer Kaltenbrunner actually offered my husband such a bet. He never made a secret of the fact that he wanted me as his mistress, but play cards on me?

"What did you tell him?"

"What do you think I told him? I told him no of course. I would never play cards on my wife. He just laughed again and said that it was a joke. But I know it wasn't."

I shook my head and helped Heinrich take his shirt off. And then I started wondering.

"Heinrich, listen. Of course it's absolutely disgusting, but think about it. You're the best card player in the whole SD. He always loses to you. And it's three hundred people we're talking about. Three hundred."

He frowned at me.

"I don't like where you're going with this."

"Just think, Heinrich. Three hundred lives. One game. Get him really drunk and they're yours. You can save three hundred people."

He shook his head, frowning even more.

"No. There's no way I'm playing on you. What if he wins? I can't risk that!"

"But he never wins!" I kneeled in front of my husband and took his hands in mine. "Heinrich, it's perfect! You could never possibly help so many people at once so easily. And there's no way that you can lose. Go tell him you'll play."

"No!"

"Heinrich, please! Think about those people!"

"I don't know those people. But I know you. You're my wife and I love you!"

"They are somebody's wives too, Heinrich. Somebody's mothers, sisters and daughters. And somebody loves them very much as well. But they are all going to die now because you didn't want to take a chance."

I let go of his hands and got up.

"I'm going to sleep, Heinrich. Good night."

He didn't say anything. Ten minutes later he got into bed where I was laying facing the wall, but didn't dare to touch me.

I turned another page of the book I was reading. Another drunken night for my husband. I couldn't wait to leave this God forsaken country already. I turned off all the lights except for the lamp on the nightstand, but sleep still wouldn't come. I finally heard the steps behind the door and put away the book, hoping that this time Heinrich didn't get too drunk. But it wasn't Heinrich who opened the door. It was Obergruppenführer Kaltenbrunner. He was very drunk.

"What are you doing here?" I already knew that drunken Dr. Kaltenbrunner was always bad news and there was no way to know what to expect from him. Under his stare I quickly snatched a robe from the side of the bed and put it on top of my night slip.

"I came to tell you that your husband is an awful man."

"Really? And why is that?"

I got out from under the blanket and off the bed. I preferred to be on my feet just in case. As if reading my mind, Obergruppenführer grinned at me and closed the door behind himself. I started to get nervous.

"I'll explain it to you in a minute." He walked towards the little cupboard where our host kept alcohol, picked a bottle of brandy and poured himself a healthy glass. "Would you like some?"

"No, thank you, Herr Obergruppenführer. I don't drink brandy. And considering your condition, I don't think you should either."

He laughed very loud and drank half of the glass in one shot.

"Where is my husband?"

"He went out."

Dr. Kaltenbrunner leaned on the cupboard and was looking at me with the expression of a wolf watching a deer. I didn't like that at all. It was a hunter's look.

"Out? Isn't it a little late to go out?"

"He said he wanted to take a ride outside the city. I think he got upset."

"About what?"

He grinned at me.

"He lost a game to me. Maybe for the fourth time in his life. But this time he lost big."

Oh no, he didn't! It's impossible! I felt blood leaving all my extremities and concentrating in my rapidly beating heart.

"How much did he lose?"

Obergruppenführer slowly finished his drink without taking his dark eyes off me, and put the empty glass on the table with a loud bang.

"You. He lost you."

I was quickly going through my options. Last time when he cornered me in the bathroom of his office, I surprised him with my slap and managed to get out. But this time I was more than sure, he was ready for something like this. He wouldn't be looking at me like that if he wasn't.

"I beg your pardon, Herr Obergruppenführer?"

I was hoping that the strategy of using an ice cold tone would work and was looking him right in the eye with my hands crossed on my chest.

"You see, like I told you, your husband is an awful man. And a terrible husband. He was so obsessed with those stupid, unworthy Jews that he agreed to bet you against them in a card game. The Jews! Against *you*. I wasn't even serious when I offered him that! But now I can't be happier that he agreed," he finished with a predator's smile.

"How nice of you two to play cards on me. Is that how high ranking officers of the Reich entertain themselves now? Playing on people?"

"Worse, Frau Friedmann. On their wives!" Obergruppenführer laughed again and moved towards me, blocking the only means of my escape. With the wall on my left and the bed on my right, I involuntarily stepped back when he slowly walked up to me. "How can someone play on his wife? I hate mine but I still wouldn't play on her, just out of respect."

He made another step towards me. I stepped back and hit the nightstand with my foot. That was it. I was completely trapped.

"And what do I have to do with all this, Herr Obergruppenführer? What do you suggest I do, pay my husband's debt just because you two made some stupid bet?!"

"No, of course not." He made the last step towards me and was now standing just inches away. "That would be an absolutely terrible thing to ask."

"What do you want from me then?"

"As I've already said, I just came to tell you that your husband is a no good husband and you should divorce him. How did he even dare to put you as a bet in a card game?" He lifted his hand and brushed the hair off my face. He distinctively smelled of alcohol and cigarettes. "You. Such a beautiful wife. If I were your husband, I would shoot a man who would only offer me that. No, you're too precious of a possession to lose. Look at you, look how goddamn gorgeous you are."

Obergruppenführer Kaltenbrunner leaned his tall body over me even more, and I leaned back, gripping the nightstand with both hands. He was looking me up and down with his hungry black eyes, tracing his hand on top of my arm, all the way to my shoulder, then to my neck and face.

"No, you are absolutely right. We both should go before the tribunal for even making such a bet. We are criminals. You can bet Jews all you want, but you can't do that with an Aryan woman." He was playing with my hair with both of his hands, laying it out on my shoulders and readjusting my locks the way he wanted. I didn't dare to move. "It's all my fault. I shouldn't have made that joke in the first place. I was very drunk and I apologize, Frau Friedmann. I would never insult you like that."

Dr. Jekyll and Mr. Hyde. Dr. Kaltenbrunner and Mr. Chief of the Gestapo. I could almost hear the two voices inside his head, one of the intelligent and respectful lawyer and another one of the despotic maniac dominating the interrogation rooms of the Secret Police. Deep inside, I was praying that the first one would win. Just to be sure, I decided to give him a little push.

"I know you wouldn't, Herr Obergruppenführer. You're an officer and a gentleman. You would never offend a defenseless woman."

He lifted his eyes from my chest and looked at me with a shade of confusion on his face. I was right in a sense: Dr. Kaltenbrunner would never do that. The Chief of the Gestapo would.

"No. Of course not," he said slowly, but then put his heavy hand on my shoulder again, his thumb caressing my collarbone. "You're so delicate. I would never hurt you…"

He licked his lips and moved his hand lower, until he reached my breast. He firmly pressed it with his hand, but then, as if he got terrified of his own instincts, quickly moved his hand to my waist.

"I respect you too much, Frau Friedmann. It's just… you have to understand how difficult it is for me to see you every day at work, so beautiful, so close to me all the time… And I just want to touch you, I want to smell your hair, and your perfume… it's so intoxicating." He moved his face even closer to mine and buried it in my hair, his hands still tightly hugging my waist. He started kissing my neck, forcing my legs apart with his knee. "I wanted you from the first night I saw you. You were so pretty in your wedding dress. And then in jail. You were so helpless, so scared… But I still didn't touch you there, even though I wanted to, really, really bad."

He was breathing heavily in his excitement, his hands now shamelessly travelling all over my body. He was pressing me hard against the nightstand, the edge of it cutting into my skin. He pushed even stronger on me and I could feel how hard he was against my hip. I knew that at that point there was no way I could make him stop.

"I've always wanted you, Annalise. And now you're finally mine."

He put both of his hands on my face and tried to kiss me, but I turned my face away from him.

"Just do it already and get it over with," I told him in cold voice. "Don't kiss me though."

He immediately let go of me and stepped away.

"No. No, I would never…" He was looking at me almost in awe. It was Dr. Kaltenbrunner's eyes, not the Gestapo guy. "Against your will… No. I wouldn't dare!"

He then stepped closer to me, picked up my hand and kissed it.

"I hope you will forgive me, Frau Friedmann. I'm very drunk. If I was sober, I wouldn't even think of… I apologize again. Goodnight."

After those words Obergruppenführer Kaltenbrunner quickly turned around and left my bedroom. I went to the door and locked it, just in case. I still couldn't believe my luck.

The next morning I was helping our host's wife with coffee when Heinrich finally came back. I guess he spent the night in his car, and judging by his look it was the worst night of his life. It was quite understandable; he probably didn't even sleep thinking of what his chief could possibly be doing to his wife. I saw him stop indecisively in the doorway; he couldn't even raise his eyes up to mine, nor to Obergruppenführer Kaltenbrunner, who was reading a newspaper by the dining table where he was sitting together with Georg and our host.

"You're late for breakfast." Dr. Kaltenbrunner noticed Heinrich, who was still standing in the doors. "Are you going to stand there like a statue all day? Sit down and eat."

Heinrich silently obeyed the order. Our host's wife quickly ran to the kitchen to serve my husband breakfast. Georg kept looking at both Heinrich and his boss, trying to understand what had happened last night that they both were acting so strange.

"I sent your Jews to Germany, like you asked me to." Dr. Kaltenbrunner finally couldn't stand the sight of his subordinate, who was moving food from one side of the plate to another for several minutes already. "Frick needs working force anyway."

Heinrich nodded and hardly whispered, "Thank you."

Dr. Kaltenbrunner couldn't care less about the Minister of Interior Wilhelm Frick and his current needs, but feeling guilty about his behavior the night before, he decided that it was the least he could do. Heinrich misinterpreted the gesture as a sort of payment for his wife's favors that his superior was supposedly enjoying in his absence, and almost buried his head in his plate completely. Obergruppenführer Kaltenbrunner rolled his eyes, finished his coffee in one shot and got up from the table.

"Stop with those miserable looks, Friedmann! I didn't touch your wife! Even though you were stupid enough to play cards on her!"

After saying that Dr. Kaltenbrunner left the room, making both our host and his wife exchange more than astonished looks. I guess in their country they weren't used to such a form of an entertainment as playing cards on each other's spouses. Georg, who saw much worse things from his boss by now, just shrugged apologetically at the Poles and smiled.

During the day that we spent at another ammunition factory, Heinrich, who finally came out of his half-suicidal state, kept following me around and begging for my forgiveness at every opportunity he had. Even my arguments that he didn't do anything wrong, and it was me who told him to accept the bet in the first place didn't seem to have any effect on him.

"I'm your husband, I swore to protect you, but instead I almost served you on a silver plate to my worst enemy."

"He's not your worst enemy. You two seem to be getting along pretty well lately."

Heinrich finally smiled.

"Well, I'll definitely have more respect for him now that he didn't use such an opportunity, even though he had every right to do so."

"I told you that he's not as bad as everybody says."

"He's worse. Because you never know what to expect from him."

It was my turn to smile.

"What do you mean?"

"Heydrich was easy to understand: he was a cold-blooded murderer, and he was enjoying being one. But Kaltenbrunner... I can't even figure out what's going on in his head. I thought that he was like Heydrich in the beginning, but now that I'm working so closely with him, he seems to be, I don't even know... human."

I smiled again and looked at that *human*, listening to the report of the director of the factory, who couldn't stop wiping his forehead and fixing his glasses at the only sight of the Chief of the RSHA towering over him. They were all terrified of Obergruppenführer Kaltenbrunner, partially because of his size, partially because of those scars on his face...

When I first asked him where he got them from, he jokingly answered that he was the Reich's most terrible fencer. He lied of course, he was a fabulous fencer; his Austrian friend Otto Skorzeny explained to me later the whole idea behind those scars. The one who would come out of a duel without marks was not considered the best fencer – everybody can move away from a sword. But it was the most fearless one, who would stand and take the hit purposely, just to show that he wasn't afraid, he would be the one deserving the utmost respect of his brethren.

Obergruppenführer Kaltenbrunner had no fear at all, and that's what terrified all his subordinates, and sometimes even superiors so much. People don't understand that absence of fear, it's unnatural and therefore frightening. You can only control through fear, but how do you control someone who has none?

Human. One time I heard the two Austrians talk in Dr. Kaltenbrunner's office through the partially opened door. They stayed late again, the second bottle of cognac was almost empty, but they weren't in their usual debauchery mood that evening.

"I envy you so much, Otto." Dr. Kaltenbrunner was resting his head on his hand; he took a drag from his cigarette wrapping himself up in a cloud of white smoke. "I wish I had a chance to fight in the Eastern front. Just think about it, what a beautiful death it is, in the actual fight, among your brothers…"

"Why die? I prefer to live!" Otto laughed, but Dr. Kaltenbrunner shook his head and remained still.

"My father fought in the Great War," he said quietly after a pause. "All my brothers are fighting now. And what am I doing? Sitting here in this fuckin office and dealing with this Gestapo shit day after day. Sometimes I'm seriously thinking of shooting myself, you know? But would it change anything, Otto?"

"Alright, you're very drunk, I see it now. Let's go, I'll take you to my house."

"No."

"No? Do you want to go to that club we like? Let's go dance with pretty girls all night, how about that?"

"No. I don't want to. I'll stay here tonight."

"In your office?"

"Yes."

"Give me your gun then."

"Why?"

"Ernst. Give me your gun. I'll bring it back tomorrow."

"No."

"You give it to me or I'll take it from you."

"Try, and I'll break your arm."

They were both staring at each other hard, and then Otto sighed tiredly and sat back into his chair.

"Fine. I'll stay here with you then."

"I don't have any more cognac."

"I'll still stay. And Ernst… you're right, it wouldn't change anything."

I cried that night. I thought of my brother for some reason.

———————————

Tomorrow we were supposed to leave for Berlin. I kept thinking about that all evening, knowing that it was my last chance to get the information for the Americans. Everything was going very smoothly, Obergruppenführer Kaltenbrunner was drinking a lot even during the dinner, and I couldn't wait for the Poles to retire to their bedroom.

But it was my husband who decided to ruin everything, and refused to leave me alone with the Chief of the RSHA no matter how persistently I was whispering into his ear that there was no way that Dr. Kaltenbrunner would talk with him in the room. After I realized that no arguments would produce any effect on Heinrich, I decided that in this case he would be the one explaining to his American superiors why we couldn't find out anything, and went to sleep leaving the two men in the smoky room.

I was already sleeping when Heinrich came back. I heard him taking his uniform off very quietly, in order not to wake me up. But then he got under the blanket with me and I realized that waking me up was in his immediate plans. I was facing the wall and never opened my eyes, but I could smell alcohol and cigarettes right away, as soon as he started kissing my neck, his hot mouth burning my skin.

"Heinrich, did you get drunk again?"

Instead of replying, he pressed himself even closer to me, pulled up the end of my night slip, put his hand between my legs and started touching me very persistently.

"Mmm, Heinrich, you're such a drunken animal. Stop it."

I could feel his breath, heavy from excitement, on my back and shoulders and by the way he was rubbing himself of my hip, I knew that he wouldn't stop. I protested a little more just out of formality, but when he slid his fingers inside of me, I couldn't help but moan. I opened my legs so he could keep caressing me as much as he wanted. I guess that excited him even more because his breath became more rapid and shallow. He was moving his hand faster and faster, and I felt how everything in my low abdomen started to tighten.

"Heinrich, please…" I wanted him inside of me. I reached for his hip with my hand and pulled him closer, rubbing my behind on his hard flesh.

I didn't have to ask him twice. In one swift move he lifted up my leg, guided himself in and started thrusting in me, rougher than usual. He even felt different. Bigger than usual. Hungrier. More insatiable, as if we hadn't made love in years. His hands were all over my body, on my thighs, breasts and neck; he was biting my shoulder and back like a wild animal. I didn't understand what had gotten into him, but whatever it was, I was enjoying every second of it, pulling on the sheets and moaning with pleasure.

And then he put his hand on my throat and the harder he was moving, the stronger his grip was getting, to the point where it was hard for me to breathe. He never did anything like that before. In fact, before he didn't do any of the things he was doing now. He was too violent with me, too rough, too controlling, as if he wanted to hurt me. Heinrich never wanted to hurt me. And then a thought crossed my mind: he didn't say a single word since he came in. It wasn't my husband.

"Heinrich?"

I gasped as I realized that it wasn't him, and tried to turn my head towards the man who was basically raping me, but he quickly pressed me down with the weight of his strong body and grabbed both of my hands. I was laying on my stomach now, my face buried in the pillow to muff my screams. But I wasn't going to scream. I knew that out of the whole house only one man would do such a thing. He couldn't fight the temptation anymore and finally got a hold on his object of desire. Obergruppenführer Kaltenbrunner.

I turned my head to the side so I could at least somehow breathe. He was hurting my wrists even though I didn't try to release myself. I knew that I didn't have a chance against him. The worst part of it all was that till the last second I thought that I was making love to my husband, and he got me very excited. Even now when my brain was screaming bloody murder, my body was clearly enjoying the rape. *I can't be possibly enjoying this*, I kept telling myself; but when he lifted my hips a little and put his hand in between my legs, my whole body involuntarily jerked. I knew that he liked that because he started moving slower now, together with his hand on my wet flesh, torturing me, teasing me, making me try to get away from his persistent fingers when I couldn't take it anymore.

"No, please!" I knew that all my pleadings would be in vain, I just didn't want him to have a complete victory over me. I could live with the thought that he raped me, but I wouldn't be able to stand the thought that it was such a pleasurable experience. That would be the most humiliating thing.

He didn't listen to me of course. Instead, he pulled my hips even higher up till I was standing on my knees in front of him, so his hand that he was touching me with wouldn't have anything in its way. In this position he could move even deeper in me and I quickly realized how big he really was, but surprisingly it wasn't hurting me. My skin was so tight around his and the sensation of him completely filling me up with every new thrust was bringing me over the edge. He wasn't holding my arms anymore and I clenched onto the pillow, trying my best not to start moaning again.

"You're so stubborn." He laughed as soon as my legs started to slightly shiver. "I know how much you're enjoying this. You just don't want to show it to me. But I'm stubborn too. I'll just keep doing it till you'll be screaming my name over and over again."

He was right, I was getting ready to start screaming. I don't think I'd ever felt such a buildup in my whole body. With Heinrich I could moan and roll around the sheets all I wanted, but with Obergruppenführer Kaltenbrunner I was trying to contain myself for so long that it played an evil joke with me. My body was more than ready to give up on me. He started moving faster and harder, together with his hand and I bit my lip very hard trying not to make a sound. It didn't help. I lost all the control over myself and did the only thing to prevent the whole house from becoming the witness of my humiliation: I hid my face in the pillow and screamed into it, my fists clenching the sheets with all the force I had.

It excited him even more. Now he wanted to enjoy his victory over me. This time he turned me on my back: he wanted me to see his face. He wanted me to look at him while he'd be doing it again, and I knew he would. He was smiling as I was laying in front of him, absolutely helpless. He pushed my legs wide apart and slowly put his fingers inside of me. I inhaled sharply as my skin tightened around his fingers, still so sensitive from the release; my body and my brain were obviously not on the same page. He played with me a little without taking his eyes off mine and then put his fingers in his mouth, savoring the taste. I hated him.

"Mmm, such a sweet girl. I should have tried you earlier. I should have been fucking you every single day since I first met you. I should have fucked you first in jail, right on the table and after I would've been done with you, you wouldn't want to go back to your husband."

He grinned at me and leaned over me, pressing his hard flesh in between my legs and slightly rubbing it on me. I tried to push him off, but he completely put his body on top of mine and all the strength that I had in my hands couldn't move his massive chest off me.

"Stop fighting me. You know that you want it as much as I do. You always did."

I let out a little cry when he forced himself inside of me again, his dark eyes piercing me with their hungry gaze, his mouth so close to mine. I wanted to look away but I couldn't. My traitor body was welcoming its conqueror again, gladly accepting his every move and ready to comply with all the demands. *I want him to get off me and disappear from my life forever*, my mind was screaming. But then he covered my nipple with his hot mouth and I forgot what I was thinking.

He wasn't rough with me anymore like he was in the very beginning. Now he was just enjoying his victim, intentionally slowly but still insistently. He was caressing my whole body with his free hand, sometimes pushing my legs further apart when he wanted to go even deeper. I dug my nails in his shoulders, partly because I wanted to hurt him and partly because of the growing heat inside my abdomen. He was going to do it to me again, make me completely lose control. Again. And again, just like he said.

I felt his heart strongly beating against my chest. He touched my lips with his fingers and then covered them with his mouth. He wanted it all from me, but I wasn't going to give in and kept my mouth pressed shut.

"Kiss me, Annalise. Open your mouth, kiss me."

"No."

"Open it." His voice was more demanding now. He put his thumb in between my lips and teeth trying to make me open my mouth, but I clenched my teeth biting it hard. He grinned at me but didn't move his finger away. Instead he just increased his tempo again and started thrusting harder and harder, already knowing what effect it would have on me. I bit him even stronger, but he wouldn't let me win. Because he was the General. Because he was the one who always wins.

When I couldn't take it anymore I shut my eyes tight and moaned loudly, letting go of his thumb. He knew that I was all his at least for this moment and covered my mouth with his lips, forcing his tongue inside. He was everywhere now, inside my body and my mouth, hungry and demanding. This time I was kissing him back, because I liked how it felt, I hated and I loved what he was doing to me at the same time. I wanted to revenge him for what he did and make him feel as weak as I was, so I hugged him tight with my legs and started moving along with him, moving my hips to meet his every move. It was driving him crazy; I knew that he was getting ready to finish, but so was I. He was moving very fast and very hard now, almost hurting me, but the pleasure taking over my body was way stronger than pain. He even stopped kissing me and was looking me straight in the eye, with his jaw line hardened.

"Say my name."

"No."

"Say it!"

"NO!"

I felt my whole body exploding, but I knew that he wouldn't stop until I did what he told me to. And I really couldn't take his thrusting anymore.

"Say it!!!"

"Ernst!"

He crushed his mouth on mine again with a loud groan and finished with me after the last several violent thrusts. Then he just laid on me, the weight of his body hardly allowing me to breathe. I pushed my hands as hard as I could against his shoulders.

"Get off me, you dirty pig! I can't breathe!"

He laughed but finally got off me and went to the chair where he'd taken off his uniform. I pulled the sheets up to my neck and was watching him getting dressed; I never felt angrier in my life. At the door he turned around and grinned.

"Don't think it was a one-time deal, sugar. You'll have to make it up to me for the lost time. From now on I'll be fucking you at every opportunity I have. I'll be fucking you good, long and hard. So better get used to it."

With those words he left my bedroom and closed the door. I never hated anyone so much.

Chapter 17

"The codename of the operation is 'Bernhard.'" Rudolf was putting my words down as I was speaking. "They're making counterfeit money in one of the camps, Sachsenhausen. Over one hundred counterfeiters are working in a secluded barrack, all of them are inmates, most are Jewish. Now the production has reached over one million British Pound Sterling monthly, part of which goes to Italy for laundering, another part to the Swiss banks. The operation is top secret and is under total control of the RSHA. All the attempts to falsify American dollar have been unsuccessful so far."

"That's amazing! Your report is even more detailed than we were hoping for originally." Ingrid couldn't contain a smile. "I told you he'd tell you everything."

He did tell me everything, the very next day on the plane, because it was the only thing I agreed to talk to him about. After he had nothing else to tell me, I turned back to my window and spent the rest of the flight in the same position. Heinrich wasn't flying with us; he had sent him away the night before together with Georg for some 'very important meeting' with some 'very important man' somewhere near Warsaw. Probably there wasn't even any man.

Our host's wife brought me the note written by my husband the next morning, saying that he had to leave immediately, and that he'd see me in Berlin. When I asked the woman why she hadn't brought me that note right away, at night, as soon as he gave it to her, she apologized a million times and explained that she thought that I was already sleeping.

I wasn't yelling this time and wasn't threatening with my resignation. I silently listened to the already familiar excuses, explanations, begging, allowed him to hug my waist when he was standing on his knees in front of me, when we were alone on the second floor; I didn't even take away my hands when he was covering them in kisses and saying how sorry he was. This time I just quietly said that since now on our relationship must be purely professional and not more than that, otherwise I'd make sure that the whole Reich will find out how the Chief of the RSHA was treating his secretary. He agreed to it of course.

Everybody finally left me alone. The Americans were happy: their dollar was safe for now, and they had a person inside the almighty RSHA who'd tell them right away if the counterfeiters would start printing their currency. Dr. Kaltenbrunner seemed to turn permanently into the kind and polite Dr. Jekyll, and wasn't even joking around me anymore, a fact that greatly surprised Otto Skorzeny.

"What happened, you kids broke up?" he asked me one evening while looking for chocolate in a cupboard. He already knew the anteroom like his five fingers, and kept eating and drinking everything he could find while waiting for his friend to finish working.

"We were never together." I shrugged indifferently, without taking my eyes off the paper on my table.

"Right." Otto finally found his chocolate. "You two are just one of those movie couples, who hate each other and can't live without each other at the same time."

"I could definitely live without your boss, and very happily."

Otto smirked.

"Is that why you were risking your life to save his?"

"Did you get your chocolate? Get the hell out of my office!"

"Yeah, that's exactly what I thought."

Laughing, he went back to Dr. Kaltenbrunner's office, to guard his master like a loyal dog for as long as he needs him to.

And at night I would curl up by Heinrich's side, feel his warm hands on my back, and try not to think of those other hands that burned through my skin right to the bones, all the way to my dark soul; I was sleeping with an angel and dreaming of a daemon. But he'd never know about that.

"It's now or never. There will never be a chance like tonight. Give me the keys from the office."

"Heinrich, it's too risky."

"No, it's not. It's a Christmas party, everybody's celebrating, I'll sneak right in and out, ten minutes at the most, no one will even notice."

I know they wouldn't; Heinrich could move like a shadow when he wanted to. The reason why I clenched the keys for Dr. Kaltenbrunner's office in my hand and was contemplating about putting them discreetly in my husband's pocket was fear. Simple as that.

"Heinrich, let's not do it." I pleaded with him again.

"The Allies need us to point them out the position of our ammunition factories. And the maps are in your boss's safe."

"Right, so they can bomb them, like they bombed Berlin already! Heinrich, I don't want them to destroy our country. I don't want to do this anymore. It's gone way too far. Let's not make it worse."

"The war is lost for Germany anyway, sweetheart," he whispered, gently tucking the hair behind my ear. "The best thing we can do is not to prolong its agony. The sooner everything is over, the better for everyone."

We were standing in the little park on the territory of the Reich Main Security Office, but I didn't even feel cold in my thin silk dress. My heart was beating way too fast. Heinrich was trying to make me look at him, but I kept looking on the snow under my feet.

"Sweetheart, give me the keys."

"I don't want them to bomb us again," I hardly whispered.

It wasn't the first time the British Air force bombed our capital, but the first significant one. The distant but overpowering roar caught the Berliners at night, in their beds, probably sitting up and freezing motionless – like I did – trying to understand what was going on. We got used to our aviation flying over the city, but this time it was too many of them, too loud, too close... And then both sirens and explosions burst through the quiet night air.

"It's not *our* planes!" I turned my head to my husband, also sitting in bed next to me, and pronounced the words together with the rest of my fellow Berliners. "They're bombing us, Heinrich. They're right here, in Berlin."

Then we were counting our losses. Over two thousand people dead and more than 175 thousand left homeless. We never thought it would come to this.

"We deserved it," Heinrich said one day in his office, looking at the Führer's portrait hanging above his table. "We brought the war to Europe, and now the war has come to our Fatherland."

In the frosty December night every breath turned into a little sparkling cloud. I turned my head back to the entrance of the RSHA building. Light music was heard through the closed doors, people were dancing inside and drinking French champagne, absolutely oblivious to everything going on outside their safe little world. It was them who brought the war to the other people's land, and now the innocent civilians would have to pay for their sins. I finally looked at Heinrich, and handed him the keys.

"What are you going to do if somebody comes?"

"I'll get out through the window. As usual."

"I'll go with you then."

"No, stay here."

"No, I'll go. If I see someone coming I'll start talking to them, and you'll hear me and will have more time to get out."

Heinrich was taking too much time in Obergruppenführer Kaltenbrunner's office, time that we didn't have. I started to nervously tap my foot on the carpeted floor, silently praying for my husband to hurry up. *He knows the safe combination, he should have long been out, what the hell is he doing there for so long?* I looked at the anteroom door behind my back and to the hallway again. And then I froze in horror: Obergruppenführer Kaltenbrunner had just turned the corner and was heading straight in the direction of his office. My heart sank.

"Herr Obergruppenführer!" I called him out loudly, loud enough for Heinrich to hear my voice and at least try to hide the papers back in the safe and get out of there as fast as possible. "I've been waiting for you."

"You have?" He stopped in front of me with an inquisitive look on his face. "What can I do for you, Frau Friedmann?"

"I've meant to ask you for a long time, but... never had a chance." I was feverishly thinking of what I could possibly ask him to prevent him from going into the office, and nothing was coming into my mind. "It's a... personal request."

He was looking me straight in the eye, and I could swear that he knew that I was waiting by his office for some other reason and was just dragging time now. Dr. Kaltenbrunner remained silent for some time as if appraising my behavior, and then finally said, "Why don't we talk about it in my office?"

I almost broke into cold sweat. *Not in the office!*

I stood quiet for longer than I should have, and I saw how he started to turn his head towards the door of the anteroom, which I knew wasn't locked. As soon as he sees it, Heinrich and I both are done for. My hands reacted faster than my brain as I caught his face and turned him to me, pressing my lips hard against his. I couldn't let him turn away from me, I had to kiss him the best I could, to throw my body into his arms and to make him forget what he came here for in the first place; my husband's life depended on that.

I grabbed his neck with both hands, clinging onto him as close as I could; I started covering his face in kisses, whispering that I couldn't lie to myself anymore and that no matter how hard I tried, I couldn't forget our night together, that I needed him and wanted to be with him again.

He was kissing me back already, on my open mouth, on my neck and shoulders, leaving wet traces on my hot skin. I moved even closer to him, until there was not an inch left between our bodies, wrapped one hand around his shoulders and ran my fingers through his hair. With my other hand I was unbuttoning his uniform jacket. This time I had to give him everything he wanted, so I put his hands on my shoulders and with my fingers on top of his pulled the straps of my dress down, until the black silk fell down to my waist.

He realized finally that I came to him myself, at last, so compliant and obedient to every request, that he could do anything he wanted to me, and it awoke some primal instinct in him; he grabbed me by my hips and lifted me up in the air, until our faces were on the same level, kissed me again while I was holding onto his shoulders, and then kicked the door open to the anteroom.

He closed the door in the same manner and pressed me against it. For a second I started panicking when he pulled up my skirt and wrapped my legs around his waist; I was almost absolutely naked, hardly breathing squeezed between the wooden door and his chest, which felt even harder than the door, with his tongue so deep in my mouth, and his insatiable hands everywhere. I dug my fingers onto his golden Obergruppenführer's shoulderboards in a last desperate attempt to push him off, but he only pressed harder into me instead.

I felt how he was undoing his pants with one hand, and closed my eyes trying to think that everything was happening not to me, but to somebody else, and very far away. I clenched my teeth when he started fucking me, not even having sex with me, but fucking me hard against the door, bruising the inside of my thigh with his holster, scratching my cheek with his – he didn't shave today again.

"Ernst!" I finally couldn't take that torture anymore. "You're hurting me!"

I called him by his name for the first time. He stopped moving immediately and looked at me.

"I'm sorry," he whispered into my mouth before kissing me again, this time more gently. "I'm sorry, I didn't mean to…"

He lowered me down to the floor and started softly caressing my tense belly with his fingertips, relaxing every muscle little by little, moving his tongue and lips along my neck down to my breasts until I closed my eyes and stopped resisting him. I knew how hard it was for him to control himself, but he was moving very slowly now, letting me get used to his size, trying to seem almost a normal human being before he could turn back into his animalistic self.

"Don't be afraid of me," he purred in my ear before slightly biting the end of it. "I want you to feel good. Just tell me what you want me to do."

"Kiss me," I asked him not even knowing why. He did, just the way I wanted him to, and I felt how my heart started beating faster. "And get rid of that gun, it's scratching me."

He grinned at me, but took the holster off and threw it on the floor.

"Since you're in command now, why don't you get fully in charge of the process?" He smiled at me again, and pulled me up until we both were sitting on the carpet, me on top of him.

No, I don't want to be in charge, before I could at least pacify myself with the thought that he was doing something to me, and I was just a helpless victim. But now he turned me into the initiator, and it was so embarrassing, so shameful… I felt the heat coloring my cheeks in light blush as I started kissing him now, slowly moving my hips up and down on his big hard flesh. *No, it wasn't shameful, it was shameless, sinful, exciting and very, very arousing.*

I pulled his uniform jacket down his shoulders, undid his tie and first few buttons on his shirt, slightly scratching my lips of his unshaven neck and cheek. He had light scars on his neck too, and I kissed every single one, and the ones on his face, and then, I don't even know why, I just wanted to do it really bad, I traced the tip of my tongue along the double one on his left cheek; I might as well have sent an electroshock through his body to get the same effect. He inhaled sharply and dug his fingers into my back.

"Annalise, what are you doing to me?" He breathed out, looking to meet my lips again. I was kissing him the way he liked it now, very deeply, holding the back of each other's necks. I started liking it too now, I liked feeling power over him, he was all mine, the man who everyone else was terrified of.

I didn't notice that I started moving faster, letting him go almost all the way inside, harder, stronger, driving both of us over the edge, until he pushed me down to the floor and attacked me again, worse than in the beginning, with all the force he had. This time I was screaming from pleasure, leaving scratches on his back and shoulders, arching my back and gasping for air, saying his name over and over again.

He wouldn't leave me alone for another hour. We gradually made our way to his office, and were laying on the carpet next to his table now, happy and completely exhausted.

"Why did you make me wait for so long?" he finally asked me gently stroking my hair as I was resting my head on his chest.

"I didn't know if I could do this to my husband," I answered honestly after a pause. "I must be a horrible, horrible person."

"No, you're not. You're a wonderful person," he answered seriously. "You're the most amazing person I've ever met."

I was aimlessly walking along one of the long corridors of the RSHA building. Deep in my thoughts, I barely noticed myself saluting to any passing agents, barely raising my hand. Ernst was having lunch with Reichsführer Himmler, and I couldn't take sitting behind my table anymore. For a month already I was carrying on my affair with him, the whole month behind the closed doors of his office with hot wet kisses, with top secret papers scattered on the floor thrown off the table in haste, Georg rolling his eyes at yet another cancelled meeting and the order not to disturb the Chief of the RSHA, winks and hidden smiles through the half opened door, and the two of us smelling of each other's perfume. And with every day I was sinking deeper and deeper in that swamp, and didn't even try to grab the ground that was right next to me. I was disgusted with myself like an alcoholic who wakes up in a pile of dirt, but crawls right back to the pub to fill himself again with the poisonous liquor slowly killing him with every new sip.

I swore to myself that I'd stop so many times, but never thought that I could possibly get so addicted. I was very discreet of course, Heinrich never found out what happened between me and Ernst that Christmas Eve – I lied to him that we were talking about the counterfeit money and my next trip to Zurich. He believed me; he always did, and it was even worse. His blind faith in me was making me suffocate with guilt every night when he would kiss me not even suspecting that the other man was kissing me just several hours ago. He was the only man who I never lied to in my life, the only one who I could trust with any secret, who I could come to for help... and now even this was gone.

I couldn't talk to anybody about my feelings: not to Heinrich for obvious reasons, not to Ursula because she'd never understand, not to my mother because she considered the whole RSHA the living hell on earth and its Chief the devil himself. I was betraying my country by working for the counterintelligence, and hurting the counterintelligence by working for the RSHA. I was betraying my husband with my lover, and betraying my lover by working for the counterintelligence. I felt like my head was going to explode soon.

I don't know how and why, but I found myself at the doors of my former boss, the Chief of *SD-Ausland* Walther Schellenberg, and asked his adjutant if Herr Oberführer (he got promoted recently) was busy.

"What a nice surprise!" The Chief of the intelligence greeted me with a handshake and a warm smile. "I can't believe that the ban on our relationship has been finally lifted and you're allowed to see me again!"

"I'm not." I smiled at the joke and sat across the table from Herr Schellenberg. "Dr. Kaltenbrunner is having lunch with Reichsführer, and I snuck out for a minute."

"Dangerous move. He'll get mad at you."

I grinned at him; I missed working with him and certainly missed his sense of humor.

"Do you have a minute, Herr Oberführer?"

"For you – always. It's not a working matter as I understand?"

I almost forgot how insightful Walther Schellenberg was. A typical spy.

"No, it's not." I didn't know why I was there and how to even start. "Herr Oberführer, with all the top secrets and intelligence that you have to deal with all the time, do you feel sometimes the need to talk to somebody?"

"Oh no. He converted you and sent you here to get something out of me."

I laughed at the serious expression on his face.

"No, no, it's not that, it's me." I paused and added, seriously this time, "I need to talk to somebody, but... I can't."

"I see," Herr Schellenberg answered simply and leaned back in his chair. "You're seeing and hearing a lot of things that you can't discuss with anybody?"

That interpretation would do.

"Basically, yes. But it's not just that. I don't even know what I'm doing here, because I can't tell you what's bothering me. You probably think that I've gone mad, right?"

"No, not at all, on the contrary I understand you quite well. I won't be asking you what is it that you can't discuss, but if it'll make you feel better, I often had the same feelings when I just started my career. Keeping your mouth shut at all times can be very... exhausting. You know what I do to make it better? I'm writing a book. Memoirs. In my head of course." He laughed. "One day, when it's all over, I'll sit down and write an actual, physical book, but now it helps me organize my thoughts, you know?"

I nodded.

"I'll start writing a diary then. In my mind also." I smiled and paused for a moment. "Herr Oberführer, do you tell your wife everything?"

"I prefer her not to know too much about my job. But you're in a slightly better situation than mine, you and your husband work in the same office. You can always talk to him."

I sighed and looked away.

"I wouldn't be here if I could."

Walther Schellenberg looked at me.

"Is it your boss?"

How does he always know everything? But I still met his eyes and answered firmly, "No."

He smirked.

"You've become a very good liar, Annalise. But I'll still always know when you lie. Go before he comes back and finds that you're gone. And don't worry, you were never here. Also feel free to come back whenever something troubles you."

"Thank you, Herr Oberführer."

I smiled, got up from my chair, shook his hand and started walking away, when the Chief of *SD-Ausland* called out my name once again.

"Annalise! Wait. Müller is investigating you. I don't know what he's looking for, but... just be careful. Go now. I never said anything to you."

I realized that I forgot how to breathe for a moment. But somehow I managed to nod in gratitude for the tip, opened the door and went back to my office where I sat without motion long enough for Georg to notice.

"Are you alright?"

I faked a smile in answer to his concerned look.

"Yes. Absolutely."

In fact I was everything but.

It was supposed to be a joyful friendly dinner with Max and Ursula, but the mood was far from cheerful. Only their little daughter Greta didn't seem to notice the suspicious silence at the table and kept playing with Sugar, because our German shepherd Rolf was still bigger than her.

"So the Leningrad siege is over with, huh?" Max nodded gratefully at Magda who had just refilled his glass, and took another sip. "Another city they took back."

"Max, honey, let's not... you promised, no war talk tonight." Ursula slightly petted her husband's hand. "That's all everyone's talking about everywhere now. Even in the hair salon!"

"Thanks to the British Air force there might not be any hair salons left for you, sweetheart."

Max took out his cigarette case and lit one. Magda quickly put an ashtray next to him. Greta was trying to wrap Sugar in napkin, but Max didn't seem to notice it.

"Greta, what are you doing to the poor doggie?" Ursula turned to the girl.

"I want to make her a dress, just like my dolly has."

"Doggies don't wear dresses, honey. Leave her alone!"

"With the way everything's going we'll lose the war altogether."

"Max! You can't say something like that!"

"What? Am I the only one who thinks so? Heinrich, don't you think that the whole campaign is going not as well as originally planned? Weren't we supposed to end the Soviet blitzkrieg by the winter of forty first? How come it's forty forth, and we're still in this up to here?" Max put two fingers on top of his throat.

"Mommy, look!"

"Not now, honey."

"What if the Führer is wrong?"

"Max!!!"

"Mommy!"

"Heinrich?"

Greta was pulling on her father's sleeve, but he was looking at his best friend, still waiting for his answer. And what could Heinrich, who knew that the war was already lost for Germany, tell him?

"Maybe everything is not so bad," my husband said softly. "Maybe it's just a minor setback. We'll regroup our armies, refill our ammunition and counterattack."

"We don't have as much ammunition as they do," Max almost whispered, biting on his nail. "We both work for the external intelligence, we both know the numbers. They exceed us both in people and ammunition. And it's only the Russians. And now count the Allies, and their air force, and ammunition, and machinery... What if they open the second front? We physically won't be able to compare to them in numbers. Somebody has to let the Führer know before... before it's too late. While something still can be done."

"He doesn't want to hear the numbers, Max. Neither does he want to listen to his generals who inform him of the situation on the Eastern front. All the talks about the only possibility of surrendering he considers a defeatism and ordered to execute anyone who only speaks of it."

"But Heinrich… It's not right. He'll make us lose our country… He'll get us all killed!"

"Max!"

"What, Ursula? I'm only pointing out the truth. And many of the commanding staff is of the same opinion!"

"Max, I'm begging you, stop saying such things!"

"Somebody has to say it, honey!"

"Papa, look!"

"Field commanders are talking about it too. I went to the meeting with a couple of people, and they were saying that if the leader is not thinking clearly blinded by his own superiority, that leader is not a credible leader anymore."

"Max!!!"

"We can't win the war just because our Führer thinks that we are a superior nation. Wars are won by guns and bullets, not by someone's birth certificate. Heinrich, come with me and listen to what they say, we need to do something to help our country while we still can."

"Like what? Kill Hitler?" Heinrich asked straight out.

"Are you seriously talking about it?" Ursula turned from the two men to me. "Are they seriously talking about it?"

"If it's the only possible solution, then yes."

"Max, you're going to get us all killed with your talking." Ursula covered her face with her hands.

"*He's* going to get us all killed! Heinrich, come with me, listen to these people, they have a plan…"

"Max. Listen to me carefully. You're not going to change anything. Please, don't get involved with this. You have a family to take care of."

"Max, listen to Heinrich, I'm begging you!"

"Heinrich, we still can do something…"

"No, we can't, Max. Trust me, we can't."

Chapter 18

"The working day is almost over."

"Mmmm, no... I don't want to go home."

"How about we go home together?"

I giggled and shook my head. I had spent the last ten minutes on my boss's lap, who was kissing me in the most provocative manner, with one hand inside my bra and another one under my skirt.

"Whose home, Herr Obergruppenführer?"

"Mine. Your damn husband is finally away, and we can spend the whole night together." He slightly bit my lip.

"I can't. What if Heinrich calls, and I'm not home?"

"Let's go by your house then."

"No, the neighbors will see your car... And besides my housekeeper's there."

"We'll take your car then." He moved the phone to me. "Here, call your housekeeper and let her go. We'll have a nice romantic dinner in a restaurant and then I'll take you right to your bedroom."

I smiled and buried my face on his neck.

"How come I can never say no to you?"

It was only the second time we ever had dinner together in a public place. The first time was almost five years ago, in Poland, when I almost got caught by the Gestapo with the radio in my hands. Tonight we decided not to talk about war, politics or anything concerning the RSHA, and just be a regular couple, no matter that both of us were still lawfully wedded to other people.

We were holding hands even while eating. I think we finished the whole bottle of champagne already, and then we danced; I was so shamelessly happy just to press my head against his shoulder while he was holding me too close to consider it decent, and we both kept smirking at other patrons' looks they were shooting at us. Ernst would make it worse of course and kiss me right on the lips – who's going to say something to Obergruppenführer?

We went back to the table where our dessert was served for us; all the staff were trying their best to immediately follow every request of their high rank guest and his... well, they were very polite and were addressing me as 'Frau.' Ernst liked that, he liked people to think that I was his wife. And now he moved his chair even closer to mine and was whispering the most indecent things in my ear, kissing my wrist and holding my knee with another hand. *Time to go*, I thought to myself still giggling, *five more minutes and he'll start undressing me right here*. And then the loud scream of sirens, even louder than music playing inside, broke down.

Ernst and I exchanged concerned looks after observing the crowd suddenly hurrying to pay their tabs and leave for the nearest bomb shelter.

He sighed. "What do you feel like doing, run with everybody else or stay here and finish their wine cellar? Or try to make it home?"

I tugged on his sleeve.

"With all respect to your bravery, Herr Obergruppenführer, I'm too young to die! Let's go!"

"You realize that we'll spend the night in the company of about a hundred people, right?" Ernst threw the money on the table, but still followed me to the exit.

"We don't have a choice!"

"Thank you, fuckin Brits, for ruining my night!" the Chief of the RSHA yelled at the night sky outside, making me burst into laughter and some people turn their heads to our direction.

"Ernst!" I tried to shush him, desperately trying to contain the laughing fit.

"What? Screw them, the fuckin Brits!"

He kept cursing out all the Allies and the British Air force in particular for the rest of the way, until we finally followed the crowd inside the closest bomb shelter. The soldiers and police officers directing the people immediately froze at attention seeing Ernst's Obergruppenführer's markings. They wanted to free a separate bench just for the two of us, but Ernst shook his head at them.

"It's fine, don't worry about us, we'll sit with everybody else."

It was very cold inside, and Ernst wrapped me up in his coat and made me sit on his lap, keeping me warm with his body. People around us were barely talking to each other, listening to the muffed explosions outside and silently hoping that their houses won't be destroyed by the bombs.

"My dogs are inside…" I whispered.

"I'm sure they'll be fine," Ernst pressed me harder to his chest. "Try to sleep."

"I can't."

"I'm sorry I'm not as comfortable as your bed." I felt warm when he quietly laughed somewhere into my hair.

"I wouldn't want to be in my bed now."

"Where would you want to be then?"

"Right here, with you," I answered simply and looked into his golden brown eyes, which all of a sudden became serious. "There's no other place I'd want to be."

"Me too." Ernst smiled, and kissed me again. I hated myself for feeling so happy with him. If the whole world would've exploded outside, I couldn't care less. I was with *him*, and that's the only thing that mattered.

I walked inside the anteroom and stopped halfway. Ulrich Reinhard was standing over my table and looking through the papers I left there before leaving for lunch. God knows where Georg was.

"What are you doing here and who allowed you to go through my documents?" I asked sternly, noticing that my hands were suddenly cold and sweaty. Why Reinhard always had that effect on me, I had no idea; I hated to admit it, but he scared me, physically.

"Hello, Annalise." He gave me the most vicious smile. "My beautiful Annalise. My brave little spy."

"What are you talking about this time?" I tried to sound as calm as I could when everything inside was slowly turning into a tight knot. *Müller is investigating you... be careful.* Reinhard works for the Gestapo. *Not good.*

"You know perfectly well what I'm talking about. You've done pretty damn well for the past several years, I have to give you that, normally people get caught after several months only. But you... I don't know how you were able to slip right through our fingers, every single time. But this time I made sure that I came prepared."

"And what am I being accused of this time?" Trying to look as bored as I could, I crossed my hands on my chest so he wouldn't see that my fingers had started to slightly shake.

"Same old, same old. Espionage." Reinhard mirrored my pose, but unlike me he was smiling wide. "You see, when the whole story with the radio and that friend of yours, the Jew, occurred, I didn't have the slightest doubt that it was you who was working with him."

"I was acquitted of those charges."

"Yes, you were. Probably because your boss can't keep it in his pants, but it doesn't matter now." *If he talks loud like that, Ernst is not in his office.* "But I have a sixth sense when it comes to cases like yours, and I personally asked Gruppenführer Müller to allow me investigate it. For a long time I've been working on it, trying to connect the dots, and something was always missing. And then guess what happened?"

I didn't ask him anything, even though he wanted me to. Reinhard smirked.

"That girl started shooting right in front of the building. Remember her?"

"Quite well, she was shooting at my boss."

"No." Reinhard shook his head and laughed. "No, and that's where the most interesting part begins. She was shooting at *you.*"

"It was a political assassination. She was trying to shoot the Chief of the RSHA, and Gruppenführer Müller closed the case."

"No, he didn't. He just said he did, so you wouldn't be able to get a fake passport that you probably have hidden someplace safe, and take off before we would finish the investigation."

I involuntarily swallowed hard, but tried to regain my composure right away.

"And why would she want to shoot me?"

"Yes. That's the question that Herr Müller and I discussed many times, before it all finally fell into place after we searched her house. Guess what we found? A small note saying 'Time's up. R.' right there, on her table. Something happened that made her change her plans, and she didn't get a chance to send it. But the handwriting, ink and paper coincide precisely with the ones you handed us yourself."

"It only proves that she wanted to kill me, but definitely doesn't make me a spy."

"Give me a minute, I'm getting there. So now we have this girl, Rebekah, the member of the Underground movement, who decides to shoot you, and not the Chief of the RSHA, and screams 'Die, you murderer!' prior to shooting. What could have you possibly done so evil that she chooses *you* as her victim instead of such a significant political figure, who was right there with you? So I started digging deeper, and guess what I found out? I found out that Rebekah was the girlfriend of the former Underground leader Josef, who suddenly went missing the same night when you were released from jail. That's a very interesting coincidence, isn't it now? And the whole following week you don't come to work because you hit your head falling off the steps in your house. But didn't you get that injury some other way? Let's say... struggling with somebody?"

He was looking me straight in the eye, and I tried to seem as unfazed as I could, even though my heart was pounding in my chest.

"Your allegations are completely ungrounded."

"You're not losing hope, are you?" Reinhard smirked. "I'll continue with your permission. Josef went missing, and his body was never found. Alright. But who would benefit from his death? Us, the Gestapo, of course. But we didn't kill him. Who did then? Someone who needed Josef to disappear, and fast. And if I remember correctly, your former dancing partner during the interrogation pointed out that it was Josef who was giving him orders. And then there is no Josef no more. Why is that? So no one would be able to interrogate him. Correct me if I'm wrong."

I didn't know what to say this time.

"Good! Seems like I'm right. And if you wanted Josef to shut his mouth once and for all so he wouldn't tell anybody that he had nothing to do neither with you or your Jew friend, it means only one thing: it was *your* radio, and it was *you* who was with the Jew that day transmitting those messages, it was *you* driving the black Mercedes, and if you two aren't connected to the Underground, it brings us to only one logical conclusion. You're working for the enemy. Oh yes, by the way, you have

202

quite a beautiful American accent according to one of our agents who followed you on your trip to Zurich. The pictures of you speaking with an American agent came out really pretty too."

The man with the newspaper lifting his head. Of course. How could I be so stupid? I stood silently on the same spot with not a single thought in my head. Except for the one – I'm dead. This time for sure.

"You don't know what to say? It's fine, I'm not here to interrogate you or anything. Just letting you know that your boss is probably thinking of the possible ways to kill you while reading your file with all this information. You have nowhere to run from here, and I wanted to give him the pleasure to officially arrest you. I bet I'll get promoted after that. I'll come watch your execution, if you don't mind."

He gave me another disgusting smile and headed to the exit.

"Oh yes, almost forgot." He stopped suddenly, walked up to me, rolled up my sleeve and took the beads and cross off my wrist. My last hope. "You're a Jew and you're wearing the Catholic cross on you all the time? I don't think so."

He quickly figured out how to open the hidden section and took a small white capsule from the inside.

"Cyanide?" He shook his head. "Goodbye, Jew-girl."

Reinhard was long gone when Georg walked inside with a stack of files in his arms.

"Annalise? Is everything alright?"

Run. The adrenaline covered me with a hot sweaty wave; I nodded, quickly grabbed my purse from under the table, said something about being right back and walked out of the anteroom. Heading to the main stairs, I kept throwing looks at the guards, trying to guess if they'd been warned about not letting me out of the building. They didn't move and I almost ran down to the third floor, the second... and then I heard *his* voice behind my back.

"Annalise!!!"

I stopped just for a second to look up and see Ernst's angry face, and ran, this time really ran, almost knocking other staff members off their feet. I knew that he was right behind me, I heard his loud steps, but for some reason he didn't scream at the guards by the garage entrance to grab me. I got that, he wanted to catch me himself, and I didn't even want to think of what he would do to me then.

Trying to make it to my car as fast as I could, I was digging inside my purse desperately looking for the car keys with my shaking hand, finally fished them out, yanked the door open and locked it from the inside, just when Ernst caught up with me and slammed his fist on the window almost breaking it.

"Open this fuckin door right now!!!"

"No!"

I put the keys in the ignition and started the car; I saw him taking his gun out. *Let him shoot me, it's still better than getting caught alive.* I pressed the accelerator and took off with a loud screeching of the tires. He didn't shoot, but didn't let me go either. On a street, in my rearview mirror I saw his black Mercedes quickly approaching my car. I pressed the accelerator harder, hoping to beat him to my house, where I had my gun. *At least I'll be able to protect myself.*

I already had my house keys ready when I jumped out of my car, as I heard him slamming his car door behind me. I didn't even bother to lock the front door, I knew by now that in his infuriated state no locks would stop him. I ran all the way up to my bedroom, yanked the top drawer of the nightstand open, took the gun out, took the safety off and aimed at the entrance right at the moment when the very menacing looking Chief of the RSHA stopped at the door. He was also aiming his gun at me.

We started screaming at each other at the same time, me warning him to stay where he was or I'd shoot him, and him yelling at me to put my gun down because I was the enemy of the state and under arrest. We kept yelling louder and louder, trying to out scream each other, but neither of us wanted to give up first.

"You lied to me!!! All this time you lied to me!!!"

"I had my reasons!!! Your government left me no choice!"

"You went against your own country!"

"You've killed half of the population of your country!!!"

"You damn Jew!!!"

"You damn Nazi!!!"

"That's exactly why all of you deserve to die!!! All of you are a worthless bunch of backstabbing rats! All of you to the gas!!!"

"The Jewish nation is the only nation that never started a single war in its history!!! It's you, you started all this! Goddamn Nazis!!! You kill innocent people!!! Children!!!"

"Because all of you are traitors!!! Look at yourself! You, Jews, made us lose the Great War, and now you'll make us lose this one?!"

"Jews fought in the Great War along with Aryans!!! And you're sending war heroes to the camps!!! Who's the traitor now?!"

"I'll take you personally to Auschwitz, I'll drag you personally right to the gas chamber and lock the door!!!"

"Not before I put the bullet in your head so nobody else suffers from you!!! You're just like Heydrich!!! All of you are with your national superiority!"

Surprisingly this time he didn't yell back at me, just clicked the safety on his gun and lowered it.

"Go ahead."

"What?" I kept looking at him and back at his gun not sure what to do next.

"Go ahead. Shoot," Ernst answered simply.

I shifted from one leg to another trying to figure out what kind of a game he was playing with me now.

"Well? I don't have all day. Shoot."

I pursed my lips and frowned at him.

"You shoot first."

"I'm not going to shoot you. If you don't shoot, I'll take you to the camp."

I turned a little sideways to him, still holding my gun high. My hand wasn't even shaking, but I couldn't for the life of me bring myself to pull the trigger. Even though it meant the camp.

"Annalise, shoot. You've killed a man before, you know how to do it. Go on, kill the Nazi. I deserved it. I'm an idiot, I believed you. If the Jewish girl tricked me so easily, I definitely deserve to get shot. You must really hate me, so do it already. After everything I've done to you."

I couldn't hear anything except for my own heartbeat. I slightly brushed the trigger with my finger for the last time, and put the gun back on the nightstand. This time Ernst looked at me, frowning and confused.

"I can't." I shrugged. "I can't shoot you. Take me to the camp."

I was waiting for him to come up to me and bring me downstairs, to his car, back to the Gestapo, but he just stood on the same spot without moving. We were looking at each other for what seemed like several hours, until I saw a faint smile touch the corners of his lips.

"You love me."

Those three words he said, or even half asked, pierced my brain like a hot needle. I shook my head, but he smiled wider now, sure of his guess.

"Yes, you do. You love me, don't you?"

"No."

"You can't shoot me because you love me. You always have."

"No…" I whispered almost pleadingly.

Ernst walked up to me and put his gun on the bed.

"Look at me." I kept staring at the floor, so he took my face in his hands and made me look him in the eyes. "You love me, Annalise. You really do."

"So what? You love me too. You couldn't shoot me either."

"I'll take you to the camp instead," he said softly, slightly brushing my cheek with his finger.

"Alright. Let's go."

"Just like that?" He moved closer to me.

"Do whatever you want to me," I whispered.

Ernst looked at me a little longer, and then slowly leaned to me and very gently touched my lips with his. I closed my eyes and kissed him back, still hardly breathing, still afraid, so small and helpless without my gun, my cover, my story. Just a young girl indecisively offering her naked soul to the enemy she fell in love with. *Do whatever you want to me.*

I was standing motionless while he was undressing me, button by button, very slowly, until I was standing absolutely naked in front of him, still fully dressed in his uniform. Nothing to hide anymore, no more lies; I let him look at me in the broad daylight as long as he wanted, until he stretched his hands to me again and took me into his arms, kissing me so deeply that I couldn't breathe, holding so tight that it was hurting every bone.

"Are you going to make love to the Jew?" I smiled at him when he lowered me onto the bed and laid on top of me.

"No. I'm going to make love to the girl I love."

I wrapped my arms and legs around him and swore to myself that I'd never let go. He was right. I did love him, with every tiny cell of my body.

Ernst was holding me in his arms while I was telling him my story from the very beginning. Sometimes he'd interrupt me with questions, but mostly he just listened quietly, gently stroking my hair. He was still mad at me for dealing with the Allies, he kept repeating that I should have told him everything from the very beginning and shook his head understanding the absurdity of his own words. He smoked too many cigarettes, still not able to comprehend how the hell he happened to fall for the girl who belonged to the race he swore to exterminate. But more than anything he was thinking of what to do with me now, now that Müller and Reinhard both had such a file on me that the only way for me would be to the gallows or the gas chamber.

"Over my dead body!" he said in a grave tone when I only mentioned that they would come and arrest me.

I was patiently waiting sitting next to him on a side of the bed with my legs crossed, while he was moving his index finger on top of his gun with a thoughtful expression on his face.

"Will you shoot me yourself? So I wouldn't suffer?" I interpreted it the only way I saw possible.

"What?" Ernst looked at me in disbelief. "Of course not! Why would you even think that?"

"They know about me. You can't get me out of the country. You can't hide me. What are you going to do with me?"

"We'll try something very risky. But you have to trust me on this one."

I nodded. "I trust you."

"Alright. Get dressed then, and… I'll have to bring you back to the RSHA."

We both got dressed in complete silence; I didn't ask him anything because I knew by now that he would never hurt me. I let him tie my hands with his tie because I had to look as if he was interrogating me all this time.

"You'll have to hit me," I told him already in the hallway.

"What?"

"Well, if you were supposedly interrogating me all this time, it has to look natural. Hit me on the face, so they could see blood."

"I'm not hitting you."

"Do it. It will look too suspicious if I come back with no marks on my face."

"Annalise…"

"Just do it and get it over with. Stop dragging time. I'll survive a little smack, don't worry."

He took a deep breath and then shifted from one leg to another indecisively.

"Alright. I'll hit you on the mouth with an open hand, not hard, but there'll be blood."

"Good. Do it."

"I can't, while you're looking at me!"

I sighed and closed my eyes. All of a sudden he took my face in his hands and kissed me.

"I'm very sorry!"

Before I could understand anything I got such a slap that I hardly stood on my feet. I'd never been hit in my life before, and it was quite a petrifying experience. I instinctively pressed my hands to my broken lips, tasting the blood quickly filling the inside of my mouth.

"I'm so sorry! Sweetheart, angel, does it hurt?"

I should feel bad for my poor lover, gently touching my cheek and covering my already teary eyes with kisses, but it hurt too damn much. If that was how he hit people 'not hard,' I couldn't even imagine how it would feel if he'd punch me with his fist and with all his force. I'd probably die of massive head trauma right there.

"I'm fine." I wiped the tears and my mouth with a sleeve and noticed several bright red dots on my white shirt. If that doesn't look like a good interrogation, I don't know what does. "Let's go."

Ernst kissed me on my forehead again, told me that he loved me and then led me out of my house by the scruff of my neck, in case Reinhard had sent the Gestapo agents to help out the Chief of the RSHA in case something goes wrong… or to spy on him. He roughly pushed me in the back seat of his car and started it.

"Now listen to me very carefully. This is what we're going to do…"

The End of Book Two

To be continued…

Thank you for reading Book Two from the series "The Girl from Berlin." I hope you enjoyed it! If you liked the story, the author and all the people who worked on the book will really appreciate it if you leave a review on Amazon or Goodreads. Annalise, Heinrich and Gruppenführer Kaltenbrunner will come back in the third and final book in the series – "War Criminal's Widow."

Made in the USA
Lexington, KY
24 March 2016